THE SORX AND THE QORX

To Jamie

With very best wishes!

John Oven

The Sorx and The Qorx

Published by The Conrad Press in the United Kingdom 2022

Tel: +44(0)1227 472 874
www.theconradpress.com
info@theconradpress.com

ISBN 978-1-914913-40-2

Typesetting and Cover Design by: Charlotte Mouncey, www.bookstyle.co.uk
The Conrad Press logo was designed by Maria Priestley.

Printed and bound in Great Britain by Clays Ltd, Elcograf S.p.A.

The Sorx and The Qorx

John Uren

With love and thanks to Helen, John and Roe,
the original Rodleyites!

'If there were no prime numbers then there would be no numbers at all!' said the Qorx.

'So prime numbers really are very important aren't they?' asked Jack.

'Yes, they are!' said the Qorx. 'Can you imagine a world without any numbers?'

Holly and Jack looked at each other and shook their heads.

The strange something

In slightly more than 43 hours plus 5, today would be a twice-upon-a-time-day but no-one had any idea that this would happen.

Holly and her brother Jack lived beside the canal in Rodley Bottoms. It was the school holidays and they longed for an adventure. But it hadn't stopped raining for a week. They were stuck indoors and bored. Then, one morning, the clouds parted and the sun finally put in an appearance.

'Come on Holly!' shouted Jack. 'I'll race you to the garden.'

They rammed their feet into their wellies and dashed out of the house.

'Hang on!' cried Holly. 'I'll just get Podge.'

She grabbed Podge, and was back with Jack before he knew she had gone.

Podge was an extremely well-loved bean-bag dog, black and brown all over with floppy ears, even floppier feet and a beautiful button nose. She was rather scruffy and not any particular type of dog, but that didn't matter to Holly.

Holly loved Podge. They talked together, listened together, slept together. They cried together, laughed together, played together. They were what together meant. Holly and Podge had been best friends for years. Holly could simply not imagine a world without Podge.

'OK! Let's go!' boomed Holly.

She and Jack quickly snail-hopped their way up the long path running by the side of their house, carefully avoiding stepping on any of the snails that had come out to say hello.

'Let's climb the Clock Tree,' said Jack, stopping for a moment.

The Clock Tree was a very old, gnarled tree, which stood in one corner of the garden. Fastened to its trunk was a clock. This was rather weather-beaten but it worked. They loved to climb the tree and watch the world go by over the high dry-stone wall that enclosed 3 sides of the garden.

'Let's go and see Zig and Zag,' Holly replied.

Zig and Zag were Holly's guinea pigs who lived in a shed just in front of the garden.

'No, you can see them later. Let's go up the tree!' demanded Jack.

Holly was determined.

'No, Zig and Zag!' she shouted.

'Clock Tree!' snapped Jack.

'No, Zig and Zag!' shouted Holly, even louder.

'OK,' said Jack, more quietly. 'Let's pick for it.'

He stooped down and gently picked up a sleeping snail in one hand, put his arms behind his back, swapped the snail from hand to hand, and then held his closed hands out in front of him.

'You choose,' he said to Holly.

Holly looked at the outstretched hands trying to see if any slime was oozing out between their fingers. There wasn't. She waved her right hand backwards and forwards over Jack's hands, paused for a moment, then put her hand on Jack's left hand.

Grinning, Jack opened his left hand to reveal an empty palm, quickly followed by his right, which contained a snoozing snail sitting in a small pool of slime.

'I win! The Clock Tree it is!' he shouted, triumphantly.

Carefully returning the snail to a safe spot, he wiped his right hand on his shorts and sauntered along the path, past the shed, and into the garden.

Holly didn't follow Jack immediately but just stood still muttering, 'Why do I never win? Jack always wins.'

She sighed, took a deep breath, and slowly set off after him clutching Podge tightly.

It didn't take long to catch him up. Jack was standing motionless in the garden pointing at something strange. Holly was just about to prod him to get out of the way when she saw what had made him stop.

Before Holly knew it, she too was motionless, and began to point at the strange something. It was the most curious creature she had ever seen.

The Sorx

The creature was facing the garden wall behind the Clock Tree, and didn't know that Holly and Jack were watching.

It appeared to be in a very agitated state, tapping the toes on all 3 of its feet on the ground. Over its shoulder was a satchel and, just above its head, a beautiful rainbow soared into the sky. But there was something very peculiar about the rainbow, the colours were the wrong way round, they went violet, indigo, blue, green, yellow, orange and red, from the top of the arc to the bottom.

The creature was shouting at the wall, '2-7-3! 2-7-3!'

It kept repeating this in a high-pitched voice, each time thumping the wall with the end of a short twisted stick it was holding in its right hand. Its voice got higher and more panic stricken as nothing happening.

In desperation, it screamed, '2-7-3!' at the top of its voice and hurled the stick at the wall. One end crashed into it. There was an enormous cracking sound, and the stick fell to the ground.

Suddenly, a stone in the wall began to move, then another and another. Holly gasped as the stone courses in the wall slid apart like opening interlocked fingers, to reveal what seemed to be a long dark tunnel.

The sound of Holly's gasp made the creature quite literally jump. When it landed, it spun round on one of its feet and stared at them. Jack and Holly stared back, while slowly lowering their arms.

'What? What are you?' stuttered Jack.

With its left hand, the creature grabbed its twisted stick from the ground, and pointed it straight at Jack as if it was about to fire it at him.

Raising itself to its full height, it proudly answered, 'I'm a Sorx, and I know what you are. You're a Hubee!'

Jack and Holly were bewildered. They turned towards each other at exactly the same time.

'Is this a dream?' asked Holly.

Jack was just about to say, 'No,' when the creature squeaked at the top of its voice, 'I hate Hubees, Hubees are bad news, bad news!'

The Sorx was small, not tiny, but small. It was covered in a thick mixture of brown, black, white and yellow hair. It was about a metre tall. It had great big feet, 3 of them, one at the bottom of each of its 3 legs, which were spread out like a tripod. Each foot had a different number of toes. One had 2, one had 7 and one had 3.

It had extremely knobbly knees and a well-rounded bottom. Above this, a slim waist opened out into a broad chest and wide shoulders with an arm at each end. These both hung down as far as the knobbly knees, or would have done if one of them was not been being used to raise the twisted stick towards Jack and Holly.

At the end of each arm was a big hand with 7 long fingers and a thumb. Those on the hand holding the stick were wrapped around it so much that it appeared to be joined to the arm by a mass of plump hairy caterpillars. Half-way along each arm was a knobbly elbow.

It had a long nose, which curved towards the ground. This had a pointed end and 2 very hairy nostrils. Below this was a wide mouth with a pair of squidgy lips, surrounding 2 rows of flat and pointed teeth. Under the mouth was a chin, or rather 2 chins, with the lower one jutting out further than the upper one.

The Sorx had 2 very large round eyes, one purple and one yellow, with long eyelashes that touched when it blinked. Over each eye were 2 very hairy eye-brows. Above these, was a surprisingly smooth forehead, given the amount of hair that it had all over its body.

Finally, on top of its head was a huge mop of hair. This stuck out from underneath a large green floppy hat with a big silver F on it, and cascaded wildly down its back as far as its marshmallow bottom. Sticking up through slits in its hat were 2 narrow cone-shaped ears. These moved independently like horses ears and, at the moment, were swirling round in a panic.

The Sorx was now extremely agitated and was getting madder by the minute. She had committed the worst sin imaginable, she had been seen by 2 Hubees, and all because the tunnel wall was faulty and had not opened quickly enough.

She looked at the 2 young Hubees. They only had 2 legs; no hair apart from a few pathetic strands on their heads, and both their eyes were the same colour. She felt sick just looking at them.

But she had no time to be sick. She had to face the facts. The Hubees had seen her and she had to do something. Unfortunately, her minds (for she had 2) were racing against each other. The aggressive one, that told her to confront them, and the peaceful one, that told her to make a run for it through the tunnel.

She was a forager, a very prestigious job, and up to this moment she had prided herself on being a very good one. She had even been commended by the forager-in-chief (a rare honour).

'You've done well 2:7:3,' the chief had said. 'You'll be after my job one day!'

'No much chance of that now!' she muttered under her breath.

Foragers were the elite, it was they who kept the Sorx supplied with vital stuff that they didn't have in their own world. They wore splendid green floppy hats, each with a silver F-shaped badge on, to show other Sorx how important they were.

Now that she had finally managed to open the tunnel she knew that it would soon close. Because of the shock of meeting the Hubees she had no idea how long it had been open. Her peaceful mind told her to get into the tunnel now.

But her aggressive mind won. She couldn't go back empty handed. That was the second worst sin imaginable. A forager must come back with something useful to hand in at the Treasure Store.

'But what?' she thought.

There was no treasure in this garden. She'd already had a good look around. She remembered her little sister, One:2:One. She'd promised to bring her something from her next forage, but that now seemed impossible. Then she saw Podge.

'Of course, that's it!' she thought. 'That will be ideal for One:2:One. I can hand it in at the Treasure Store and then buy it back. And I'll get a discount for finding it!'

She was a very greedy Sorx.

But there was no time to lose. Even as she was thinking, the tunnel wall was beginning to vibrate gently as if it was about to close. This made her panic even more, but finally her training kicked in.

'What did it say in the Panic Section of the Training Manual? Oh yes, when in doubt show your smile,' she remembered.

Opening her mouth she revealed 2 rows of brilliant white flat and pointy teeth, which shone like stars. These lit up Holly and Jack like searchlights and had a very odd effect on them.

Without thinking, they began to smile back and their teeth began to glow a lovely white light. Just like a yawn, the Sorx smile was infectious, and soon they were smiling as broadly as she was.

They were now both in a Sorx Trance.

2:7:3 put her stick in her satchel and reached out to Holly with her left hand, smiling all the time. Holly began to raise her left hand and Podge towards her. Jack stood motionless, still locked by the Sorx's smile.

The Sorx shuffled closer to Holly. Reaching forward she wrapped her plump hairy fingers around Holly's hand and tickled her wrist. Holly shivered and released her grip on Podge.

2:7:3 slipped Podge out of Holly's hand.

Keeping her teeth firmly pointing towards Holly and Jack, she began to step quietly backwards towards the tunnel. She was only a few steps from the entrance when a very loud rumbling noise from behind her made her jump. She turned her head towards it. The entrance was closing.

But now the beam was broken, and Holly and Jack began to come out of their trances. Holly reacted quicker and, looking down, saw that her hand was empty.

'Where's Podge?' she thought, in a panic.

The Sorx looked back and saw that Holly was awake. She dashed headlong towards the closing gap, waving her arms to help her move. Holly saw that she was carrying Podge.

'Podge!' she screamed, and ran after the Sorx.

This sudden commotion awoke Jack from his trance. He'd seen what had happened, but hadn't been able to move. All that changed in an instant. Quick as a flash he sprinted after Holly and the Sorx.

The entrance was closing quickly. The Sorx got there first and let out a high-pitched whistle. The odd rainbow flashed out of the sky and slithered into her satchel. She rammed Podge in beside it and dived into the tunnel. Holly was still a few steps away from the entrance.

Seeing this, Jack shouted, 'Stop Holly! Don't go in! Stop! You can get another Podge! Stop!'

'There's only one Podge! I can't leave her!' shouted Holly. 'She's my best friend of all!' and crashed in after the Sorx.

'Don't Holly! Stop! Come back!' shouted Jack, as the layers of stones moved closer together.

Jack reached the wall and knew he had to help Holly. Without thinking he forced himself through the narrowing gap. Almost through, he felt the walls tightening on his wellies making him fall to the ground just inside the tunnel. He grabbed the tops of his wellies and tugged hard.

His wellies and feet came through with a loud popping noise, as the layers of stone crashed together like thunder. He was lying on the tunnel floor inside the tunnel. There was no light anywhere but there was a faint sound, the sound of running water.

The tunnel

Inside the tunnel, Jack scrambled to his knees and looked around. At first he could only see darkness, but as his eyes adjusted he could make out a very faint orange glow. He reached towards it nervously with his right hand and touched it. It seemed to be a flower.

Looking further in the distance, he could see more faint orange glows on both sides of the tunnel. The ones near to him were beginning to fade. He stood up and held his arms above him feeling for the top of the tunnel. He felt nothing so he set off, slowly following the orange glows.

Up ahead, Holly was running as fast as she could after the Sorx. Like Jack, she was also following the glows. But she could also hear the sound of the Sorx running. It sounded like a steam train: da-da-da-dum, da-da-da-dum, da-da-da-dum.

She could also see a brighter white light, not far ahead, bouncing around the flat floor and curved ceiling of the tunnel.

Soon the floor rose and fell as it crossed a bridge. Under the bridge was the sound of running water, and there was a horrible stink in the air.

The Sorx was getting tired. Clutching Podge in her left hand, she was also running as fast as she could. But she wasn't very fit. It also didn't help that she had to smile all the time to use her teeth as a torch; this was sapping her strength.

Her teeth were causing the bouncing white light that Holly could see, and also making the flowers along both sides of the tunnel glow orange.

'I wish those Lion's Teeth would stop smiling,' thought 2:7:3.

Back down the tunnel, Jack was moving quicker, guided by the orange glows. His eyes had now fully adjusted, and he could see the glows quite easily. As he ran, the sound of running water grew louder. He soon reached the bridge and gasped at the horrible smell coming from underneath.

Crossing the bridge he began to notice the bouncing light. He could just make out Holly and the Sorx silhouetted against the white beams.

Holly was closing on the Sorx. This spurred her on. There was light at the end of the tunnel, and she could just make out a big gate at the entrance.

The Sorx was shattered. She was slowing down with every stride, but was now very close to the gate. This was the Rodley Bottoms Portcullis. It was always kept locked. Unlike Hubee locks, it had 5 keyholes.

The Sorx reached the gate, put Podge on the ground, and grabbed the lock with her right hand. To open it she had put her right thumb and the correct fingers of her right hand into the holes. She had done this many times before and knew exactly what to do.

Unwinding her fingers from each other, she stuck her left thumb and the ends of the 2nd, 3rd, 5th and 7th fingers of her left hand into the 5 keyholes. Nothing happened. She pulled them out and tried again. Still nothing happened.

'Open, please open!' she screamed, in panic.

The lock didn't open.

She looked at the lock, and then looked at her fingers.

'I'm using the wrong hand!' she screamed. 'How stupid I am!'

Quickly changing hands, she pushed her right thumb and the ends of the 2nd, 3rd, 5th and 7th fingers of her right hand into the 5 keyholes. The lock sprang open. The portcullis rumbled into motion and rose quickly.

The Sorx dashed through, and almost immediately the gate crashed down and the lock snapped shut. She was out of the tunnel.

She let out a big sigh of relief and started to walk away from the gate. But something was missing, what was it?

'Oh no!' she thought. 'I've left my treasure in the tunnel!'

She spun round and ran back to the tunnel. There on the floor just inside the portcullis was Podge, and just behind her came Holly.

2:7:3 fell to the floor in front of the portcullis and reached inside through one of the gaps. Her fingers wrapped round Podge's body just as Holly grabbed one of Podge's legs. They both held on firmly.

The Sorx looked up at Holly and smiled, trying to put her in a trance. But Holly just looked at Podge. 2:7:3 pulled as hard as she could. Holly held on tightly.

But poor Podge was in trouble. The leg Holly was pulling was starting to come away from her body, stitch by stitch. Holly saw this and couldn't bear to think of Podge losing a leg, she loved her too much.

She let go.

The Sorx pulled Podge through the bars, waved cheekily at Holly, and ran away from the tunnel.

'Podge! Podge! Podge!' screamed Holly, bursting into tears

and falling to her knees just as Jack arrived at the gate. He had seen what had happened and knelt down beside her.

'I had to let her go,' sobbed Holly. 'Her leg was starting to tear. I didn't want it to come off. We must get her back. I can't bear to think of her all alone in this strange place.'

At that moment Jack realised how much Holly loved Podge. He had to help her get Podge back.

'Don't worry,' said Jack. 'We'll get her back. I promise.'

'Thank you,' sobbed Holly. 'But how?'

'There's always a way,' said Jack, who loved a challenge.

He stood up and inspected the portcullis lock. It had 5 keyholes and was fastened tight. Just below the keyholes was a narrow slit running the full width of the lock. Above the slit was an arrow pointing to the right, and below it an arrow pointing to the left.

Grasping the top of the lock in one hand and the bottom of the lock in the other, he pulled them in the opposite directions. The bottom of the lock slid open and a key fell out.

Jack gasped.

'Look Holly!' he said. 'It's a key!'

Jack looked at the key and the lock, but couldn't see where the key should go. It was a strange key. It looked like the end of a finger and it had number 3 stamped on one side of it. Jack looked at the lock again. He brushed some dust off it, and noticed that under the middle keyhole there was a tiny number 3.

Holding the key, Jack pushed its finger end into the middle keyhole. Nothing happened. He took the key out and looked at it, turning it over in his hand. On the other side was a number 5.

He looked at the lock again. He brushed more dust off, and under the keyhole furthest to the right he felt a slight bump. He rubbed it hard to reveal a small number 5. He rubbed under the other keyholes. None of them had any numbers.

He pushed the finger key into keyhole 3, pulled it out, and pushed it into keyhole 5. Nothing happened. He tried again. Nothing happened.

Holly had been watching him.

'Try it the other way round, 5 then 3,' she said.

He pushed the finger key into keyhole 5, then into keyhole 3. The lock sprang open and the portcullis shot upwards.

'You must have to use the big number, 53, not thirty-five,' shouted Holly as she rushed out of the tunnel.

Jack, feeling proud that he had opened the lock, watched her leave. The portcullis crashed down behind her and the lock snapped shut. She was outside, he was inside! Jack was in shock!

'Try it again Jack!' shouted Holly, from outside the tunnel.

Jack pushed the key into 5 then into 3. The lock and gate both opened.

'Quick! Get out!' screamed Holly.

Jack grabbed the key and dashed out of the tunnel. The portcullis crashed down and the lock snapped shut. They were out but that was all they were. They didn't know where they were, and they didn't know where they were going.

'What do we do now?' asked Holly.

'We go and get Podge back!' said Jack, boldly.

He looked at the finger key.

'I think I'll keep this,' he said to himself. 'It might be useful.'

He put the key into the back pocket of his shorts and walked over to Holly, who was pointing down a road heading into a forest.

'The Sorx went that way,' she said. 'I wonder where it goes.'

'To SǪorxville, according to that signpost,' said Jack, pointing away from the tunnel entrance.

Not far from the entrance was a small house that looked like a tree. It seemed to be a guardhouse, but there were no guards.

Near the guardhouse was a large wooden signpost set in a clearing where several roads met. It was painted white and had 5 white direction signs with neat black lettering. One read:

RODLEY BOTTOMS TUNNEL 53p, 163d.

This pointed directly into the tunnel they had just escaped from. 2 others pointed along roads leading into some woods on the right. These read:

WOODPECKER WOODS TUNNEL 443p, 1327d.
FARSLEY TUNNEL 661p, 1993d.

2 others pointed along a road leading towards high ground. These read:

BRAMLEY TUNNEL 2347p, 7039d.
QŜORXVILLE 2213p, 6637d.

On one of these, the 'S' had been crossed out with red paint and replaced by a badly drawn red 'Q'.

The last sign pointed along the road that 2:7:3 had taken. It read:

S**Q**ORXVILLE 1109p, 3323d.

Here, the 'Q' had been crossed out with red paint and replaced with a badly drawn red 'S'.

'I wonder why the "Q" and "S" have been crossed out, and I wonder what "p" and "d" mean?' asked Holly.

'I don't know,' said Jack. 'But we'd better get going if we are to find Podge, and it looks as though we will have to walk 1109p or 3323d to get there.'

So, keeping close together, they set off on the road to S**Q**orxville.

Into the forest

At first the road was straight, but soon it began to twist and turn as it entered a deep, dark forest of very tall trees. Holly and Jack were frightened and moved forward very carefully, not saying a word. Holly was in front looking forward and Jack was just behind, often turning back to see if anyone or anything was following them.

'The Sorx must be a long way away by now,' said Jack, breaking the silence.

'Yes, and so is Podge,' sobbed Holly, although she was now more angry than sad.

'We must find her and get her back,' she said, gritting her teeth.

'We will,' said Jack, positively. 'We'll definitely get her back.'

They were now right in amongst the trees; lots of them, close together. Most were high and mighty, with really gnarled tall trunks topped with branches reaching sideways and upwards. These locked together like a huge net. The wind in the tree tops made them sway and rub against each other. They made an eerie swooshing sound.

The sky only peeped out occasionally through small gaps; it was a lovely shade of blue. As they went deeper in the forest, however, it began to change from blue to brown. There was also a stink in the air, just like the one from the river they had crossed in the tunnel.

'Can you smell that Jack?' asked Holly. 'And did you smell it in the tunnel?'

'Yes, I can and yes, I did. I thought it was you!' Jack said, laughing a few steps behind her.

Holly picked up a big piece of bark and threw it at Jack, hitting him right in the middle of his chest.

'Ooowww!' yelled Jack.

'No more than you deserve!' said Holly, pleased that she hadn't missed him.

Jack leant over and picked up an even bigger piece of bark. He was just about to throw it when Holly said, 'Sshh! Listen!', holding a finger to her lips.

Above the sound of the rustling branches, they heard a noise. They grabbed each other, jumped sideways into a nearby straggly bush, and lay flat on the ground behind it. The sound got louder.

Holly recognised it at once: da-da-da-dum, da-da-da-dum, da-da-da-dum. It was a Sorx.

Peeping through the bush they could see a Sorx scampering up the road using its feet and hands. Its feet were making the da noises, and it was using its long fingers on both hands at the same time to push itself forward. These made the dum sound.

Like the other Sorx, it was wearing a large green floppy hat with a silver F-shaped badge on. Its ears were sticking up through the hat and twitching as it moved along the road. Over its shoulder was a satchel with a stick protruding from it.

The Sorx seemed to be in a hurry. It shot passed them leaving a trail of fresh multi-toed footprints and long finger marks. Jack and Holly waited for a while until the sound disappeared, then crept back onto the road.

'That was close,' said Holly.

'It sure was,' said Jack. 'We'd better keep going, but let's keep our eyes open.'

'And our ears,' said Holly.

They crept forward along the road keeping their eyes and ears open, and their mouths shut. They trudged on becoming more and more worried. They seemed to be getting nowhere.

'Let's just stop and have a think,' said Jack.

'OK,' said Holly, very relieved to do so.

They moved away from the road and sat down on a large bank of moss next to a small stream, resting their backs against a tree, and hiding behind a big clump of ferns.

'We must be nearly somewhere,' said Jack, trying to raise their spirits. 'It's just that we don't know where! And somewhere is better than nowhere!'

They both laughed, then suddenly stopped. They could hear a rustling sound.

'What was that?' whispered Holly.

'I don't know,' said Jack. 'But it came from over there.'

He pointed to some ferns on their right.

They looked over and just caught sight of a brown furry creature. It was mainly hidden by the ferns, and they couldn't see its face or how big it was. It didn't move.

All of a sudden a soft gentle voice said, 'I love you!'

'Did you hear that?' exclaimed Holly. 'Something loves us!'

The voice spoke again, 'I really love you!'

Then without warning the brown furry creature vanished, and a very large bird-shaped shadow passed over the ferns. The shadow disappeared then returned. They held their breath and held each other.

Through a gap in the ferns they could see a huge bird circling over them. It was bright green with a white tail and very large yellow wings, big black claws, piercing blue eyes and a long pointed red beak. It made no sound at all. It swooped low, gliding silently through the air. Its black claws brushed the top of the ferns. Then with a huge swish of its wings, it landed on a branch no more than half a metre away from them. It looked around and began to preen itself, pulling out one or 2 small yellow feathers from its wings, letting them float away in the air.

Jack and Holly were scared stiff and kept as silent and as still as they could. The bird seemed to stay on the branch forever. It continued to preen then stopped, raised its tail, and fired a huge stream of bright-yellow poo out of its bottom. This flew into the air and hit the ferns next to Jack, splashing his face. Biting his lip tightly, he managed to stop himself from shouting.

Satisfied that it had had a good poo, the bird launched itself into the air, flapping its huge wings so fiercely that the ferns protecting them waved like flags in a gale. Just as quickly as it had arrived, it was gone.

They held onto each other for some time before Jack shouted, 'Aaaargggh!', finally able to speak safely as he started to wipe bright-yellow poo off his head.

'What was that?' said Holly, in a very shaky voice.

'I've no idea,' said Jack, angrily. 'But it sure knows how to poo, my face is covered in it. It stinks!'

'It certainly does!' said Holly, as the slimy yellow poo ran down Jack's face. 'You'd better wash it off. Come on. I'll help you.'

The stream was right next to them. Jack pushed his face into it, pulled it out and shook his head. Bits of poo flew everywhere. Holly grabbed handfuls of water and threw them at him. She quite enjoyed it. When most of the poo had gone, Jack reached out, grabbed a couple of ferns and used them to dry his face.

'How do I look?' he asked Holly.

'Not too bad,' said Holly, thinking about what had just happened and trying not to laugh.

She picked a fern and brushed away a few remaining globs of poo and water from his face.

'There!' she said. 'You'll do. But wasn't that bird was amazing! And what was it that said "I love you"?'

'I've no idea,' said Jack. 'But this is a very strange place. We've got to find somewhere safe before that bird comes back.'

Jack sighed deeply and raised his head above the tops of the ferns. He leant back against the trunk of the tree, and looked upwards towards the brown sky above the road snaking ahead.

'But what is that just sticking up through a gap in the tree tops?' he wondered. 'It looks like a chimney!'

'Holly!' exclaimed Jack, pointing to the gap. 'Look over there, it's a chimney!'

Holly looked. Sure enough it was a chimney, shaped like a letter T, appearing black against the brown sky. It seemed to be coming out of the top of a tree.

'Come on, let's go and look,' said Jack.

'Oh!' said Holly. 'But we may get into more trouble. What if a Sorx lives there? I'm scared!'

'So am I,' said Jack. 'But we need to get off this road in case a Sorx sees us. That could be somewhere we can hide and rest.

We need to do something, and we need to do it now!'

'I suppose so,' said Holly, reluctantly.

So, slowly, and even more carefully, they made their way along the road towards the chimney. There was no sign of any Sorxes.

The Lonely Sweet Shop

A short distance ahead was a clearing in the forest, and on the edge of it was a very odd looking tree. It was similar in height to all the other trees, but had an enormous thick trunk and a great big knobbly round top. It looked like a huge green cauliflower on top of a giant stick of brown celery.

As they crept nearer they could see that it was not a tree, but a house. It had windows and a very tall door. Above the door was a faded pale-pink and sky-blue sign hanging at a crazy angle. It had flaking white lettering on it which read:

THE LONELY SWEET SHOP.

From their position, they could see four windows in the vast trunk and 2 larger windows in the big cauliflower on top. This had a chimney with a big letter T on its end sticking out of it at a crazy angle with smoke coming out of both sides of the T.

The house was very, very high and its trunk formed a great big circular shape. It was made out of dark brown wood and covered in bark. It looked as though the outer layers of lots of trees had been sliced off, and then joined together to form the trunk.

The door was much higher than it was wide, with straight sides and a curved top. There were big hinges down one side, and a very big handle about a third of the way up on the other side. This presented a great problem since the door was so tall that only a giant could reach the handle.

Having now seen 2 Sorxes, Jack and Holly could not imagine them opening the door with this handle, unless they used a very long ladder. However, at the bottom of the big door, was another door in exactly the same style as the big one, with hinges and a handle, but much smaller. A Sorx could easily get into the house through this. There seemed to be a small sign hanging on it.

Jack and Holly crept up to the side of the house and hid behind a big clump of giant orange flowers.

'What shall we do?' asked Jack. 'It looks as though there is something living there, but we could do with somewhere to hide and make some plans.'

'Yes,' said Holly. 'We could. But if we go in we may get caught. What shall we do?'

As they were pondering this, their minds were made up for them as the sound of, da-da-da-dum, da-da-da-dum, da-da-da-dum, came drifting through the air.

Heading down the road in the distance towards them was a Sorx. It hadn't yet seen them, but it was very likely that it would as the orange flowers weren't hiding them very well. To make matters worse, it was beginning to get dark, and the Sorx was smiling to illuminate the road.

Like the first Sorx they'd seen, it had a floppy green hat on and was carrying a satchel holding a stick. As it got nearer, the flowers started to glow, just as they had done in the tunnel. The light from them was shining on Jack and Holly, making them much easier to see.

'Come on Holly,' whispered Jack. 'Don't look at the Sorx. We've got to get off this road. The only place to go is into this tree house.'

'OK,' said Holly, trying hard not to look at the Sorx shining teeth.

Sliding carefully around the trunk, keeping low, they edged towards the little door. There was indeed a sign. It was hung on a rusty nail in the middle of the door. It read:

A MONSTER LIVES HERE!
DO NOT ENTER – EVER!

There was a big lock on the door just below the handle, like the one on the tunnel portcullis.

'What shall we do?' whispered Holly.

The da-da-da-dum, da-da-da-dum, da-da-da-dum rhythm grew louder and louder by the second.

'We've got no choice,' Jack whispered back, getting to the lock first.

He saw immediately that it was like the other lock. Grabbing it with both hands, he slid the top half away from the bottom half and out fell a finger key. He picked it up, and turned it over in his hand. There was a 3 on one side and a 2 on the other.

'Thirty-two or 23?' he thought to himself. 'Use the larger number.'

He pushed the key into keyhole 3, then into keyhole 2. Nothing happened.

'I've done it the wrong way round again,' he said, panicking.

He pulled the key out of keyhole 3, pushed it into keyhole 2, quickly pulled it out and stuck it in into keyhole 3. The lock sprang open, falling onto the ground. The finger key fell out beside it.

'Yeesss!' he gasped.

He grabbed the door handle, turned it and pushed. Nothing happened. He pushed again. Still nothing.

'Help me Holly!' said Jack, trying not to shout.

Da-da-da-dum, da-da-da-dum, da-da-da-dum, got nearer.

Holly stepped back and gave the door an almighty kick. It moved a tiny bit.

Da-da-da-dum, da-da-da-dum, da-da-da-dum, got even nearer.

Pushing and kicking together, the door suddenly flew open and they tumbled inside, Holly falling on top of Jack. The sign on the door fell off, and made a loud crashing sound on the ground outside. They scrambled onto their knees, put their hands on the inside of the open door, and pushed as hard as they could. It moved quickly then stuck, slightly open. They sat behind it pressing their backs against it, pushing even harder, trying to close it.

From the road outside they heard a loud, da-da-da-dum, then a second, da-da-da-dum, even louder. Then there was silence, which was soon broken by the sound of a Sorx breathing heavily. Jack and Holly looked at each other and made the shushing sign. They sat quite still pushing hard against the door.

The Sorx had seen that the little door was slightly open and had dadumed over to it.

'That shouldn't be open,' he said to himself. 'No-one is allowed in there. Why has the sign fallen off? Why is the lock on the ground?'

He curled his long fingers round the little door handle making it completely disappear, and pushed. Nothing happened. He kicked it hard 3 times, once with each foot. Jack and Holly felt the kicks but they didn't move and, more importantly, neither did the door.

'Humph!' said the Sorx. 'That's never going to open. I'd better close it.'

He pulled the door handle hard, but the door wouldn't close. Looking down, he saw that a pile of soil was stopping it. He reached down with his long fingers and moved the soil. After 3 big pulls the door closed. He picked up the sign and hung it back on its rusty nail. He saw the lock with its finger key on the ground. Thinking it was broken, he reached into his satchel and pulled out another lock. A forager always carries spare locks in case of an emergency. He fitted it in place, and snapped it shut.

'There, that should do it,' he said, picking up the key and the broken lock and putting them in his satchel. 'I'd better get going. I've got foraging to do!'

Satisfied that all was well, he returned to the road. Soon, the da-da-da-dum rhythm began again, then slowly faded into the distance, as he headed towards the Rodley Bottoms Tunnel.

Back in the house, Jack and Holly looked at each other and breathed a huge sigh of relief. They were safe for now, or so they thought.

The Qorx

Holly and Jack slowly stood up, dusted themselves down and looked around. The light coming through the windows was beginning to fade, but there was enough for them to see. The floor was made of soil and marked with lots of dusty footprints. There seemed to be only one enormous room, which was roughly circular in shape.

In the middle of the room was a large stove with a chimney going up through the ceiling. This was a long way above them; much higher than the big door. There was a faint red glow from the stove, and the room felt warm.

On the curving wall to the left of the big door were shelves running from the floor almost to the ceiling, with a large ladder leaning against them. Most of the shelves were filled with big glass jars. They were full of what looked like sweets. On other shelves there were piles and rolls of paper and very large books. In front of the wall was a long wooden counter.

Beside the curving wall to the right of the big door there was a huge spiral staircase, which ran up through the ceiling to the floor above.

In front of the stove were 2 chairs and a table. Jack and Holly walked over to the stove. They picked up the chairs and sat down exhausted, enjoying the warmth from the glowing fire.

'Why did 23 work, when thirty-two didn't?' asked Jack

'There seems to be no pattern to those finger keys.'

'I don't know,' said Holly. 'But what are we going to do now? We don't even know where we are.'

'I do!' said a deep voice from behind the stove.

Holly and Jack jumped up and dashed to the other side of the stove. They gasped when they saw a huge metal cage stretching up as far as the ceiling. The cage had thick horizontal and vertical bars in a square pattern such that each square was only big enough to put your head through.

In the front part was a caged door about the same size as the big door to the house, but it didn't go right down to the floor. There was a gap at the bottom less than a metre high. Fastened to the cage on the right-hand side of its door was a long metal ladder leading up to a big handle, which was held in position by a large padlock.

In the cage was a very high table, a very high chair and a huge bed with very high legs.

Sat on the chair, was a very high creature that looked nothing like a Sorx.

Holly and Jack looked at each other completely shocked, and then looked at the creature.

'Who are you?' Holly asked very nervously.

The creature looked down towards them from its lofty position and folded its 3 arms together.

'I'm a Qorx,' it said. 'And I know what you are. You're a Hubee. I haven't seen one of your kind for a tumble of time. Welcome to Qorxville in Highlow. Or I suppose I should say SQorxville these days.'

Holly and Jack looked at the Qorx. For the second time that day, they couldn't believe what they were looking at. The

Qorx was enormous. Even sitting there in its cage it towered over them.

'If it stood up, I don't think I'd be able to see the top of it,' thought Jack to himself.

And, as if to prove Jack right, the Qorx stood up. Its top almost touched the ceiling way up above.

The Qorx was at least ten metres tall. Unlike the Sorx, which had 3 legs and 2 arms, the Qorx had 2 legs and 3 arms. Starting at floor level, it had 2 feet, each with 7 large rectangular toes, all about the same size. Coming out of each toe was something that looked like a smooth snake, which ran down the front of the toe and entered into the ground, as if to anchor it in place.

Its legs were very long and looked like tree trunks. There was a knee half way up each leg.

The legs joined into a body shape that was also like a tree trunk. This stretched upwards, getting wider and deeper until it reached a triangular shape, with one of the corners pointing outwards. Its neck and head rose from the middle of the triangle. From the corners of the triangle sprouted 3 sturdy arms: one in the middle, one on the right and one of the left. Each of these had an elbow.

At the end of each arm was a hand with six long fingers and a thumb. The Qorx was opening and closing these like human fingers as it stood looking at Jack and Holly. It then bent lower to look more closely at the 2 Hubees.

Holly and Jack could now see the upper part of the Qorx more clearly. On top of its neck was its head. This looked like a huge upside-down pineapple out of which had been carved 2 brown eyes. It had a very wide mouth and gentle lips that were formed into the shape of a smile. Inside its mouth were 2 rows of brown teeth.

Growing out of each side of its head were 3 giant leaves, one above the other. Between its eyes and its mouth was a very long nose, which stuck straight out and ended in a point. From the top of its head sprouted dozens of thin branches, each covered with small leaves, some green and some brown.

But the most unusual thing about the Qorx was that it seemed to be entirely made of wood, rough wood, like bark on an old tree.

Despite its sheer size and strangeness, it looked very kind and gentle.

The Qorx continued to lean forward. It pushed its nose through the bars of the cage until its end was now almost touching Holly's head. The nose sniffed, and Holly saw that, on its end, there was a little branch with a leaf on.

The Qorx looked Holly up and down, sniffing all the time, and then turned to Jack and sniffed him.

'I'd forgotten how Hubees smell,' it said, sniffing even more. 'You smell like rosemary.'

'That's funny,' Holly exclaimed. 'My mum is called Rosemary!'

'That doesn't surprise me,' said the Qorx. 'Hubee children often smell like their mothers.'

'How did you get here?' asked the Qorx.

'It's a long story,' said Jack.

'That's good,' said the Qorx. 'I love long stories. Please go and get the 2 small chairs from the other side of the stove and bring them here.'

Holly and Jack went to get the chairs.

By the time they got back, the Qorx had sat down on its very high chair.

'Come in under the gate and bring the chairs with you,' it said.

They bent down and scrambled under the gate dragging the chairs behind them.

'Sit in them, and I'll lift you up,' said the Qorx, leaning forward on its chair.

Holly and Jack sat in their chairs.

The Qorx reached down and picked up Jack's chair in its left hand and Holly's in its right hand. They held on tight as they and their chairs were raised high into the air, and carefully lowered onto the top of the table.

Sitting there, the floor seemed a long way down.

On the table were 3 large wooden bottles. 2 had corks in the top. The cork for the third one was lying next to its bottle.

The Qorx picked up the cork less one with its middle hand, put it to its mouth and took a big swig. It put the bottle back down on the table, then looked at Jack and Holly.

'Would you like a drink?' it asked.

'Oh yes please,' said Holly.

'Yes, I would,' said Jack.

Reaching across, it picked up the 2 corked bottles with its right and left hands.

'Here,' it said. 'You can drink this.'

It handed each of them a bottle.

'What is it?' asked Holly.

'It's Perx,' said the Qorx. 'It's made from herbs mixed with fresh stream water. I hope you enjoy it.'

The bottles were small for a Qorx, but very large for a Hubee.

They had difficulty holding them.

Holly carefully held her bottle against her body with one hand, slowly pulled out the cork with the other and dropped it onto the table. Then holding onto the bottle with both hands, she lifted it to her lips and had a drink.

'That's great!' she exclaimed. 'Try some Jack!'

Jack held onto his bottle with both hands. He pulled out the cork with his teeth, spitting it onto the table. He took a very large swig, leant back, and burped very loudly.

'Lovely!' he said.

'Jack!' shouted Holly, trying hard not to burp herself. 'Don't be so rude!'

'Pardon me!' he said. 'Sorry.'

'There's no need to be sorry,' said the Qorx. 'It has that effect on me as well!'

It laughed a huge laugh, like a happy foghorn, then burped. It leant forward, placing its 3 forearms on the table in front of where they were sitting. They looked like old tree trunks.

'OK,' said the Qorx, looking straight at them. 'Please tell me your tale. I'm all ears.'

At that point the 3 giant leaves on each side of its head swung outwards and cupped themselves towards Jack and Holly.

They were its ears.

Lion's Teeth

So Jack and Holly told the Qorx about everything that had happened that day. While they were telling their tale, the Qorx would occasionally stop them and explain what things meant and why they had happened.

It told them that rainbows were made in Highlow for Hubees to enjoy after rain.

'But aren't rainbows formed when the sun's light passes through rain drops?' asked Jack, who loved studying science.

'Well, that's what Hubees think. But in fact we made them!' said the Qorx, laughing. 'We used to make them in the Rainbow Factory in Qorxville and take them through our tunnels into your land.'

It paused and scratched its nose.

'But the Sorx took the factory from us and now they make rainbows,' it continued. 'They carry them in their satchels, and release them in the Hubee lands. But they misuse them. While Hubees are looking at them, the Sorx steal things.'

'Shouldn't that be Sorxes?' asked Jack.

'What do you mean?' asked the Qorx.

'Well you said, "The Sorx steal things",' said Jack. 'Shouldn't you have said, "The Sorxes steal things"?'

'No,' said the Qorx. 'Sorx is correct. You see the words Sorx and Qorx are used if there is one of them or lots of them. So we say, "One Sorx, 2 Sorx, 3 Sorx, one Qorx, 2 Qorx, 3 Qorx", and so on. I think you do the same in Hubeeland with some of your names for animals. Don't you say, "One sheep, 2 sheep, 3 sheep", for example?'

'Oh yes, we do,' said Jack.

'And we have a lot more words like that,' said the Qorx. 'Usually ending in the letter x.'

'So the Sorx took the Rainbow Factory from us,' continued the Qorx. 'But we knew that they were going to do that, so before they did we changed the rainbow-making machines so that the colours were reversed.'

'Oh!' said Holly. 'The rainbow that the Sorx had in our garden was like that.'

'Yes, and they never realised what we had done,' said the Qorx. 'The machines can't be changed back so now all the rainbows they make at the Rainbow Factory are wrong ones. We call them wobniars!'

It laughed its foghorn laugh then continued, 'If you ever see a wobniar you know that there is a Sorx close by foraging and probably stealing things. If you ever see a rainbow you know that a Qorx has put it there to cheer you up. We now make them at a new factory in Woodpecker Woods. If we make too many we release a double rainbow.'

'That's amazing!' said Jack.

The Qorx then explained that the giant flowers they had seen were called Lion's Teeth, because their petals look like them.

'They look like our Dandelions,' said Jack. 'Only much bigger.'

'Yes, they are related to each other,' said the Qorx. 'I think Dandelion means Lion's Teeth in one of your Hubee languages.

And because any teeth light up when a Sorx smiles at them, Lion's Teeth will start glowing. When the smile stops their glow fades away.'

It tweaked the branch on the end of its nose.

'But you mustn't look at a Sorx when it smiles at you,' it said, firmly. 'The Sorx smile is dangerous. They use their smiles as weapons to disarm their enemies. That's why you went into a trance.'

'Yes, we realised that,' said Holly. 'We try not to look at them now when they are smiling but it can be difficult not to.'

'I know,' said the Qorx. 'Their smiles are extremely hypnotic.'

When Jack mentioned the finger key the Qorx nodded.

'Ah yes, the finger keys,' it said. 'These are emergency keys fitted to all Sorx locks in case they forget the finger code. But they only work with prime numbers.'

Prime numbers

'Prime numbers are very important to the Sorx,' said the Qorx. 'Many of their activities are based on them.'

It paused and stroked its chin.

'For example, when a finger key is used it must be in the form of a prime number,' it continued. 'That's why 51 and 23 worked, and fifteen and thirty-two didn't. And when your Sorx opened the lock, it would have put its right thumb and the 2nd, 3rd, 5th and 7th fingers of its right hand into the 5 keyholes. They are its prime number fingers.'

Holly had heard of prime numbers, but wasn't too sure about them.

'Can you remind me what a prime number is please?' she asked.

'Yes,' said the Qorx. 'A prime number is a number bigger than one, which can only be divided by the number one and itself. For example, number 7 is a prime number because only the numbers one and 7 can divide into it.'

'So number four isn't a prime number is it?' asked Holly.

'That's right,' said the Qorx. 'It can be divided by one, 2 and four.'

'So why are prime numbers important?' asked Jack.

'Prime numbers are the building blocks of all numbers,' said the Qorx.

'What do you mean?' asked Jack.

'Well, let's take an example,' said the Qorx. 'Number twelve isn't a prime number because it can be divided by one, 2, 3, four, six and twelve. Any number that isn't a prime number is called a composite number. So number twelve is a composite number.'

'OK,' said Jack.

'But a composite number can be made by multiplying together 2 or more prime numbers,' continued the Qorx. 'And number twelve can be made by multiplying 2 by 2 by 3. Numbers 2 and 3 are prime numbers.'

'And that applies to all numbers?' asked Holly.

'Yes,' said the Qorx. 'Think of a number.'

Holly thought and said, 'Number thirty-nine.'

'OK,' said the Qorx. 'Number thirty-nine is a composite number because it can be divided by one, 3, 13 and thirty-nine. And it can be made by multiplying 13 by 3, both of which are prime numbers.'

'Try another one,' said the Qorx.

'Number one thousand one hundred and twenty-seven,' said Jack, deliberately thinking of a big number to try and catch the Qorx out.

The Qorx thought carefully about this number before speaking.

'That is a composite number,' it said. 'Because it can be divided by one, 7, 23, 49, 161, and one thousand one hundred and twenty-seven. And it can be made by multiplying 23 by 49, or by multiplying 7 by 161. All these four numbers are prime numbers.'

'Wow, you're very good with numbers,' said Jack.

'Thank you,' said the Qorx. 'But I've had a lot of practice working them out while I've been trapped in The Lonely Sweet Shop.'

'So any composite number can be made by multiplying prime numbers,' said Jack.

'Yes, any composite number,' said the Qorx. 'If there were no prime numbers then there would be no numbers at all!'

'So prime numbers really are very important aren't they?' asked Jack.

'Yes, they are!' said the Qorx. 'Can you imagine a world without any numbers?'

Jack and Holly looked at each other and shook their heads.

'No, we can't,' said Holly.

After explaining about prime numbers, the Qorx nodded when they mentioned the stinky river and the signpost, and said it would tell them more about those later. But when Jack mentioned the silent bird, the Qorx drew in its breath.

'Oh!' it said, 'You had a very lucky escape there!'

This frightened Holly.

'What do you mean?' she asked.

Cacawkers and Drongles

The Qorx looked at her and twitched the branch on the end of its nose.

'That was a Cacawker,' it said. 'They are very dangerous. They're the only birds left in Highlow. We used to have so many different types of birds, but the Cacawkers have eaten them all. They are silent in flight; they can hover and seem to come out of nowhere. Cacawkers will eat anything that moves or grows. They rummage around in the undergrowth, in waste bins, and piles of rubbish looking for food.'

Holly shivered.

'They sound horrible,' she said.

'Yes, they are!' said the Qorx. 'They have lived in Highlow longer than any other animal, and they are not scared of anything. They have eaten not only all the birds, but also almost all the animals that used to live here.'

Holly shivered even more.

'So are there some animals left in Highlow?' asked Holly.

'Yes,' said the Qorx. 'The Cacawkers have eaten everything apart from one species, the Drongles, and that is only because they don't like their taste, which of course is good for the Drongles.'

'What are Drongles?' asked Jack.

'Oh, they are very funny and inquisitive creatures who love

life, although this can get them into a lot of trouble,' said the Qorx.

It paused then continued, 'When they meet you, they instantly fall in love with you and always want to be your friend, but this can be rather annoying. It can be difficult to shake them off, because they have such an amazing sense of smell they can always find you even if you are a long way away.

They used to love everyone in Highlow, but now they are very wary of the Sorx since they drove the Qorx out of Qorxville. Drongles and Qorx have always been great friends. The Drongles used to live all over Highlow but now they tend to stay in the forested areas. Because of this they are quite shy, but the voice that you heard saying, "I love you", was definitely a Drongle. I am sure you will meet them again!'

It laughed its foghorn laugh.

'I do hope so,' said Holly. 'They sound very interesting!'

'Indeed they are,' said the Qorx. 'Now where were we? Oh yes, Cacawkers.'

It cleared its throat with a deep booming cough and then continued, 'Cacawkers live in the forest and have been trained by the Sorx to glide around Highlow to find strangers. When they find anyone they suspect, they inspect them to see if they are true Sorx. If they think you are a Sorx, they do an odd Cacawker Ceremony, and let you go.'

It stopped and shook its head then went on, 'If your Cacawker had seen you it would have known you were Hubees, and it would have let out a very loud high-pitched shriek which sounds like, 'Cacaw!' This gives them their name, and is known as the Cacawker Call. The Sorx would have heard it and they would have started hunting for you. Those ferns must have hidden you well. But you said it had a white tail, so it was probably a young Cacawker and it would not be so experienced at finding strangers. Fully grown Cacawkers don't have white tails. Nevertheless, you were very lucky.'

Holly and Jack continued their tale and when they finished the Qorx looked at them in amazement.

'What a day you've had!' it said. 'But tell me? Is there a tree in your garden which has a clock on it?'

'Yes, there is,' said Holly. 'How do you know that?'

'Because I used to live in that tree when I was young!' exclaimed the Qorx. 'I loved that tree. Your mum was always kind to me by watering the flowers around the tree, and I used to drink it! She didn't know she was doing it, of course, because she didn't know I was there!'

It laughed loudly then continued, 'After all your adventures today you must rest. You can stay here tonight and sleep upstairs in my bed. I will sleep down here in my chair.'

'That's very kind of you,' said Holly.

She was beginning to relax now that she had met the Qorx, who seemed to be very nice, and the warmth from the stove was very pleasant.

'But please tell us about Highlow,' she said. 'We have so many questions. We can't understand what is happening, we don't know where we are and we don't know how to get Podge back.'

Highlow history

'OK,' said the Qorx. 'I'll give you a history lesson about Highlow. Before I do, however, I think we should introduce ourselves. What are your names?'

'I'm Holly, and this is my brother Jack,' said Holly. 'We're very pleased to meet you.'

'I'm very pleased to meet you also,' said the Qorx, bowing its head down towards them. 'I'm Hornbeam, a male Qorx.'

'Hello Hornbeam,' said Holly. 'That's a lovely name. Did you choose it yourself?'

'No,' said Hornbeam. 'Every Qorx is given the name of a tree. My mum and dad chose Hornbeam, because it's a beautiful and mighty tree.'

'Just like you!' said Holly.

'Why thank you!' said Hornbeam. 'That's kind of you, but I don't think I'm very beautiful or very mighty.'

He looked at Holly then said, 'And you're named after a tree as well! I do like the holly. It's a very clever tree; it never sheds its leaves. But they are very prickly!'

He laughed his foghorn laugh again.

'Now, are you ready for your lesson?' he asked.

'Yes,' said Jack and Holly at the same time, looking forward to finding out more about the strange world that they had entered through the tunnel.

'OK,' said Hornbeam. 'Here we go! Please feel free to ask questions at any point.'

Hornbeam coughed gently to clear his throat and began to speak, 'You're now in Highlow, which originally consisted of 2 towns, Sorxville and Qorxville, where the Sorx and the Qorx lived. Highlow lies beside Hubeeland. These are joined but can only be entered through tunnels that the Sorx and the Qorx built tangles of time ago.'

'Sorry,' interrupted Jack. 'But what's a tangle of time?'

'Oh, that's a Qorx expression for time, which that means an unknown amount of time,' said Hornbeam. 'We have many expressions like this for time, depending on how long the time is. Going from a long time to a short time, we say, tangle, tumble, tremble, tickle and touch. The Qorx and Sorx don't have the same concept of time as Hubees do. Time to us is based on solar and lunar periods. We use Enzor time, Cora and Turq time, Lightness and Darkness. We don't measure it using clocks or watches like you do. But we do have continuums and solars.'

'What are Enzor, Cora and Turq?' asked Holly.

'And what is a continuum and a solar?' asked Jack.

'Oh sorry!' said Hornbeam. 'Forgive me. I forget that you cannot speak Qorxish.'

He laughed then continued, 'Most of our words are the same as Hubeeish. That's what we call your language. But we do have many words of our own. Enzor is the name of our sun, and Cora and Turq are our 2 moons. Continuum is our word for what you call a year and solar is our word for what you call a day, although they are not the same in terms of time. The Sorx also speak mainly Hubeeish but they have lots of words and expressions in their own Sorxish language, for example, their words for time are squall, squage, squidge, squodge and squig.'

Hornbeam intertwined his 3 arms, which looked very comfortable, leant back in his chair and began the history lesson.

He started at the beginning.

'There've been Sorx and Qorx in Highlow since before we had any words for time,' he said. 'They were always friendly towards each other and got along very well. It also helped that they lived in different parts of Highlow, so they only had to meet up with each other when they wanted to!'

He laughed his foghorn laugh.

'Now that you have seen us you will know that we look very different,' he continued. 'The Qorx are about 11 times taller than the Sorx, and they each have a different number of arms and legs. This is because of where they live.'

He paused, unfolded his middle arm, and reached up and tickled the little branch sticking up at the end of his nose. He then refolded his arm with the other 2 and continued his tale.

'You see the Sorx lived in the high parts of Highlow, where there are no trees and it is often very windy,' he said. 'They like to be in fresh air and fields with low hedgerows and to have plenty of space to run around, and they can run very quickly. The Sorx being small makes them ideal to cope in such an open environment, and their 3 legs enable them to stand up better in the wind. They live from crops they grow in their fields.'

He unfolded his arms and put his 3 hands on the table.

'The Qorx, on the other hand, lived in the low parts of Highlow, where there is a dense forest full of huge trees,' he continued. 'We live off what the forest and the land can provide. We call ourselves Forlandarians. We identify closely with the trees and love walking slowly amongst them, enjoying their company. Our 3 arms make it much easier for us to move the branches as we travel through the forest.'

Hornbeam paused again, leant forward and sat quietly for a touch of time.

'Are you OK?' asked Holly.

'Yes, I'm fine,' said Hornbeam. 'I was just thinking of how good it was in the past.'

'So, have things changed?' asked Jack.

'Oh yes,' said Hornbeam, as he straightened himself up in his chair. 'They've certainly changed. Let me continue with the history.'

'So, the Sorx and the Qorx got along very well and often helped each other out. Together we built high tree houses for the Qorx and low wooden houses for the Sorx. Because of that we called our land Highlow. We also built windmills to provide power for the Sorx to light and heat their homes, and all the roads and tunnels leading from Highlow to your land and the Other Lands. The Qorx have no need for power, they get all they require from the forest and the land.'

'What other lands?' asked Jack.

'Oh there are several Other Lands near Highlow where creatures similar to the Sorx and Qorx live.' said Hornbeam. 'There is Nearfar, Updown, Backforth and Inout, to name just a few.'

'So the tunnels are designed for the Qorx as well as the Sorx,' said Holly. 'But the Rodley Bottoms Tunnel doesn't seem big enough for a Qorx to pass through.'

'Well they are, up to a point,' said Hornbeam. 'Or should I say, up to a height. The tunnels to the Other Lands are big enough for Sorx and Qorx. So is the tunnel to Woodpecker Woods, which is tall enough for a full grown Qorx to go and visit the trees there. In fact, it was specially built for the Qorx by the Sorx who gave it to them as an act of friendship. However, the others are only about 3 metres high. so I could certainly not stand up in one now, and I would not even be able to crawl through them. But I could when I was a Qorxling.'

'What's a Qorxling?' asked Holly.

'That's a Qorx who is less than 3 metres tall, usually up to 11 continuums old, although that depends on how quickly they grow.'

'Are there such things as Sorxlings?' asked Jack.

'Oh yes,' said Hornbeam. 'But that's got nothing to do with height. It has to do with the number of toes they have on each of their feet. When they are born they have one toe on each foot, and as they get older further toes grow at random. Until they have 2 toes on at least 2 of their feet they are known as Sorxlings. They get their names from their toes. For example if a Sorx had nine on its left foot, 13 on its middle foot and 7 on its right foot it would be called, Nine:13:7!'

'That's a lot of toes!' exclaimed Jack.

'It sure is!' said Hornbeam. 'And they can cause them a lot of problems. The more toes they have the more difficult it is for them to walk upright like Qorx and Hubees do. They can manage a short distance upright, but if they want to travel quickly, they drop onto their hands and dadum along.'

Dadums and Pedarcs

'What's a dadum?' asked Holly.

'A dadum,' said Hornbeam. 'Is a Sorx measurement equal to the distance a fully grown Sorx moves forward when it uses its 3 feet and its 2 hands at once. When you saw a Sorx coming up the road earlier you probably heard it first. When it runs, it puts its feet down in turn making a da-da-da sound, and then it pushes itself forward with both hands making a dum sound. These combine to give a very distinctive da-da-da-dum rhythm. Have you heard it?'

'Yes we have,' said Holly. 'So does that mean that a da-da-da-dum is one dadum?'

'Exactly!' said Hornbeam. 'One da-da-da-dum is one dadum. They use dadums to measure distances and put them on signposts. Did you see the signpost at the crossroads near the entrance to the Rodley Bottoms Tunnel?'

'Oh yes,' said Jack. 'I think it has Rodley Bottoms Tunnel 53p, 163d written on it.'

'Yes, it does,' said Hornbeam. 'The "d" on the sign stands for dadums, so it is 163 dadums to the entrance to the Rodley Bottoms Tunnel from that sign.'

'What does the "p" stand for?' asked Jack.

'That's a Qorx measurement in which "p" stands for pedarc,' said Hornbeam. 'A pedarc is the distance between the heel of one foot and the heel of the other foot, when a fully grown Qorx does one stride.

So it is 53 pedarcs to the Rodley Bottoms Tunnel from that sign. One pedarc is about 3 dadums. All the old signposts still have "p" distances on them. But any new ones put up by the Sorx only show "d" distances. Let me show you a pedarc. Please stand up.'

Jack and Holly stood up from their little chairs on top of the table. Hornbeam stood up and leant towards them. Lifting first Jack, then Holly, he placed them very carefully on the floor.

'Please go outside the gate,' he said.

They scrambled through the opening at the bottom of the gate, and looked back into the cage.

Up to this point, the Qorx had never moved his feet since Jack and Holly had fallen into his house. Even when he had placed Jack, Holly and the chairs on top of the high table, his feet had always stayed in the same spot on the floor.

'Excuse me while I get moving,' he said. 'Watch my feet.'

Holly and Jack watched his feet.

Hornbeam shouted, 'Retract!'

The smooth snake-like things coming out of each toe, and which ran into the ground began to move. Like toothpaste going back into its tube, they slid back into the toes, with little bits of soil flying off them as they came out of the ground.

Very quickly they vanished altogether, and soon there was no evidence of them ever having been there.

Jack looked at Holly in astonishment.

'Did you see that?' he said.

'Yes, but I don't believe it!' said Holly.

'What did you do?' Jack asked Hornbeam.

Hornbeam smiled.

'Oh, that's nothing!' he said, and started to laugh.

This echoed round the room like a happy foghorn. Jack and Holly started to laugh.

'I've just stopped feeding, that's all!' said Hornbeam. 'I eat through my foot roots, and I retract them when I've finished. Qorx get most of their food and drink from the ground, that's why we have no need for power.'

He looked down at his feet.

'Watch,' he said.

Holly and Jack watched his feet again.

'Engage!' he said, loudly.

The foot roots reappeared and started to burrow into the ground.

After a touch of time he shouted, 'Retract!'

The roots disappeared back into his toes.

Jack and Holly started to clap.

'Thank you,' he said, bowing low. 'I get most of my food through those roots. I mainly only use my mouth for talking and for drinking Perx.'

Hornbeam stepped forward and put his right hand on the big door of the cage. He pushed it and, to Jack and Holly's great surprise, it opened with a deep grinding noise.

'You can open the door!' exclaimed Jack. 'I thought you were locked inside the cage.'

'So did I!' said Holly.

'I used to be when the Sorx kept me a prisoner here,' said Hornbeam. 'But they haven't been back for tumbles of time. That's why the little door you finally managed to open was stuck; it was all clogged up with dirt. The last time they came, they unlocked the cage door and ran away. Since then they haven't bothered me. I think it's because they know that they've won, and that I won't cause them any trouble.'

Hornbeam gave a very long sigh.

'I think they're frightened of me,' he continued. 'They see me as a dangerous giant, so I keep the stove burning to let them know I am still alive, and they keep away. They think the big door to the tree house is locked, but I managed to break the lock a tumble of time ago. I sneak out at night to get branches and bark that have fallen from the trees to keep the stove going all the time.'

'So can you escape whenever you want to?' asked Holly.

'Yes, I suppose I could, but I don't want to,' said Hornbeam. 'Where would I go? All my Qorx friends have gone, and there are only Sorx left in Highlow. I'm much better off here on my own.'

'That's so sad,' said Holly, patting the Qorx's left foot.

'Thank you, you are kind,' said Hornbeam. 'But don't feel sorry for me, I'm quite happy! Now where were we? Oh yes. I was going to show you a pedarc. Watch carefully.'

The Qorx walked across to the wall and turned round. He stood up straight so that his head almost touched the ceiling. He dug his right heel into the ground, and stepped forward into a huge stride. His left leg arched into the air and seemed to go on forever, as his left foot rose high above them, and came crashing down almost halfway across the vast floor. He dug his left heel in, and brought his right foot up to join it.

'There!' he said, proudly. 'That's a pedarc. Impressive, isn't it?'

'It sure is!' said Holly, and she and Jack started to clap again.

'Thank you again,' he said, bowing even lower than before.

'Would you like me to continue with the history lesson?'

'Yes please,' they said almost together, completely fascinated by Hornbeam and what he was telling them.

'OK,' he said. 'Let's go back into the cage and sit down. It's a bit more comfortable in there.'

They went in, Hornbeam lifted them back onto his table, and they all sat down.

'Now where were we before we got distracted?' he asked, folding his forearms together in a comfortable knot.

'You had just explained how the Sorx dadumed when they ran with that da-da-da-dum rhythm, which I find very scary,' said Holly.

'And it's meant to be scary,' said the Qorx. 'They use it to frighten their enemies. When a lot of Sorx dadum together it sounds like a thunder storm.'

'That's very clever,' said Jack.

'Yes it is,' said the Qorx. 'Sorx are very clever, sly creatures. They can also be very rude and grumpy. As a general rule, never trust a Sorx.'

He scratched his nose then continued, 'So, as I was saying, in the beginning and for tangles of years the Sorx and Qorx rubbed along quite happily, each living in their own worlds in Highlow, and interacting with each other as required to make life easier. They even shared a hospital and 2 schools. Then one day everything changed.'

'What happened?' asked Holly.

'The Great Upheaval happened,' said Hornbeam.

The Great Upheaval

'One fine morning, the Sorx were rushing around quite happily in Sorxville, and the Qorx were just getting about their business slowly and steadily in Qorxville,' said Hornbeam, leaning further back in his chair. 'Then it happened.'

He paused, put his right hand on his forehead, and closed his eyes.

'The Great Upheaval,' he said, quietly.

Hornbeam opened his eyes, refolded his arms, and continued, 'There was a huge booming sound under the high ground in Sorxville, and the whole of Highlow moved from side to side and up and down. The trees in the forest shook violently and lots of them came crashing down, knocking others over as they fell.

In Sorxville, giant cracks opened up in the ground. Many of the Sorx stocky houses and windmills fell into them. At the same time, there was an incredible storm with hurricane winds and torrential rain. This flattened what was left of Sorxville, wiping it from the face of Highlow.'

'On no!' said Holly. 'What happened to the Sorx?'

'Very sadly, some of them got washed into the cracks and were never seen again,' said Hornbeam. 'Fortunately, most of them ran away. They managed to get out of Sorxville and make their way to Qorxville. But they didn't have time to collect any of their things, so they arrived here with nothing.'

'That's terrible,' said Jack.

'Indeed it was,' said the Qorx. 'But it got worse. You see there were so many of them, and they were so desperate that they began to overrun Qorxville. There have always been a lot more Sorx than Qorx. The Qorx offered help and shelter in their tree houses, but the Sorx took advantage of this. At first they said they were very grateful to the Qorx, and thanked them for taking them into their homes. But Sorx are very sly creatures and quickly took over the tree houses. You must remember that Sorx have 2 minds, which they have difficulty choosing between, an aggressive one, that always wants to win, and a peaceful one, that doesn't want to cause any trouble. The aggressive one will not change its ideas, whereas the peaceful one is more reasonable, and usually keeps the other one in check. But when the Great Upheaval happened, panic set in. The aggressive minds of all the Sorx acted as one completely overruling the peaceful minds. They decided to get rid of the Qorx and take over Qorxville.'

'Was there a battle?' asked Jack.

'No,' said Hornbeam. 'The Sorx were cleverer than that. They changed the tree houses in Qorxville to make them impossible for Qorx to live in. Even worse, they ran out of fallen trees and they forced the Qorx to chop down living ones to get them enough wood. Sorx are not strong enough to do this.

The Qorx did this as gently as they could but the poor trees were in terrible pain. We hated doing this, because we love trees and always want to protect them. But if we didn't, the Sorx said they would set fire to the whole forest; and we believed them.'

Hornbeam paused and sighed deeply, then continued, 'From

the moment the Sorx invaded, Qorx began to leave. It is not in our nature to fight, we just want a gentle life, so more and more joined them.'

'Where did they go?' asked Holly.

'Well,' said Hornbeam. 'They couldn't go through the tunnel to the Other Lands because the Great Upheaval made it collapse. They couldn't go through the tunnel to Nearfar because the Sorx blocked it off when they took over Qorxville. They don't like the Nearfar creatures, who are much more like Qorx, and their capital Corxville is very like the old Qorxville.

So the only way was the Woodpecker Woods Tunnel. The Sorx left this open deliberately until all the Qorx had escaped, and it has never been used since. Many of the Qorx now live in Woodpecker Woods amongst the trees. You may see them there next time you walk along the canal from Rodley Bottoms'

'We've done that loads of times,' said Holly. 'But I can't remember seeing any Qorx in Woodpecker Woods.'

'Oh they're there,' said Hornbeam. 'But they can hide themselves well amongst the trees.'

He leant forward, put his middle forearm on the table and held his head with his other 2 hands.

'I'm the last remaining Qorx in Highlow, he said. 'I do miss my fellow Qorx. I often wish that I was with them.'

'So why did you stay?' asked Jack. 'Was it to fight the Sorx?

'Oh No,' said Hornbeam, straightening himself up and leaning back in his chair. 'I'm not that brave!'

He smiled gently, then continued, 'No, when things started to get really bad I went deep into the forest and hid where the trees are tallest and densest, too dense for any Sorx to enter. I stayed there for trembles of time. Even that deep in I could hear screaming and crashing and banging. Then one day it stopped.

I waited for several solars, and then crept out of the forest. I reached the edge of the trees and looked across to Qorxville. I could hardly recognise it. All the tree houses had been changed with new floors, small windows and little doors. Where there had been one home, there were now 2, 3 or four, one on top of the other, with ladders leading up from the ground to the each one.

There were Sorx everywhere. And every Qorxville sign had been changed to SQorxville and every Sorxville sign to QSorxville.'

'So that's why the sign was altered outside the Rodley Bottoms Tunnel,' said Holly.

'Yes,' said Hornbeam.

'So the Qorx were kicked out of their home town,' said Jack.

'Yes they were,' said Hornbeam. 'They were forced out with nowhere to go, except through the Woodpecker Woods Tunnel. Qorxville was completely changed by the Sorx.

Even the sky was no longer blue, it was a dirty-yellowy-brown colour and the whole place smelt of Crudax. We Qorx have very sensitive noses and the smell was overpowering. You smell like rosemary and other Hubees have different smells, usually nice ones, but all Sorx smell of Crudax!'

'What's Crudax?' asked Jack.

Crudax

'Crudax is what the Sorx call the waste material they produce in their bodies,' said Hornbeam. 'There are 3 types. Crudax One is the liquid that they produce, Crudax 2 is the solid they produce and Crudax 3 is the gas that they produce. But they usually call them Number Ones, Number 2s and Number 3s.'

'They sound like our wee, poo and farts!' said Jack, laughing.

'Jack!' shouted Holly. 'Don't be so rude!'

'On don't worry!' laughed Hornbeam. 'I know what you Hubees call them, and that's exactly what they are!'

'So, is the colour of sky and the smell caused by Crudax?' asked Holly.

'Yes,' said Hornbeam.

'How?' asked Holly.

'Well, the Sorx need energy to power SQorxville and they have to get it from somewhere,' continued Hornbeam. 'They can no longer use windmills, and they don't know how to get energy from Enzor. All the Qorx have gone, so there is no-one to chop down the trees. At least that's one good thing to come out of this disaster.'

He paused, thinking about the trees, then continued, 'They have used up all the fallen ones and now the only source of energy is the gas that comes from their own bodies. So they built a Thunder Works that generates power from Crudax. All Sorx donate to it. It is quite disgusting.

There are Thunderboxes set up in the town where Sorx go to donate their Crudax into holes which lead into big pipes. The Crudax from their toilets at home also goes straight into these pipes, which carry it underground to the Thunder Works. There, Crudax 3 is separated from Crudax One and Crudax 2 and processed into gas, which is burned to provide power. It is stored in a huge balloon inside the Thunder Works. During the process, some of the Crudax 3 escapes into the air, and this causes the colour of the sky and the horrible smell.'

'What happens to the rest of the Crudax?' asked Jack.

'Crudax 2 and 3 are of no use to them,' said Hornbeam. 'So, after they have filtered out Crudax 3, these are taken by an over-ground pipeline, the Crudax Line, which runs from the Thunder Works past this tree house and into the River Crudley. That is the one you crossed when you came through the Rodley Bottoms Tunnel. Eventually it goes underground into a bottomless pit.'

'Ugh!' cried Jack. 'That is gross!'

'It certainly is,' said Hornbeam. 'And the final straw for me was when I saw the Treacle River.'

'The Treacle River!' shouted Holly.

'Yes!' shouted Hornbeam back. 'They've made a river of treacle to counteract the smell from the Thunder Works!'

He paused then continued, 'Between Sorxville and Qorxville is the Telecar Mine, which had not been opened for a tangle of time, so long in fact that everyone had forgotten about it, and didn't remember what it was used for. But, when the Great Upheaval occurred, the mine cracked open, and some very sweet smelling thick liquid, which tasted like treacle, started to seep out. No-one knows why this is, it just is.'

He paused and scratched his nose, then continued, 'Now, the Sorx have a very sweet tooth. They say it is because their teeth shine brightly when they smile, and sweet things help them to shine. So they dug a channel out of a dried-up stream that used to run from the Telecar Mine. This became the Treacle River that flows into the old Telecar Lake just outside SQorxville. The Sorx renamed it the Treacle Lake and have become addicted. They spend many tickles of time by the river and beside the lake just licking the treacle.'

Holly thought about this, she liked treacle but couldn't imagine licking a lake of treacle.

'I don't fancy that!' she said.

'But the Sorx do!' said Hornbeam. 'They say they do it to take away the smell of Crudax, but they really are addicted. Unfortunately, it makes them smell even worse. A mixture of Crudax and treacle, can you imagine!'

Jack and Holly couldn't.

'Because of this, I decided that I had to get away,' said Hornbeam. 'I packed my satchel, and set off to escape through the Woodpecker Woods Tunnel. I got there in just a solar; it isn't very far from here. I waited until it was dark, and headed for the tunnel entrance.

But when I got there, I couldn't get in. The Sorx had fitted a huge portcullis, which was closed and locked. I thought I'd better get away from the entrance. But, just as I turned to go back, a large group of Sorx appeared and captured me. They tied my hands, and took me to the Jail House in SQorxville. I was interrogated for several solars. They wouldn't let me fall asleep, and kept me on a stone floor so I couldn't use my foot roots.'

'Weren't you frightened?' asked Jack.

'No,' said Hornbeam. 'I wasn't frightened, I was terrified! They wanted to know if there were any more Qorx living in Highlow. I said that I was the last one, but they didn't believe me and kept on beating me.

Eventually, after they didn't find any more Qorx, they threw me into a small dark cell in the Jail House, which was not even high enough for me to stand upright.'

'So how did you end up here?' asked Holly.

'All because of a keesceptre and a Quadruple Prime,' said Hornbeam, mysteriously.

'What are they?' asked Jack.

Keesceptres

'You said that the Sorx you saw in your garden had a stick, didn't you?' asked Hornbeam.

'Yes, it did,' said Holly. 'It kept hitting it against our dry-stone wall.'

'Well that stick is called a keesceptre,' said Hornbeam. 'They are only carried by foragers, and are very powerful short twisted pieces of wood that are extremely important to Sorx.'

'Why?' asked Holly.

'Well,' said Hornbeam. 'According to ancient Sorx documents that I have read, 127 Sorx arrived in Highlow in Sorx continuum 673 after travelling from the Other Lands. When they arrived it was winter on the high ground, and they needed somewhere to live. There were only 11 trees growing up there so they chopped them down, and used them to make a long low communal house in which they all could live. They called this the Super Bremmin Hoose, and it enabled them to survive the winter. Bremmin is a Sorx word for family. The Sorx believe they survived because 673, 127 and 11 are all prime numbers, and they have tried to model their lives on prime numbers ever since.

Once the spring came, they began to move through Highlow. They met the Qorx and became friendly with them. The Qorx provided them with wood from their forests, and the Sorx used this to build their own low wooden houses and to set up the old Sorxville. The Super Bremmin Hoose fell into disrepair. All the Sorx had moved out of it to live either on their own or with their families.'

'So what happened to the communal house?' asked Jack.

'One very windy solar, it blew down and the wood was scattered all over the ground,' continued Hornbeam. 'Rather than use it to build new houses, the Sorx decided to save this as a memory of their safe arrival in Highlow. As they began to journey into Hubeeland they needed sticks to help them get around in the undergrowth. At first they used to make them from fallen wood from the forest, but this didn't last very long. So they decided to use wood from the Super Bremmin Hoose. They started to do this and they found that these sticks had great powers.'

'That's amazing,' said Holly. 'But why are they called keesceptres?'

'They had a competition to give the sticks a name, and the winning entry was keesceptre, because no one knew what it meant, and everyone liked the sound of it!' said Hornbeam, laughing his foghorn laugh. 'Later, the word was discovered in one of the ancient Sorx documents and found to mean, keep secret, and that's exactly what a keesceptre does.'

'How do they work?' asked Jack.

'They are twisted in the middle. They have a flat end and a pointed end, and have many powers,' said Hornbeam. 'For example, they can open doors and hidden entrances to tunnels. To do this, the creature holding the keesceptre bashes its flat end against the door or tunnel wall, and chants the number of toes they have on their feet, in order from left to right.'

'Yes,' said Holly. 'That's what the Sorx in our garden was doing.'

'Can they open a portcullis?' asked Jack.

'No,' said Hornbeam. 'There is only one keesceptre that can do that; the first one ever made from the wood of the Super Bremmin Hoose. But I have never seen it and I don't know where it is.'

'Can only foragers use keesceptres?' asked Jack. 'Could Holly and me use them even though we are not Sorx?'

'It doesn't matter who or what you are. Keesceptres will work for anyone who commands them,' said Hornbeam. 'But they don't belong to anyone. They have minds of their own, and will do whatever they think is best in the circumstances.

When you fight using a keesceptre you can feel great power flow through your body. If you hit your opponent with the end of your keesceptre, the power passes into them and they experience great pain. The flat end is extremely dangerous, but the pointed end is even worse. All the power is concentrated at the point.'

Hornbeam shivered as he remembered being hit by a keesceptre in the Jail House.

'But after a while the keesceptres will take over and fight on their own,' he continued. 'They want to make the decisions. When you are fighting, you must hold them very firmly and keep control; never let your keesceptre be the boss or they will start to control you!'

'Will it really?' said Jack.

'Oh yes!' said Hornbeam. 'Keesceptres have great powers. The Sorx believe that these powers come from the 3 prime numbers associated with the Super Bremmin Hoose. But some of the keesceptres' powers are not yet fully understood by the Sorx. They still keep some of their secrets. I only discovered one of them when I was a prisoner.'

'What was that?' asked Jack.

'Well, believe it or not,' said Hornbeam. 'They can make wishes come true!'

'How can they do that?' Jack asked.

'When you make a wish in their presence, and 3 prime numbers coincide to form a fourth prime number,' continued Hornbeam. 'I call it a Quadruple Prime. It is extremely rare, and I did not know about it until it happened to me.'

'What happened to you?' asked Holly.

The Quadruple Prime

Hornbeam moved position in his chair to get more comfortable, and then continued, 'When I was held in a cell in the Jail House, I had 3 Sorx guarding me: a forager and 2 prison guards. They took it in turns to interrogate me. Once they all came into the cell and all hit me at the same time. The forager used a keesceptre and the Guards used wooden branches.'

'Oh how horrible,' said Holly.

'I noticed that one of them had a total of 19 toes on its feet, one had 11 toes and the other had 13 toes,' said Hornbeam. 'These are all prime numbers and I added them up while they were attacking me to try to take my mind off the pain. I got 43, another prime number.'

He stopped and sighed very loudly, then continued, 'The Sorx were very cruel. They kept saying, "We're going to hit you all day until you tell us where the other Qorx are hiding". They started hitting me again and were hurting me so much that I snatched the keesceptre from the forager, held onto it as tightly as I could and cried out, "I wish it was tomorrow!" All of a sudden the 3 Sorx disappeared and I was alone in my cell. Even the keesceptre had gone. It was tomorrow!'

'You must have been so happy!' said Holly.

'Yes, I was!' said Hornbeam. 'The keesceptre had made time

move forward as far as I had wished. The Quadruple Prime had worked!'

'That's amazing!' said Jack. 'But are you sure the keesceptre did that?'

'Yes, because it worked again,' said Hornbeam.

He adjusted his position in his chair.

'You see they came back to interrogate me,' he went on. 'They wanted to know what had happened, and started to beat me.'

'The same Sorx?' asked Holly.

'With the same keesceptre?' asked Jack.

'Yes,' said Hornbeam. 'The same forager with the same keesceptre and the same guards, but this time they had truncheons.'

'What happened?' asked Holly.

'Just like before, as they were beating me, I snatched the keesceptre from the forager, held it tight and made a wish,' said Hornbeam. 'This time I wished to be in The Lonely Sweet Shop.'

'What happened?' asked Holly.

'I was suddenly all alone in The Lonely Sweet Shop!' said Hornbeam.

'So the Quadruple Prime worked again with the same keesceptre!' said Jack.

'Correct!' said Hornbeam. 'Those 3 Sorx came to The Lonely Sweet Shop to see if I was there. When they found me they were very frightened. They thought I had magic powers that I could use against them, but in fact it was all due to the powers of the keesceptre. I had been saved twice by a Quadruple Prime.'

'Why did that work?' asked Jack.

'That's a good question. I also wondered why,' said Hornbeam.

'Then I remembered the 3 prime numbers associated with the Super Bremmin Hoose: 127 Sorx, continuum 673, 11 trees. If you add them together you get 811 which is also a prime number. That's a Quadruple Prime.'

'That's amazing!' said Jack, who loved numbers.

'It is!' said Hornbeam. 'And I think it's the reason why keessceptres can make wishes come true. That Quadruple Prime was passed into the keessceptres made from the Super Bremmin Hoose, and they kept its secret. Then, whenever one of those keessceptres is in the presence of a Quadruple Prime, that secret is revealed and is able to make a wish come true.'

'So can keessceptres make time go backwards?' asked Holly.

'Yes,' said Hornbeam. 'They will grant any wish. But you must be in the presence of a Quadruple Prime, and you must be holding a keessceptre when you make your wish.'

'That could be very useful,' said Jack.

'Yes, it could,' said Hornbeam. 'But you must be careful. Both my wishes were granted, but remember that I only made one wish each time.'

'What do you mean?' asked Holly.

'My first wish was for it to be tomorrow and it was granted,' said Hornbeam. 'I don't know if it would have been granted if I'd wished for it to be tomorrow, and also for Enzor to be shining.'

'So you think you can only ask for one thing to happen in a wish?' asked Jack.

'I don't know,' said Hornbeam. 'But it's not worth the risk. So if you are ever lucky enough to be able to use a Quadruple Prime, please make sure you only wish for one thing. Do you understand?'

'Yes,' said Holly and Jack at the same time.

'So that's how I ended up here,' continued Hornbeam. 'In the old days it was known as The Lonely Sweet Shop, because it used to be a sweet shop, and is some distance outside of Qorxville. The Qorxlings loved to come here.'

'So are those glass jars on the shelves full of sweets?' asked Holly.

'Yes,' said Hornbeam. 'They are, but they have been there for several continuums. so I wouldn't eat any of them if I were you!'

He laughed his foghorn laugh.

'The Sorx built this cage,' he continued. 'Put me in it, and locked me inside. At the beginning they put in a couple of grumpy Sorx to be my guards, but after a touch of time they soon got bored and often left me on my own. Occasionally, they would come back but one day they left and never returned. They put a big sign on the door outside warning Sorx to keep away, and never came back.

I have not spoken to anyone in here since then until you 2 fell in. I like being on my own, but I must admit that I enjoy your company. I am pleased that you are with me, but also sorry that you find yourselves here. I do like Hubees.'

He paused and looked at Jack and Holly, rather sadly.

'Well, there you are,' he said. 'Now you know some of the history of Highlow.'

16TH PRIME: NUMBER 53

Bad news Hubees

When Hornbeam finished his history lesson, Jack and Holly clapped.

'What an amazing tale,' said Holly.

'Thank you,' said Hornbeam.

'Yes it is,' said Jack to Holly. 'But history only tells us about the past, we need to think about how we can get out of here. All 3 of us: you, me and Hornbeam.'

'No,' said Holly. 'All four of us! Don't forget Podge!'

'Oh, of course Holly, I'm sorry,' said Jack.

'Thank you for including me,' said Hornbeam. 'But it won't be easy because there are Sorx everywhere and they hate Qorx and Hubees.'

'But why do they hate Hubees?' asked Holly. 'The one who took Podge said that Hubees were bad news. Why?'

'Sorx don't like Hubees partly because they don't like any other creatures, and also because they don't even always like each other,' said Hornbeam. 'But the real reason they don't like you is because of what Hubees did to them, or rather what Hubees did to Hubeeland.'

'What did we do to our own land?' asked Holly, very confused.

'Well,' said Hornbeam. 'You destroyed a lot of it, particularly the parts of it that Sorx love.'

He paused, and looked at Holly and Jack as if he was going to tell them off.

'You see Sorx weren't always sly,' said Hornbeam. 'They were in fact very trusting creatures, who just wanted to run around in the open air and grow their crops. They loved to forage in hedgerows and wild flower fields. They liked the wind, particularly how it felt in the long fur that covers their bodies.'

He paused then continued, 'They loved Hubeeland and they used to move in and out of it through the tunnels quite often, not causing any trouble, just enjoying its natural environment. But that was a tangle of time ago.'

He sighed then carried on, 'Now, very sadly, Hubees have covered much of their land with roads and concrete and tarmac and buildings. They have ripped out many of the hedgerows that Sorx loved to forage in. Those that are left are full of paper, plastic and other rubbish abandoned there by Hubees. You really are a most untidy race! Sorx hate that because they are a very tidy species.'

He put his middle hand to his head and sighed even deeper than before.

'Hubees have turned their quiet villages into busy towns, and their busy towns into concrete cities,' he continued. 'The Sorx got very angry about this and became sly and crafty. Even before the Great Upheaval, they took against Hubees and decided to go on foraging raids to take whatever they could, in return for the Hubees destroying their favourite hedgerows and ditches.'

Hornbeam paused and sighed again.

'Soon,' he went on. 'They became obsessed with this. They are obsessive creatures who are easily addicted, remember the Treacle River, and they became addicted to annoying the

Hubees. Because, as your first Sorx said, to them Hubees are bad news. Now they carry out raids whenever they can. In SQorxville they have a Treasure Store where the things they have stolen are put on display and sold. That is probably where Podge will be.'

'I hope so,' said Holly, quietly.

'So you see,' continued Hornbeam. 'Although they have overrun the Qorx and forced them out of Highlow, it's really because of Hubees that Sorx are now the way they are. If you hadn't destroyed your own land, they may have even moved into it after the Great Upheaval. But you changed it so much, it was impossible, so they took over Qorxville instead. Hubeeland would have been much better for them, because they're not made for living in a dense forest.'

'So is it all our fault?' asked Holly.

'Yes,' said Hornbeam. 'I'm afraid it is, and it makes me very angry. Things could have been so much better.'

'OK,' said Jack. 'Sorx hate Hubees and Qorx. We are stuck in probably the last proper tree house in SQorxville and there are Sorx everywhere. None of us wants to be here. We need to find Podge and we all need to get out of Highlow and return to Hubeeland. Me and Holly through the Rodley Bottoms Tunnel, and you through the Woodpecker Woods Tunnel. How are we going to do that?'

'I don't think we can,' said Hornbeam. 'I've tried, and it didn't work.'

'Do you mean we are stuck here forever?' asked Holly.

'Probably,' said Hornbeam, very unhappily. 'Just like me.'

'Oh come on,' said Jack, anxiously. 'There must be a way. Can't you help us escape? Please Hornbeam, help us!' he pleaded.

Hornbeam looked at Jack and Holly and felt ashamed. He had been on his own far too long and had become self-centred.

Here were 2 strangers asking for his help. It had been a long time since anyone had done that. He really must try to help them to escape. It would take some planning, but he liked a challenge.

His mood changed. He leant forward, put his 3 elbows on the table, rested his head on his hands, and thought very carefully. While he did this his leaf ears flapped backwards and forwards.

'I'm sorry for being so negative, please forgive me,' he said, after a tickle of time. 'I'd love to help you.'

'Oh thank you!' said Jack.

'And you are quite right,' continued Hornbeam. 'There probably is a way but it won't be easy. In order to get Podge back you'll have to go to the Treasure Store, but that is right in the middle of SQorxville.'

He stood up, retracted his feet, and lifted Jack and Holly from the table placing them gently on the floor beside his huge toes. He opened the cage.

'Come with me,' he said, as he headed across the floor to the enormous spiral staircase. 'We need to go upstairs.'

Up the spiral staircase

Hornbeam reached the bottom of the spiral staircase in one pedarc, with Jack and Holly not too far behind him. Moving surprisingly quickly, he stepped up the staircase as it curved through the ceiling. Jack and Holly had much more difficulty. The steps were very high. They just about managed them one at a time, and then only by using their hands to help. Jack counted the steps as he climbed up them. There were only 13 in all, a prime number yet again, but it felt like many more. Eventually, they joined Hornbeam upstairs. By the time they got to the top, Jack felt shattered, and so did Holly.

The staircase led to a big flat wooden floor that stretched up to the edge of the wooden wall. This ran round the room in a roughly circular shape, exactly like that on the ground floor. There were four large windows in the walls through which the forest and the road could be clearly seen.

'What a great view!' said Jack, beginning to get his breath back.

'Yes, I love it,' said Hornbeam. 'I often come up here just to watch the world go by.'

Right around the top of the wall, were large wooden beams that supported the wooden roof. The stove pipe ran upwards from the floor below, through the middle of the room, and out through the roof.

The walls were very high, as high as those on the floor below, and Hornbeam could stand up straight without any difficulty. Up against the walls were several wooden boxes and some wooden cupboards with drawers in them. One of the walls bulged out into the room and was covered in well-worn knot holes. There was also a table, 2 chairs and a bed. They were all very large, big enough for Hornbeam to use. Jack and Holly we fascinated by the enormous size of everything.

'We've got to get you into SQorxville, and safely out again with Podge before someone buys her at the Treasure Store,' said Hornbeam. 'But you can't go looking like Hubees. You'll get caught and taken to the Jail House to be questioned before you can say, "Sly Sorx", and, believe me, that is not very nice.'

'But how else can we go?' asked Jack. 'We are Hubees after all!'

'That's true,' said Hornbeam. 'But Hubees like to do something that might be very useful now.'

'And what is that?' asked Holly.

'If I remember right, Hubees like to dress-up,' said the Qorx.

'Yes, we do,' said Holly. 'But I don't see how that can help.'

'Neither do I,' said Jack.

He wasn't very keen on dressing-up. He used to be, but he now felt that he was too old to take part in such childish things.

'I don't want to,' he said. 'I'm too old.'

Hornbeam looked at him.

'OK, Jack,' said Hornbeam, very sternly. 'That's fine. You and Holly can just stay in SQorxville forever. I don't mind. I live here already.'

Jack was surprised by Hornbeam's strong voice. He didn't know what to say.

'I thought you wanted my help, and I thought you wanted to help Holly to get Podge back,' continued Hornbeam.

'I do,' said Jack.

'Well this is the only way I can think of,' said Hornbeam. 'Sometimes we have to do things we don't want to do, in order to do the right thing.'

Now Jack felt ashamed, he knew he was being selfish.

'OK,' he said. 'I'll do it. I'm sorry for being selfish.'

'That's great!' said Hornbeam. 'Who knows, you might even enjoy it!'

He walked over to one of the wooden boxes, and lifted its lid with his left hand. He reached in, grasped some of its contents in his other 2 hands, and pulled out a vast pile of the weirdest clothes they'd ever seen.

'Here! Try these on for size!' said Hornbeam, dropping the clothes in front of Jack and Holly.

Holly looked at them in amazement.

'I've never seen costumes like those!' she said.

'I'd be very surprised if you had,' said Hornbeam. 'They are made for Qorx and Sorx, not Hubees. In the old days we used to have fancy dress parties, and the Qorxlings and Sorxlings would wear these.'

While Hornbeam had been talking, Jack and Holly had been digging around in the pile in front of them.

'Look at this!' cried Holly, holding up a costume which appeared to have 5 legs in it. 'It's a Sorx!'

'Yes,' said Jack, who was now getting quite excited. 'And this is a mini Qorx!'

'That's right,' said Hornbeam. 'The Qorxlings and Sorxlings used to dress-up as each other!'

'But how did they fit into them?' asked Jack. 'Sorx and Qorx have different numbers of arms and legs.'

'That's true,' said the Qorx. 'So we altered the costumes to make them fit. You'll see what we did when you try your Sorx costumes on. They always looked good, and it was often difficult to tell the real Sorxlings or Qorxlings from those in the costumes. In fact, that's what I am hoping will happen when you go to SQorxville.'

'What do you mean?' asked Jack, anxiously.

'I think he wants us to dress-up in these Sorx costumes and go into SQorxville wearing them,' said Holly.

'Correct!' cried Hornbeam. 'That's exactly what I want you to do!'

'You must be joking!' cried Jack. 'Holly might be OK, but I am too tall to be a Sorx! I'll never get into a costume!'

'That won't be a problem,' said Hornbeam. 'The costumes are made of very stretchy material. They can fit any Qorxling, even big ones.'

'But I really am too tall!' complained Jack.

'No,' said Hornbeam. 'Some of the older Sorx are taller than you. Other Sorx sometimes mock them, calling them, "SQorxy", saying they are as big as Qorx. That may happen to you so just ignore it. And if you bend down to make yourself look smaller, you should get away with it. But you will need to practise a lot before you go into SQorxville.'

'I sure will,' muttered Jack, under his breath.

'And so will I,' replied Holly, excited at the idea of dressing-up, but scared by what might happen when they went into SQorxville dressed as Sorx.

'Right, let's get started!' said Hornbeam. 'Find a Sorx

costume and put it on. Each costume consists of a head, a body and hands. But before you do you should take your wellies off.'

They took their wellies off and handed them to Hornbeam.

'I'll look after these for you,' said Hornbeam, walking over to the wall and putting them in a drawer.

Dressing-up

Jack and Holly dug into the pile and chose 2 Sorx costumes. They tried to put their bodies on first. Each of these had 2 arms, one solid leg, which was covered in a white bandage and 2 hollow legs. The arms were OK because they had 2 of them just like the Sorx, but their legs got all mixed up.

'Ooofff!' cried Jack, as he collapsed in a heap of arms, legs and fur on the floor in front of Holly.

Holly laughed at him then came crashing to floor herself with one leg sticking up in the air, as she tried to put her other one in the solid leg by mistake. This made Jack laugh. They both tried again and fell over again. They did this several times, and soon they were having a fit of giggles lying next to each other on the floor.

'This is going to take longer than I thought,' said Hornbeam to himself.

'OK,' he said. 'Please stand up, hold the bodies of your costumes in front of you, and sort the 3 legs out.'

Jack and Holly rolled around on the floor until they had freed themselves from their costumes. They stood up and shook the bodies so that the 3 legs were hanging in front of them. Jack had a costume which had a bandaged solid left leg, and Holly had one with a bandaged solid right leg.

Holly noticed that a flap was built into each costume just

below the Sorx bottom.

'What's this flap for?' she asked.

'Oh that's for your Crudax,' said Hornbeam.

Holly pulled a funny face.

'Oh!' she said.

'Right! Hold up your bodies,' said Hornbeam.

They held up their bodies.

'Good,' said the Qorx. 'Now do your legs first. Holly, you must put your right leg into your middle body leg and your left leg into your left body leg. Jack, you must put your right leg into the right body leg and your left leg into your middle body leg.'

They did as they were told, and managed it without falling over. The third legs of their bodies, the solid ones, hung down on the left-hand side for Jack and the right-hand side for Holly, both wrapped up in bandages, as if they had been injured.

'That's good!' said Hornbeam. 'Finally we are getting somewhere! Now find the left arm of your body and push your left arm in. Then do the same with your right one.'

Bending their backs and shrugging their shoulders up and down, they pushed their arms in. Then, grabbing the front of their costumes, they stretched the material right up to their necks. They looked at each other, covered in fur with a vast bottom, huge feet, big knobbly knees and elbows, and laughed.

'Now put your heads, on and pull them down until they click,' said Hornbeam.

They picked up the costume heads, and stuck them on theirs until they clicked. They could see out of 2 eye holes.

'Under the fur behind your left ear is a button,' said Hornbeam. 'Press it.'

They felt for their buttons, found them, and pressed them. Nothing seemed to happen.

'Now put on the hands,' said Hornbeam.

They picked up the costume hands. These had furry forearms running into long plump caterpillary fingers. They pushed their hands in, and their fingers went right to the ends of the plump ones.

'We should be able to pick things up if we need to,' thought Jack.

'That's it!' said Hornbeam. 'You are in! Come and look at yourselves.'

Hornbeam walked across to the part of the wall that bulged out into the room, and pressed one of the knots. A long mirror came sideways out of the wall and turned to face them. Holly limped over to it followed by Jack. They looked into the mirror. What they saw amazed them. There, in the mirror, were 2 Sorx, one a little bigger than the other, each with a white bandage wrapped round one of its legs.

'What do you think?' asked Hornbeam.

'We look like Sorx!' said Holly, in a very high voice, just like a Sorx.

'We do, and you sound like a Sorx, Holly!' said Jack, in a high Sorx voice.

'So do you!' said Holly.

'That's your heads,' said Hornbeam. 'They are fitted with voice-changers that make whoever is wearing them sound like a Sorx. But you must press the button every time you put on the head, otherwise it won't work.'

'You really do look and sound like Sorx,' said Hornbeam. 'I think you'll be able to get away with it, and your bandaged legs will help you to identify each other in a crowd. You are very unlikely to see another Sorx with a bandaged leg.'

He paused for a moment, and twitched the little branch on the end of his nose. Holly loved it when he did this.

'Now you need to practice moving like Sorx,' he said. 'You have seen how they dadum, and you have to be able to move like that as well. So start practising. Remember, they use their feet first and then their hands. You won't be able to do it properly, of course, because you have a bandaged leg, but that will help if it looks wrong because they will think it is because of your bad leg.'

He pointed to the legs of their costumes then continued, 'Your 2 good costume legs will help you to dadum. They are fitted with springs that push you along to make it easier, and to stop you getting tired. But you will still need to practice.'

So for many touches of time all that could be heard from the upstairs room was a variation on, da-da-da-dum, da-da-da-dum, da-da-da-dum, and the sound of Hornbeam's deep voice shouting, 'Again! Again! Again!'

In fact, their dadums sounded more like, da-da-thump-dum, da-da-thump-dum, da-da-thump-dum, because of their poorly legs. But that wasn't important. The main thing was that they dadumed like Sorx with poorly legs, and after a lot of practice they did. The springs certainly helped. They also practised putting on and taking off their costumes, and after a while became quite good at it.

'OK,' said Hornbeam. 'That's enough. You're ready. You can take your costumes off. Now we need to plan your trip to SQorxville. It's too dark to do anything more now and I need to sleep. Qorx go to bed when Enzor goes down and get up when it rises. You are very welcome to sleep in my bed up here. I can go downstairs and sleep in my cage. I will also be able to feed while I am there.'

Holly took off her costume, folded it as neatly as she could, and placed it on the end of the bed.

'That's very kind of you,' said Holly, yawning. She was beginning to feel tired.

'Yes it is,' said Jack. 'But do you have anything we can eat please? We haven't eaten since breakfast.'

He took off his costume, folded it up not quite as neatly as Holly's, and placed it beside hers.

'Oh, how rude of me,' said Hornbeam. 'I should have offered you something. Please forgive me; I'm not used to having visitors. Now let me see.'

Oodax

Hornbeam walked over to the wall and pressed another knot. A drawer slid out. He reached in. With his left hand he pulled out a brown paper bag, and with his other 2 hands he pulled out 2 small wooden bottles of Perx. He shuffled back to the bed. He handed one bottle to Holly and the other to Jack.

'Is there anything in there that you would like?' he asked, handing the bag to Jack.

Jack opened the bag and looked in. Inside, there seemed to be a number of small rugby balls. He showed the bag to Holly. They each took one out. They were striped yellow and brown.

'What are these?' asked Holly.

'They are Oodax,' said Hornbeam. 'I pick them in the forest and they're very tasty. I use them to supplement my root food. I picked these a couple of solars ago. They last for a tremble of time. Try one.'

They looked at each other, and then bit into their Oodax. They were not like anything they'd ever tasted before. The yellow stripes tasted sweet and juicy like a mixture of all kinds of fruits, and the brown stripes tasted like a mixture of all kinds of nuts and spices. The overall taste was of sweet and savoury together. They were delicious!

Jack and Holly quickly scoffed down their Oodax and reached into the bag to take another, then another. After a short time, they'd each eaten four and they felt wonderful. They washed them down with more Perx, and they both burped very loudly.

'You certainly like your food and drink!' said Hornbeam. 'But don't eat too many Oodax, they will help you to sleep, but they will also give you wind!'

He laughed his foghorn laugh.

'Now it's time for bed,' he said. 'So come on, I'll help you on.'

They walked over to the enormous bed. Hornbeam reached down slowly and lifted them onto it very carefully. There were huge pillows and a lovely thick soft duvet. They snuggled under the duvet and rested their heads on the pillows. They looked like cuddly toys that had been placed very comfortably in a huge bed!

'Early tomorrow you will be off to SQorxville and we'll need to plan what needs to be done. So have a good sleep,' said Hornbeam. 'Night, night! I'll call you early in the morning.'

'Night, night,' said Jack, very faintly as the Oodax kicked in. Holly had already drifted off, and they were both soon fast asleep.

Hornbeam looked at them, and then turned to go down the spiral staircase. All he could hear was the sound of steady breathing and the occasional deep sound of a long Oodax fart coming from beneath their duvet.

Yumbax

'Rise and shine!' called Hornbeam, pushing up and down on his huge bed. Jack and Holly bounced on the thick mattress, gently snoring.

'Come on young Hubees!' he shouted. 'You'll soon be off to SQorxville!'

Holly stirred.

'What? Where am I?' she said, before giving out a great big yawn. It was still dark outside the window.

'You are in my bed, and Enzor will soon be up,' said the Qorx.

'What's going on?' muttered Jack, grumpily, turning his head on one of the vast pillows. He was not at his best whenever he woke up.

'It's time to get up,' said Holly, who was more of a morning person.

'Oh,' said Jack. 'Just 5 more minutes please.'

'No!' boomed Hornbeam, in his foghorn voice. 'You have to get up and get going! So come on, get out of bed both of you! Now!'

This shocked Jack and Holly so much that they both jumped out of bed at the same time, crashed into each other, and fell onto the floor.

'Ow!' shouted Holly, as Jack landed on top of her. 'Get off!'

Hornbeam reached down and picked Jack up in his right hand and Holly in his left hand. He leant on the bed with his middle hand and pushed himself upwards. Straightening his back, he shuffled across to the table and placed Jack and Holly on top of it.

He crossed over to the wall and stood by one of the cupboards with drawers in. He pressed a knot in the wood on the front of the drawer. The drawer slid open. He reached in and pulled out something that looked like a light blue cucumber. He broke it into 2 pieces, crossed over to the table, and gave one piece to Holly and the other piece to Jack.

'Eat this,' he said. 'It will wake you up, and give you some energy ready for your big solar ahead.'

'What is it?' asked Holly.

'It's fresh this morning,' said Hornbeam. 'I picked it in the forest. You will love it. Enjoy!'

Jack took his piece, smelt it, and nibbled at its end. It tasted just like his favourite breakfast, porridge with sugar and warm milk. It was delicious and he quickly finished it off.

Holly took her piece, smelt it, and nibbled at its end. It tasted just like her favourite breakfast, corn flakes with cold milk and grapes on top. It was delicious and she quickly finished it off.

'Wow!' said Jack, not knowing how it had tasted to Holly.

'Wow!' said Holly, not knowing how it had tasted to Jack.

'Wow indeed!' said Hornbeam. 'It tastes of whatever your taste buds want it to taste. To me it tastes like wild mushrooms picked early in the solar. I love wild mushrooms! It only grows on one tree in the forest, and only I know where it is. I call it Yumbax.'

'It's great!' said Holly, who was now wide awake.

'It sure is!' exclaimed Jack, who was almost wide awake.

'Right, now that you've had breakfast,' said Hornbeam. 'Let's look at some maps.'

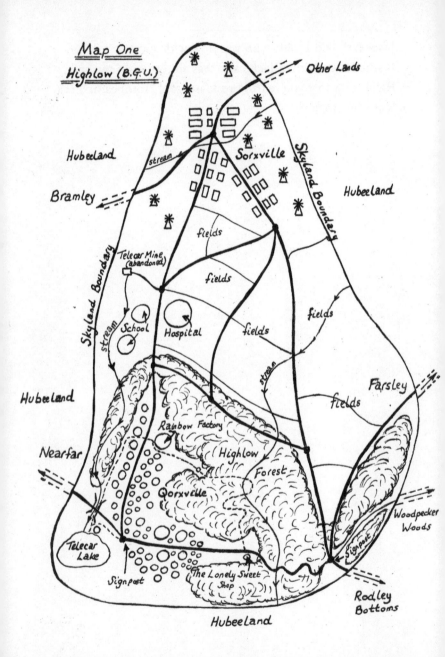

Map One
Highlow (B.G.U.)

Other Lands

Hubeeland

stream

Sorxville

Skyland Boundary

Hubeeland

Bramley

fields

Skyland Boundary

Telecar Mine
(abandoned)

fields

School

Hospital

fields

fields

Hubeeland

stream

fields

Farsley

Rainbow Factory

Highlow

Forest

Nearfar

Qorxville

Woodpecker
Woods

Telecar
Lake

Signpost

Signpost

The Lonely Sweet
Shop

Rodley
Bottoms

Hubeeland

96

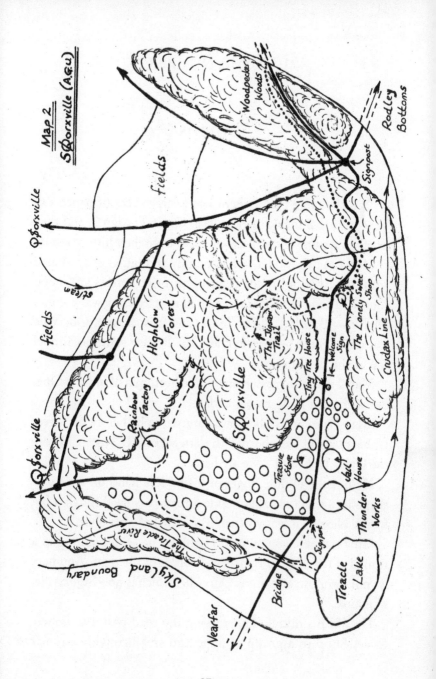

Map 2
SPorxville (A.G.u)

Woodpecker Woods

Rodley Bottoms

Signpost

The Lonely Sweet Shop

Crudax Line

PPorxville

fields

Stream

fields

Highlow Forest

SPorxville

The Jigsaw Trail

Tiny Tree House

Welcome Sign

QPorxville

fields

Rainbow Factory

Treasure Store

Jail

Thunder House Works

The Treacle River

Skyland Boundary

Signpost

Bridge

Treacle Lake

Nearfar

97

2 maps

On the table beside them was a large sheet of paper. On it were 2 maps, marked Map One and Map 2, and they recognised some of the places on them from their history lesson.

Map One showed a large, roughly triangular-shaped area with a network of roads running through forests and open country. Along the top of the map in neat lettering was written: Highlow (B.G.U.). Sorxville was towards the top, Qorxville was towards the bottom left, and the Rodley Bottoms Tunnel was at the bottom right.

Map 2 was a larger drawing of the bottom half of Map One, but with a lot more names added.

'Map One shows Highlow as it used to be before the Great Upheaval,' said Hornbeam. 'The letters "B.G.U." mean "Before the Great Upheaval". We are here.'

He put the middle finger of his middle hand on a circular shape in a small clearing beside a road passing through a big forest. Next to it was written: The Lonely Sweet Shop.

'This is where you entered Highlow,' he said, pointing to a tunnel at the bottom right-hand corner of the map. 'And here is your signpost, and this is Qorxville, which is now SQorxville, of course.'

He slid his middle finger along the road past The Lonely Sweet Shop to a group of large and small roughly circular buildings. Beside these, written in very neat lettering, was the word *Qorxville*.

'It's 683 pedarcs from here, so it should not take you long to get there even in your Sorx costumes,' said Hornbeam.

He pointed to the forest and the Rainbow Factory.

'And this is Highlow Forest,' he said. 'It surrounds Qorxville on 3 sides and almost touches the Rainbow Factory.'

He pointed to the signpost where several roads met in Qorxville, and ran his finger upwards.

'This is the road to Sorxville,' he said. 'It runs past the schools that the Qorxlings and Sorxlings use to share, and the hospital where anyone who lived in Highlow could be treated. Then it goes near the abandoned Telecar Mine from which a stream used to flow into the Telecar Lake. Before the Great Upheaval, this stream and Telecar Lake had dried up.'

He ran his finger down the dried-up stream to the lake, and then back up to the mine.

'Then it reaches Sorxville,' he added. 'These symbols show the windmills where they used to generate their power.'

His finger reached 3 groups of rectangular buildings. Next to these, in the same neat lettering, was the word *Sorxville*. The whole area around Sorxville was in open countryside well above the tree line, and dotted over it were symbols that looked like little windmills.

In the middle area of Map One, the road from Sorxville to Qorxville was joined by several narrower roads running from one side of Highlow to the other.

Defining the boundary of Highlow was a thick black line beyond which was written *Hubeeland*, at regular intervals.

Skyland Boundary was written at several places along this

line, and each road that reached it led into a tunnel marked with the name of the place it led to in Hubeeland. The one they had entered through simply read: *Rodley Bottoms*.

'What's the Skyland Boundary?' asked Holly.

'That's the edge of Highlow where the Sky meets the Land,' said Hornbeam. 'They're joined together all around Highlow so that no-one can come or go except through the tunnels. That's the way it has always been.'

'That's amazing!' said Jack. 'So Highlow is like a big bubble with tunnel holes in it?'

'I've never thought of it like that,' said Hornbeam, laughing. 'But yes, I suppose it is!'

Jack and Holly continued to look at Map One very carefully and began to understand exactly where they were. They recognised the names of Farsley and Bramley, which were villages not far from Rodley Bottoms, and they often cycled along the towpath to Woodpecker Woods.

'When I came out of hiding in the forest, and when I was taken to the Jail House, I noticed some changes that the Sorx had made,' said Hornbeam. 'So I made Map 2.'

He pointed to Map 2. It was entitled: *SQorxville (A.G.U.)*.

'I added "A.G.U." to show it was "After the Great Upheaval",' he said.

He paused and sighed.

'And sadly, to be accurate,' he continued. 'I changed the name of Qorxville to SQorxville.'

With the first finger of his right hand he pointed to some place names in SQorxville that he had added.

'Here are the Jail House, the Thunder Works and the Treasure Store,' he continued. 'I've also added the Rainbow Factory, the

Treacle River, the Treacle Lake and the Crudax Line. After the Great Upheaval, the Treacle Lake became much larger than the old Telecar Lake.'

He moved his finger to a small circular shape on Map 2.

'I also noticed this Tiny Tree House when they were taking me back into SꝊorxville,' he said. 'It was on the left just before we entered the town. I don't know what it is, but it may be important. You will know when you are near to SꝊorxville because there is a Welcome Sign just before the Tiny Tree House.'

He pointed to the Welcome Sign.

'What's this line?' asked Holly, pointing to a dotted-line running from The Lonely Sweet Shop to the Woodpecker Woods Tunnel.

'Oh, we don't need to talk about that at the moment,' said Hornbeam, mysteriously.

'Now before you go we need to make sure you get you back here safely with Podge,' he said, very seriously. 'To ensure this, I have drawn up a 7-Point Plan that you must follow. Please pay attention!'

Hornbeam cleared his throat and began to set out his plan.

Hornbeam's 7-Point Plan

'First,' said Hornbeam. 'You must make sure you press the button every time you put your costume head on. If you don't, and you speak to a Sorx, you will sound like a Hubee. Then you will be in big trouble. Do you understand?'

'Yes,' said Jack.

'Yes, I understand,' said Holly.

'Second, you will need Sorx satchels and Sorx money,' he said.

He took 2 satchels and a small leather bag from a drawer and handed the satchels to Holly and Jack.

'These satchels can hold much more than you think,' said Hornbeam. 'They are almost bottomless!'

He opened the small leather bag and tipped a pile of chunky purple stones onto the table. They were all the same size and shaped like a letter K.

'These are Sorx coins, they are called Kalex,' he said. 'You will need them to buy Podge from the Treasure Store. They are made by the Sorxville Superior Bank.'

'That sounds like a very important bank,' said Holly.

'Yes, it does,' said Hornbeam. 'But it's the only one in Highlow!'

He laughed his foghorn laugh.

Jack and Holly counted the Kalex. There were forty-eight of them. They shared them and put them in their satchels.

'Third,' continued Hornbeam. 'You will need some identity discs.'

From the same drawer he took out 2 thin pieces of wood, circular in shape, about the size of a saucer.

'All Sorx carry one of these at all times to prove that they are Sorx,' he said, handing one to Jack and one to Holly.

'They have the numbers of toes on their feet marked on it, for example, 3-Six-Four,' he continued. 'These ones were left here by the Sorx who used to guard me. They discarded them because they each grew more toes, so they had to get new identity discs. These ones have 3-3-2 and 3-1-3 marked on them, but they are very faded.'

Holly looked at hers. It was the one marked 3-1-3. She turned it over and on the other side was a drawing of a windmill and the word *Sorxville*.

'We need to change the numbers,' said Hornbeam. 'How many toes do you each have on your costume's feet from your left foot to your right foot?'

'3-2-3,' said Jack.

'3-3-3,' said Holly.

'Oh, that's not bad,' said Hornbeam. 'We only need to change 3 numbers.'

He walked over to the open drawer, took out a rough piece of wood, and what looked like a pointed piece of tree root.

'Pass me the discs please,' he said, walking back to the table.

Jack and Holly handed them to him. He laid the discs carefully on top of the table with their faded numbers upwards.

Using the rough piece of wood like sandpaper, he rubbed out the wrong numbers. He then took the pointed tree root and began writing the new numbers.

Soon the correct numbers were written on the discs. He then rubbed them in his hand for a tremble of time. This smudged them slightly.

'There,' he said. 'They now look genuine and well-used. They will do nicely.'

Satisfied with his work, he handed the discs to Jack and Holly.

'Keep these safe in your satchels,' he said to them. 'If anyone stops you they will want to see these discs. You must carry them with you at all times.'

Jack took the 3-2-3 disc, Holly took the 3-3-3 disc, and they put them in their satchels.

'Fourth,' said Hornbeam. 'You must become familiar with SQorxville as much as you can before you go. So let's look at Map 2 again.'

They all peered down at the map.

'Remember, I made this from memory, so it may not be correct,' said Hornbeam. 'The Jail House and the Treasure Store may not be exactly where I have drawn them, but they are opposite each other near the centre of town.'

He pointed to the centre of SQorxville.

'But you should not have any difficulty finding the Thunder Works. It is the largest tree house in SQorxville, and it will stink to the heavens! You might be able to earn some more Kalex there if you need any.'

Jack and Holly laughed rather nervously at this. They

were getting very anxious about what was to come, and they wondered what they would have to do at the Thunder Works to earn any more Kalex.

'You should not need to go to the Treacle River or to the Treacle Lake, as they are on the other side of town,' said Hornbeam.

Holly was disappointed by this; she would love to see the Treacle River and the Treacle Lake, but she said nothing.

'But you will need to go to the Rainbow Factory,' he said. 'It's on the main road to QSorxville near the edge of the town.'

He pointed to the Rainbow Factory.

'Fifth,' continued Hornbeam, 'You must get Podge back. Hopefully she will be in the Treasure Store, and you will be able to buy her with your Kalex. If not, you will have to find her. You must ask the Sorx running the Treasure Store who bought her, and then track them down. Remember you must use any means possible to get her back, that's the whole reason why you are here.'

Jack and Holly looked at each other and nodded grimly.

'We will,' said Jack.

'We sure will,' said Holly.

'Sixth, you must not waste any time,' said Hornbeam. 'You need to be back here before one solar has passed otherwise your Sorx costumes will start to wear out. They are not meant to be worn for a long time, they are just fancy dress. You will also become very hot and tired wearing them, even with the springs in your legs. So, you must get back here tonight.'

'Seventh, and most importantly,' he said. 'You must get back here without being spotted. That will not be easy. You must keep off the main roads. They will be busy with foragers heading for the tunnels. Instead you should be able to sneak back here along this trail.'

He leant over Map 2 and ran his finger down a very faint snaky line, which ran from the Rainbow Factory to The Lonely Sweet Shop.

He paused then said, 'On this path, not far from the Rainbow Factory, is a long abandoned trail that Qorxlings made a tangle of time ago through the forest to The Lonely Sweet Shop. They would watch rainbows being made, then play on the trail before buying some sweets.'

He stopped his finger at a small circular shape on the snaky line.

'It is known as the Jigsaw Trail and this is the starting point,' he said. 'It is marked on the ground by a tree-like shape cut in the surface on the path from the Rainbow Factory. You must find a jigsaw piece that will fit into this. It is hidden nearby. When you find it the route will open up to you, and you will have to find other pieces to help you on your way.'

He paused again, and then his voice became sterner.

'Whenever you find a piece, you must put it back where you found it,' he said. 'If you don't, you will not be able to proceed. The Qorxlings arranged this so that they could use the trail again and again. You can only go one-way along the trail, and you mustn't cheat. If you do you will be in serious trouble. The trail finishes in a tunnel that goes under the road outside The Lonely Sweet Shop, and comes up through a trapdoor in the floor downstairs. No Sorx has ever taken the Jigsaw Trail, and they do not even know that it exists.'

Hornbeam leant back in his chair.

'So,' he said. 'That is my 7-Point Plan. Do you have any questions?'

Leaving Hornbeam

Jack and Holly looked at each other. The plan seemed to be very complicated. They were not sure they could complete it successfully.

Holly spoke up, 'The Jigsaw Trail sounds scary.'

'Oh, don't worry,' said Hornbeam. 'Once you find the first piece you will enjoy it!'

He laughed his foghorn laugh.

'What happens if we manage to get back with Podge?' asked Jack, trying to be positive. 'How will we get back to Rodley Bottoms?'

'Don't worry,' said Hornbeam. 'I'll form another plan for that while you are away. You just make sure you get back here before the end of this solar. Just stay calm, and all will be well. Are you OK?'

Jack and Holly nodded back to him, but they didn't feel OK at all.

'Good!' said Hornbeam. 'I'll get your costumes, while you have a final look at Map 2.'

Jack and Holly, kneeling on top of the table, looked at Map 2 very carefully, trying to remember all the names and places.

Hornbeam came back with the costumes in his left hand. He also had some Yumbax and Oodax in his middle and right hands, and 2 small wooden bottles tucked under his arms.

'So, are you ready to go?' he asked.

'Yes,' said Holly, nervously.

'Yes, I suppose so,' said Jack.

'OK. Let's go downstairs and put your costumes on,' said Hornbeam. 'And here are some Yumbax, Oodax and Perx.'

'Thank you,' said Holly.

They shared out the Yumbax and Oodax and put them in their satchels, together with a bottle of Perx each. Hornbeam picked up the satchels in his left hand. With his middle and right hands he gently lifted Jack and Holly off the table and put them on the floor.

'Now, you must concentrate on getting back here safe before nightfall with Podge. Follow me,' said Hornbeam, handing them their satchels.

He walked over to the spiral staircase and quickly stepped down to the ground floor. Jack and Holly followed him down, jumping from one big step to another.

When they reached the bottom, Hornbeam told them to stand to one side. He looked down to the floor and wiped away some of the dirt with his feet. Clouds of dust flew into the air. He kept wiping and revealed a trapdoor with a ring-pull handle and a locking bolt.

He reached down, unlocked the bolt and pulled on the handle, raising the trapdoor. Jack and Holly peered into the darkness, and could just make out what seemed to be another spiral staircase going deep into the ground.

'This is where the Jigsaw Trail ends,' said Hornbeam. 'When you get back tonight you will come up this spiral staircase. You can open the trapdoor from underneath. I will be waiting for you.'

He closed the trapdoor, locked it, and wiped the dirt back over it until it could not be seen. Dust again flew everywhere. He then went across to the small table and put the costumes on it.

'Right,' he said. 'Put these on and get going. Enzor is up, and you will need as much of this solar as possible to finish your task.'

Holly and Jack slipped into their costumes, and pressed the buttons in their heads. They put their satchels on, and looked at Hornbeam.

'You really do look like Sorx with poorly legs! This could very well work!' said Hornbeam.

'I do hope so,' said Jack, in a high Sorx voice.

'So do I,' said Holly, in an equally high voice.

'Good, your voice-changers are working,' said Hornbeam. 'Remember to press the button every time you put them on.'

'But don't we need keesceptres?' asked Jack. 'The Sorx we saw in our garden had a keesceptre.'

'No,' said Hornbeam. 'Only foragers carry keesceptres, so you do not need them. If you can find any please bring them back. But I'll be surprised if you can. The foragers guard them very carefully.'

Hornbeam walked across to each of the windows and looked out. There was no sign of any Sorx.

'It's all clear,' he said. 'Now, before you go remember to beware of the Cacawkers. They have marvellous eyesight and incredible hearing. If they see any damage to your costumes, they will know that you are not Sorx, and then you will be in trouble. If they hear you talking in Hubeeish, they will hunt you down.'

Jack and Holly nodded. They didn't want to be attacked by Cacawkers.

Hornbeam moved over to the big entrance door, grabbed the large handle halfway up it, and pulled hard. It swung open raising a lot of dust.

'Off you go then!' he said. 'And Guid Lukio!'

Holly and Jack walked over to the door and stepped outside. Hornbeam closed the door behind them and walked back to his cage. He sat down in his chair, shouted, 'Engage', and began to feed through his feet.

'I hope they will be safe,' he said to himself. 'I do like those 2 young Hubees.'

Affable

Outside the tree house, Jack and Holly looked at each other very nervously. They were on their own in a strange world. They walked over to the road. There was no sign of any Sorx, but the smell of Crudax was quite strong.

'OK Holly!' cried Jack. 'Let's do this!'

They quickly got into the Sorx dadum rhythm: da-da-thump-dum, da-da-thump-dum, da-da-thump-dum, and after a while they hardly noticed that they were doing it. The springs in their good legs were working well, and they moved quickly side-by-side along the road, which was dipping slowly into a valley.

They reached the lowest point on the road and it began to rise up in front of them. After a while, even with the springs, they could feel their legs hurting as they dadumed up the increasingly steeper slope.

'Are you OK, Holly?' asked Jack, slightly out of breath.

'Yes, I'm fine, but my legs are beginning to ache,' said Holly. 'How are you doing?'

'I'm OK. But I hope we get to the top of this slope soon, my legs are hurting as well, and the smell of Crudax is getting worse,' said Jack. 'I could do with a drink. Do you fancy some Perx?'

'Yes,' said Holly. 'That's a good idea.'

They stopped, sat down by the side of the road, and took the bottles of Perx from their satchels. Several gulps later they started to burp and laugh.

'That tastes really good,' said Jack. 'But we'd better not drink it all, we may need some later.'

They put the stoppers back in the bottles, put the bottles in their satchels, and stood up.

'Are you ready?' asked Jack.

'Yes, and it can't be far now,' said Holly.

'I love you!' said a very gentle voice from some bushes beside them. 'I shouldn't, but I really love you!'

'Did you hear that Jack?' asked Holly.

'Yes, I did,' said Jack. 'It came from over there.'

He pointed to the bushes.

'Who's there?' asked Holly, nervously.

She was starting to feel frightened.

'Just me,' said the voice.

'Who's me?' asked Holly.

'I'm me, and I love you,' said the voice, as the bushes parted to reveal a wondrous creature.

Holly gasped as the creature walked towards her. It looked so cute.

It was mainly light brown, with four large floppy feet covered in black fur, and a lovely spiral tail in the most brilliant yellow colour. Down the middle of its back was a soft ridge, also covered in black fur.

Its head was as yellow as its tail, and it had 2 black fluffy ears which looked as if they had simply been stuck on. Holly noticed that there was a chunk out of one of its ears. It had a gentle face with great big brown eyes, and a black button nose above a beautiful upwards curving mouth.

'You are so cute!' cried Holly. 'I love you!'

'And I love you,' said the creature. 'But I don't think I should.'

'Why not?' asked Holly.

'Because you're a Sorx,' said the creature. 'And I don't like Sorx.'

The creature came closer and sniffed the air.

'But you don't smell like Sorx. You smell like rosemary,' it said. 'Sorx always smell of Crudax.'

This made Jack very worried. He didn't want their cover to be blown.

'Well, we are Sorx,' he said, very firmly. 'I'm 3:2:3, and this is 3:3:3.'

The creature looked at their feet.

'OK,' it said. 'If you say so.'

But it wasn't convinced.

'So, what are you?' asked Jack, trying to change the subject.

'If you are a Sorx, you should know what I am,' it said.

'Don't be silly 3:2:3,' said Holly. 'You know what it is. It's a Drongle! Don't you remember what Hornbeam said?'

She suddenly realised what she had said, and knew that she shouldn't have mentioned Hornbeam.

'Of course!' said Jack. 'Silly me!'

'Oh!' said the Drongle. 'You know Hornbeam the Qorx! So do I. He is a friend of mine.'

'Yes,' said Jack, thinking quickly. 'We often guard him in The Lonely Sweet Shop.'

The Drongle knew that Jack was lying. Hornbeam had not been guarded for several continuums. She often saw him in the forest at night.

114

'OK,' it said. 'If you say so.'

But she now knew for certain that these were not Sorx.

'Do you have a name?' asked Holly.

'Yes,' said the Drongle. 'I am Affable.'

'That's a good name,' said Holly.

'Thank you,' said Affable. 'I really love you. Where are you going?'

'To SƠorxville to find a friend,' said Holly. 'And I love you too.'

'Well, I wish you luck in your search,' said Affable. 'But SƠorxville is a bad place. I don't like it. There are Sorx everywhere.'

'Of course there are,' said Jack. 'It's where we live!'

'And there are Cacawkers!' said Affable.

'Yes, they live in SƠorxville as well,' said Jack,

'No!' shouted Affable. 'There are Cacawkers! I love you!'

It raised one of its front paws off the ground, and pointed it in the direction of SƠorxville. Jack and Holly looked up the road. 5 huge dark shadows appeared on the ground in front of them. Cacawkers were moving towards them in a V-formation like swans in flight. They were still some distance away, but they had clearly spotted the 2 Sorx with poorly legs.

Holly looked round to thank the Drongle for warning them, but Affable had vanished.

The Cacawker Ceremony

Gliding quickly and silently the Cacawkers swooped down. 2 landed on the road and began hopping towards them. Jack and Holly could clearly see their blue eyes and red beaks. These were opening and closing like pairs of scissors, making terrible Click-Clack sounds. They could also see the long sharp claws at the ends of their black feet.

The other 3 swooped backwards and forwards, inspecting them, and almost brushing their heads. Occasionally, they hovered over them like huge birds of prey. Jack was frightened that their claws might rip open their costumes, but they never quite touched them.

After a while, these 3 joined the other 2 on the road in front of them. All 5 then formed a closed circle with their heads inwards and began to make a Click- Clack sound with their beaks; first on their own, and then together. As they did this, the circle rotated slowly, and Holly noticed that they did not have white tails. These were fully grown Cacawkers.

After a tickle of time, the circle opened out, and spread itself in a straight line across the road, blocking their way with one in the middle and 2 on each side. The Cacawkers then all bowed low, stamped their claws on the ground, flapped their wings, and nodded their beaks slowly up and down. While they were doing this, the 2 at each end of the line moved sideways further away from the road. Suddenly they all stopped moving.

The Cacawker in the middle turned sideways, bowed low, and with one of its wings beckoned to Jack and Holly to continue their journey. The other Cacawkers also bowed.

Holly and Jack looked at each other and, without saying a word, knew instinctively what they had to do. They bowed low to the birds, and then slowly dadumed past them, keeping their eyes fixed on the road ahead. They continued daduming up the slope for about thirty dadums, then stopped and looked back. The Cacawkers had vanished.

'What was that all about?' asked Holly.

'I've no idea,' said Jack. 'But I think we have been accepted by the Cacawkers, so that can't be bad. Maybe they won't bother us again.'

'Let's hope not,' said Holly. 'They're really scary. All that bowing must have been the Cacawker Ceremony. Come on, let's keep daduming up this slope.'

They quickly set off again, hoping that the Cacawkers wouldn't return. The road and the slope seemed never ending. Then something appeared in the distance.

Jack stopped and stared hard ahead. He dadumed ahead of Holly and reached the spot first. There, held up by 2 posts with Lion's Teeth growing beside them, was a big neatly painted white sign with black lettering reading:

WELCOME TO SϴORXVILLE.

The 'Q' was crossed out in red paint and a red 'S' added. Underneath, another sign read:

This had also been crossed out in red paint.

Jack looked ahead, he was now at the top of the slope, and the road began to fall away gently into a valley.

'Holly! Look at SΩorxville!' he shouted, as Holly dadumed up to him.

Ahead of them was an amazing sight. About fifty dadums further on, both sides of the road were lined with tree houses. But these were not like The Lonely Sweet Shop. Even from this distance they could see that they had been altered in all sorts of ways. Most had ladders going up to different floors and small doors and windows had been added. It was just as Hornbeam had described.

'And what is that up ahead?' asked Holly.

She pointed along the road.

On the left-hand side there was a much smaller tree house, with a pointed roof. Next to it, a long branch of a tree stretched out across the road blocking the way. It was supported at each end by a wooden tripod.

'This must be the Tiny Tree House that Hornbeam saw,' said Jack. 'It looks like a Check Point. We'll have to pass through it to get into SΩorxville. We'll need our identity discs.'

They reached into their satchels and took out their discs.

'OK. Let's do this!' said Holly.

The Check Point

Holly and Jack slowly dadumed towards the Check Point and then stopped a few metres away from it. There was an open window on the side next to the road. They walked over and looked in. Behind a counter sat a Sorx, fast asleep and snoring loudly. Covering part of its head was a very large floppy light-blue hat with a silver S-shaped badge on it.

'Hello!' said Jack, quite cheerfully.

The Sorx snorted, grunted, and fell off its chair. Its floppy hat landed on top of it. It picked up the hat, scrambled to its feet, and dusted itself down. It put its hat back on, popped its ears through the slits, and looked at Jack through the window.

'Hello! You're very early!' it snapped, trying to regain its composure. Its ears were rotating in opposite directions, making its hat wobble.

'Hello!' said Holly to the Sorx, trying not to laugh at its wobbly hat, which really was far too big for it.

'Hello!' said the Sorx to Holly, seeing her beside Jack. 'You're the first ones through the Check Point today. Give me your ID discs!'

It was now shouting quite angrily.

Holly and Jack put their ID discs on the counter. The Sorx picked them up and looked at them very carefully. It then looked at Jack.

'You're a bit of a SQorxy aren't you!' it said, very rudely.

Jack ignored this, remembering what Hornbeam had said. The Sorx then looked at both of them.

'Your feet! Let me see your feet!' it shouted, and waved at them to move further back from the window.

Jack and Holly stepped back into the road. The Sorx looked at their feet.

'OK, come back!' it shouted. They moved back to the window.

'That all seems to be in order,' it said, handing their ID discs back to them. 'But what have you done to your legs?'

Jack panicked at this question. In all their preparations, they hadn't thought what to say if someone asked about their bandages. He looked at Holly blankly, and she looked back at him in exactly the same way. This lasted for what seemed like a long time, then Holly had an idea.

'We broke them when an old tree fell on us in the forest several solars ago,' she said. 'We were very lucky not to get killed. They were badly broken and we may have to keep these bandages on for squidges of time, but they will get better.'

'Oh, that's awful,' said the Sorx. 'That must have been very painful. But your bandages are getting dirty, you should get new ones. While you are in SQorxville you can get some from the Farmer.'

Jack and Holly looked at each other, knowing exactly what the other was thinking: *Why should we go to a farmer for new bandages?*

'OK, you can go through,' said the Sorx. 'That will be one Kalex each.'

'What?' asked Jack. 'Do we have to pay?'

'Normally, you wouldn't,' said the Sorx. 'But today is a market day and we are expecting many Sorx to come into town. We always charge on market days. Didn't you know that?'

'Oh yes, of course,' said Jack, thinking quickly. 'I just forgot that it's market day.'

He and Holly reached into their satchels and handed over one Kalex each.

'Thank you,' said the Sorx.

It stood up, came out of a door in the side of the tree house, walked over to the barrier, and lifted up one side of it.

'Please go through.' it said. 'Enjoy the market, and have a good solar. Guid Byo!'

'Guid Byo!' said Holly, instinctively, as she passed under the barrier, quickly followed by Jack.

The Sorx lowered the barrier and walked back into The Tiny Tree house.

They walked on a few steps and looked at each other. Inside their costumes they smiled. They were in SQorxville!

'Come on Holly,' said Jack. 'Let's go and find Podge.'

High above, 5 Cacawkers watched them as they dadumed into town.

Into SƟorxville

Jack and Holly dadumed slowly into SƟorxville, and stopped in front of the first tree house on the left. They stood up and looked at it. At one time it would have looked very like Hornbeam's Lonely Sweet Shop, but not now. The big Qorx-sized door had been crudely boarded over and a much smaller Sorx-sized door added. A number 3 was fixed to it.

3 new Sorx-sized doors had been cut out of the trunk. One a quarter of the way up on the left was number 7, one halfway up in the middle was number 13 and one three-quarters of the way up on the right was number 19. Each had a long rickety ladder reaching up to it from the ground. Extra windows had been added. Going upwards from the ground, they could see four sets of 2, there may have been more at the back.

As there were four doors, it was likely that each floor was a separate home for a Sorx family. The roof had the same cauliflower-like shape as The Lonely Sweet Shop, but there were now four T-shaped chimneys. A tree house for one Qorx had been turned into a home for four families of Sorx. But the elegance and beauty of the original tree house had gone. This tree house looked like exactly what it was, a very bad conversion.

'That looks so wrong,' said Holly.

'That's because it is wrong,' said Jack. 'They've made a right mess of what was a lovely tree house.'

Just as he said that, the door to number 19 opened and a Sorxling stepped out. It was wearing a very large yellow floppy hat without a badge, and holding a toy keesceptre.

Putting the keesceptre in its mouth, it stepped backwards onto the ladder, grabbed each side of it, and slid all the way down to the ground.

'Weeeeeee!' it shouted, in a very high voice.

It landed on the ground in a heap, jumped up, and skipped off into town making strange high-pitched noises while waving its keesceptre.

'That Sorxling is very lively,' said Holly.

'She certainly is and she drives me mad!' said a grumpy voice from door number 3 at the bottom.

The voice continued, 'She's off to see her friends and then she'll be going to the market but she makes so much noise about it.'

Jack and Holly turned to see a normal-sized Sorx standing in the doorway also wearing a hat that was too big for it, a pink one, without a badge.

The sight of the Sorx scared them.

'Hello,' said Holly, trying to sound calm.

'Hello,' snapped the Sorx. 'I suppose you're going to the market as well are you?'

It looked very grumpy indeed.

'Yes,' said Holly, thinking quickly. 'And we're also looking for the Treasure Store. Can you tell us where it is please?'

'Oh, are you from out of town?' asked the Sorx, very inquisitively. 'Everyone in town knows where the Treasure Store is, why don't you?'

'Yes,' said Holly, panicking slightly. 'We live in a tree house in the forest.'

She hoped that was a good answer.

'Ah yes,' said the Sorx, enviously. 'More and more Sorx are doing that nowadays to get away from the smell. Lucky you! I wish I could move away from this dump.'

'Yes, we're very lucky and I hope you will be able to soon,' said Holly, sympathetically.

'Not much chance of that!' exclaimed the Sorx. 'I'm number 193 on the Rehousing Waiting List! It'll take me squalls of continuums, and I'll be long gone when I finally get to the top of the list. It's just not fair!'

It stamped its middle foot on the ground and waved its left arm in the air.

'At least I'm living on the edge of town where the smell isn't so bad,' it went on. 'But my life is plagued by those noisy Sorxlings upstairs.'

It paused then continued, 'So, the Treasure Store is it, why the Treasure Store?'

It really was very nosy, in both senses, as its long nose was now twitching up and down.

'We are hoping to buy a present for one of our cousins,' said Holly, thinking on her 3 feet. 'We've heard there are some good ones there.'

'Yes, there are, if you can afford them. But I can't!' it grumbled.

And with that it stamped its middle foot on the ground again, turned back into the tree house, and slammed the door behind it.

'That Sorx was very rude,' said Holly, who didn't like rudeness. 'And it didn't even tell us where the Treasure Store is.'

'That's true,' said Jack. 'But remember what Hornbeam told

us. Sorx don't really like each other very much! Come on. Let's keep walking.'

The next tree house they came to, which was also on the left, solved a mystery. It too had been altered. At ground level there was a shop. Its entrance was a very neat Sorx-sized door. On either side of this were 2 large windows with shelves behind them, full of glass jars containing different coloured liquids and pills. Above the door was a large green sign, with white lettering reading:

29 SORXVILLE FARMACY.

'So that's why the Check Point Sorx told us to go and see the Farmer,' said Jack, laughing. 'This is a Pharmacy but they've used an "F" instead of "Ph"!'

Outside the Farmacy was a life-size wooden statue of a Sorx with a big hole in its head. Attached to it was a sign reading:

KEEP SORXVILLE TIDY!
PUT YOUR LITTER IN HERE!

It looked very neat and was definitely tidy.

'I like their litter bins,' said Holly.

She looked down at their dirty solid legs.

'Should we get some new bandages?' she asked.

'No,' said Jack. 'We've got to get to the Treasure Store. We mustn't waste any time. Let's keep walking.'

They walked on. Now there were converted tree houses on both sides of the road. The smell of Crudax was getting stronger. Their nostrils were starting to itch.

'What a pong!' exclaimed Holly. 'We must be getting near to the Thunder Works.'

'We are,' said Jack, remembering Map 2. 'But I think the stink is coming from that Thunderbox over there.'

He pointed across the road to a small tree house with a sign sticking out the top of it, which read:

THUNDERBOX.

There were 2 Sorx waiting to go in.

As they walked on, SQorxville was beginning to wake up. Sorx began to come down ladders and walk down the road. Most completely ignored them, but occasionally, one would look at their bandaged legs as they passed by. Fortunately, no-one spoke to them.

Soon, they came to a tree house on the left that looked very strange, even compared to the other converted tree houses. This one was painted dark-blue with a black roof. On top of it was a big light like the ones on top of lighthouses. But this light was blue, not white.

It had the original Qorx-size door, but this had not been boarded up and it had a smaller Sorx-size door cut into it. Like the other conversions it had four sets of 2 windows going upwards, but there were no smaller doors and no ladders. All the windows had big set of bars on the outside.

Above the large Qorx-size door was another very large green sign with white lettering reading:

59 SORXVILLE JAIL HOUSE AND POLICE STATION.

Lower down, on either side of the Sorx-size door were 2 smaller signs, each reading:

No Loitering!

Jack and Holly stopped in front of the Jail House and gasped. It looked evil.

'That looks scary,' said Holly, feeling frightened even more.

'It's meant to be,' said Jack. 'It's a Jail!'

'Poor Hornbeam being locked up in there,' said Holly.

'Yes, I wouldn't want to spend any time locked up in that,' said Jack, shivering slightly.

Just then the small Sorx-size door opened and 2 Sorx came out, each wearing a dark-blue floppy hat with a silver P-shaped badge on it. One of them carried a thick wooden truncheon. It saw Jack and Holly standing there.

'Hey! You 2! Can't you read?' it snapped.

It pointed to one of the smaller signs with its truncheon.

'Which part of, no loitering, don't you understand?' it asked, menacingly.

Jack and Holly looked at each other. They weren't sure what loitering meant, but clearly they were doing it.

The Sorx raised its truncheon over its head as if to hit them.

'Sorry,' said Jack, very humbly. 'We're from out of town, and we're looking for the Treasure Store.'

'It's right behind you, can't you see it?' it squeaked, angrily. 'But it doesn't open for a squodge. Now stop loitering! Move on!'

With that it lowered its truncheon, and dadumed off down the road with the other Sorx.

'Do you think they were the police?' asked Holly. 'They had a silver P on their hats.'

'Probably,' said Jack. 'The one with the truncheon was rude, but it was very helpful.'

Jack turned round and pointed across the road.

'For there's the Treasure Store,' he said.

Outside the Treasure Store

Holly turned round and saw what Jack was pointing at. Set back slightly off the road was an amazing conversion. It had originally been a very big tree house, but the Qorx-size door had been completely removed and filled in so carefully, that there was no trace of it at all. It had 2 Sorx-size doors at ground level. The left one had ENTRANCE written very neatly in white lettering on a green sign above it, and the right one had EXIT written on a red sign above it.

There were windows running equally spaced around the trunk, and these were at 5 levels. All the windows appeared to have shelves fitted on their insides.

Its main trunk was painted in a series of vertical and horizontal stripes of different colours. The horizontal ones were blue and white, and the vertical ones were yellow and red. Around each window were fairy lights that twinkled in similar colours.

The roof was painted in vertical red and white stripes, and there was a huge green triangular flag with yellow edges, flying from a flagpole at the top. It really looked like a treasure store, and just to confirm this,

23 TREASURE STORE

was written in neat white letters on a green sign, halfway up the trunk between 2 rows of windows.

Jack and Holly walked over and looked in one of the wider windows on the ground floor. They couldn't see very far in because it was dark inside, but on the shelves was a world of delights.

'Look at the telescope and glove-puppet,' said Jack.

'And look at the skittles and deck-chair,' said Holly.

This continued for some time, with each exchanging expressions of delight as they spotted one thing after another, and moved from window to window.

'These must have been foraged from Hubeeland,' said Jack, forgetting for a moment that he himself was a Hubee.

'You mean from our land!' exclaimed Holly, laughing.

'Oh Sorry! Of course I did. I must be turning into a Sorx!' said Jack, laughing at himself.

'Have you noticed that everything has a price tag on?' asked Holly.

'Yes, I have,' said Jack. 'And some of them seem to be expensive. That big seashell is 23 Kalex. I hope we will have enough for Podge.'

'I hope we do as well. But we have to find her first, and I can't see her in any of these windows,' said Holly, sadly.

'Don't worry Holly, this is a big shop, she'll probably be inside somewhere. We'll find her soon,' said Jack, reassuringly.

'But it doesn't open for a squodge, whatever that is,' said Holly. 'What are we going to do until then?'

'A squodge doesn't sound too long,' said Jack. 'So it should open soon, but while we are waiting let's see if we can find the Rainbow Factory.'

Outside the Thunder Works

Holly and Jack stepped back onto the road and continued walking through the town. Slightly further on, on the opposite side of the road to the Treasure Store, was the biggest tree house they had yet seen. It was enormous, and it was obvious what it was. Hornbeam had been right; they couldn't mistake it because it stank. This was definitely the Thunder Works.

In its front were 2 Qorx-size doors, and next to these were 2 Sorx-size doors. There were no other doors, no windows and no ladders. It looked like a factory. It was painted in a light-yellow colour, which was badly faded in places and covered in brown patches. Its roof was black, and there were several black pipes going in and out of its upper half.

Holly counted at least 7 chimneys sticking out of its roof. Some of these were belching out brown smoke, which was only slightly darker than the air above them. Halfway up its vast front, between the Qorx-size doors, was a long dark-blue sign with faded white lettering reading:

67 SORXVILLE THUNDER WORKS.

There were 2 smaller signs next to the 2 Sorx-size doors. One read:

Paid Volunteers Wanted.

The other read:

Come in and Win a Medal!

Between the doors, about 2 metres off the ground, a big golden trumpet stuck out into the street. A pipe coming out of the Thunder Works led into its blowing end. Even in the gloomy air, the trumpet was shining. It looked as though it had been polished very recently.

'I wonder why that's there?' said Jack, looking at the trumpet.

'I've no idea,' said Holly. 'But the stink is really bad now, my throat is getting sore.'

'Yes, so is mine,' Jack replied, coughing. 'Let's move on.'

They stopped walking and began daduming.

Passing yet another Thunderbox, they dadumed further down the road to an open area where 3 roads met, and where there was a large wooden signpost about 2 metres high. It was similar to the one that they had seen outside the Rodley Bottoms Tunnel. It had 5 signs on it. One read:

Rodley Bottoms Tunnel 1163p, 3491d.

and pointed directly back along the road they had just come. 2 others, each pointing along different roads, read:

Bramley Tunnel 2437p, 7309d.

~~Nearfar~~ Tunnel 347p, 1031d.

NEARFAR had been crossed out with red paint.
Another read:

QSORXVILLE 2099p, 6311d.

and pointed along a wide road to the right, in the same direction as the sign to Bramley. Once again the 'S' had been crudely crossed out with red paint and been replaced by a badly drawn red 'Q'.

The last one read:

TREACLE LAKE 397d.

and pointed in the same direction as the sign to Nearfar.

'I'd love to go to the Treacle Lake,' said Holly.'

'Maybe later if we have time,' said Jack. 'But first we need to find the Rainbow Factory, so that when we get Podge back, we know how to get onto the Jigsaw Trail.'

Jack thought about Map 2.

'Let's go up there,' he said, pointing along the QSorxville road.

A lot of Sorx and Sorxlings were heading in that direction. Jack and Holly quietly sneaked in beside them, and followed them up the road. None of the Sorx noticed them do this. Very soon they were in a street full of altered tree houses and tree shops on both sides. This seemed to be the main shopping street. In front of the shops were long lines of stalls spilling into the road, with Sorx wandering up and down a central row between them, stopping to look at what was for sale.

'This must be the market we paid one Kalex for,' said Holly.

'Yes,' said Jack. 'And it's very busy which is good for us. We can get lost in the crowd and no-one will notice us.'

'I hope you are right,' said Holly, nervously.

'Come on Holly we can do this,' said Jack, encouragingly. 'Just follow me.'

The Market

Jack set off walking up the line of market stalls, and was soon in amongst the crowd. Holly followed him, but Sorx kept crossing in front of her to get from one stall to another. It was difficult to keep up with him. As she followed him, she noticed some of the shops behind the market stalls. Over their doors were very neat signs reading:

SORXVILLE GREENGROCERS.
SORXVILLE CANDLESTICK-MAKERS.
SORXVILLE NUMBER ONE SWEET SHOP.
SORXVILLE NUMBER 2 SWEET SHOP.
SORXVILLE NUMBER 3 SWEET SHOP.

'That's lot of sweet shops,' Holly thought to herself.

Each shop in the street had a number, but the numbering didn't seem to follow a normal pattern. The first shop on the right-hand side of the street was number 2. The next one was number 5, then: 11, 17, 23, 31, 41 and 47. On the other side of the street the shops were numbered: 3, 7, 13, 19, 29, 37, 43, and 53.

In the candlestick-makers there were candles shaped like Qorx and Hubees. Signs in the window read:

Burn a Qorx!
Melt a Hubee!

Toy stalls offered models of Qorx and Hubees doing silly things, shelves full of jigsaws, make-your-own-Cacawker kits, miniature tree houses and models of an odd-looking long house. There were toy keesceptres, and pink and blue moons on sticks. Hanging from the awning, were soft toy Drongles in all different sizes.

One stall, in particular, was very unusual even amongst these odd stalls. It just sold numbers. It had a handwritten sign hanging from its awning, which read:

Prime Numbers.

Its awning was covered in numbers: 181, 2739, 7, 1481, 61, 2063, 5, 7757, and many more. They were printed in gold against a dark-blue background, and glowed as Enzor shone on them. On the table below were numbers in all colours, shapes and sizes.

Hanging from the awning were charts listing: The First Hundred Prime Numbers, The First Thousand Prime Numbers, and what looked like a roll of wallpaper that listed: The First Million Prime Numbers.

Looking at these, she understood what Hornbeam had said about the Sorx and prime numbers. She realised why the shops had their strange numbering pattern, they were in the order of the prime numbers.

One other thing she had noticed was that almost every Sorx

was wearing a big floppy hat, with their ears sticking out of them.

'Of course, their hats!' she thought, realising that she and Jack didn't have hats. 'I must buy some.'

Every third stall seemed to be a hat stall, each loaded high with hats of many colours. Stopping at one of them, she rummaged through the piles and found an orange one that she liked, and a dark-blue one for Jack. There was a star-shaped mirror hanging from the stall. She put her hat on and looked into it. It completely covered her head. There were 2 slits in it, so she reached up and pulled her ears through them. It was perfect; she felt more like a Sorx. While she had been doing this the stallholder had been looking at her. It was wearing a purple floppy hat.

'That looks good!' it said, trying to make a sale.

'Thank you!' said Holly. 'How much are they?'

'They are six Kalex each,' said the Sorx. 'But 2 for 11 Kalex.'

'I'll take these 2,' said Holly.

She reached into her satchel and pulled out a handful of Kalex. She counted out 11, handed them over to the stall holder, and put the rest back. She put her orange hat on, and put Jack's hat in her satchel. She had to admit that Sorx satchels were very useful things.

The next stall was selling coloured liquids in glass bottles. These seemed to be drinks. Sure enough, several Sorxlings came up and bought some of the bottles containing a blue liquid. They drank them, started laughing and made burping noises as they talked to each other.

'We need some more drinks,' she thought.

She noticed a sign reading: 2 Kalex. She reached into her

satchel and took out four Kalex. She picked up 2 bottles like the ones the Sorxlings had drunk.

'I'll have these please,' she said to the stallholder, handing her bottles over.

It held onto them while she gave it four Kalex. It handed her the 2 bottles and then gave her four more.

'There you are! Six bottles of Burpz!' said the stallholder.

She looked at her six bottles.

'I think you've made a mistake,' she said. 'You've given me six bottles.'

'No I haven't,' it said. 'It's 2 Kalex for 2 bottles and on market days you get another one free.'

'Oh thank you,' said Holly.

She thought quickly, and decided to keep the extra bottles.

'They may come in useful,' she said to herself.

She put the bottles into her satchel and looked round for Jack. He was a couple of stalls away. She set off after him. As Hornbeam had said, he could easily be spotted by his bandaged leg. She came up behind him and tapped him on the shoulder.

'Hi Jack!' she said. 'I've bought you a hat.'

Jack turned round, except it wasn't Jack.

'Hello!' said a Sorx. 'Who are you?'

'Hello!' said Holly, panicking. 'Oh I'm so sorry I thought you were someone else.'

'Who'd have thought there'd be a real Sorx with a bandaged leg,' she thought to herself, as she rushed away from the stall.

Up ahead, Jack ploughed on through the crowd, finally reaching the second last market stall. This sold strange shaped cushions in very bright colours. He picked up one or 2 while waiting for Holly. The Sorx behind the table on which the cushions were stacked watched him.

'Hello! Can I help you?' asked the Sorx. 'Do you like my cushions?'

'Hello! Yes,' said Jack, lying (he thought they were awful). 'But I'm just looking.'

'Oh that's fine,' said the Sorx, rather sadly. 'There's no charge for looking. Please take your time.'

At that point Holly arrived.

'I like your hat!' said Jack. 'But quick, let's get away from here before I end up buying a cushion.'

'What?' asked Holly, not sure she had heard him properly. 'A cushion?'

'Never mind,' said Jack. 'I'll tell you later.'

They quickly walked away, and Holly began to tell him about the real Sorx with the bandaged leg. But before she could complete her tale, they were both startled by what they saw on the last stall.

It looked the same as the other stalls; it was covered in a yellow and brown striped awning with a rolled up cover at the front, and had a table with a Sorx behind it in a floppy hat. But there was only one thing on the table. There, in a tatty cage with a bashed corner and a bright red handle, was a Drongle.

'Look at that Drongle!' cried Holly. 'I love it!'

The creature heard what Holly had said, moved one of its ears, and looked towards the Sorx who had just said it loved him. It sniffed.

'That looks like a Sorx,' it thought to itself. 'But is smells like rosemary not Crudax.'

It looked carefully at Holly, and knew she wasn't a Sorx.

'And I love you too!' it said, in a soft gentle voice.

139

The stallholder saw Holly and Jack looking at the Drongle.

'Do you want to buy it?' he asked. 'It's only 127 Kalex.'

'Oh, no thank you,' said Jack. 'We've got nowhere to keep it.'

'Please buy me,' said the Drongle, in its soft gentle soft voice. 'This Sorx is not very nice to me!'

'Shut up you stupid creature!' shouted the stallholder.

He grabbed an old blanket and threw it over the cage.

'Stall closed!' he shouted.

He reached up, and pulled down the cover over the front of the stall. Behind the cover, they could hear the Drongle crying as the stallholder began to hit it.

'Oh Jack,' said Holly, tearfully. 'Can't we do something to help it?'

'I'd love to Holly,' he said. 'But what can we do? I know it's tough but we have to stay with our plan, we haven't got much time. Come on, let's get away from here.'

Holly knew he was right, but was very sad about the Drongle.

'I've got a surprise for you!' said Holly, breaking the gloom caused by the sight of the poor Drongle. 'I got you a hat as well! I thought they'd make us look more like Sorx.'

She reached into her satchel, took out the dark-blue hat and handed it to him.

'Thank you!' said Jack.

He put the hat on, and pulled his ears through the slits.

'Come on,' he said. 'The Rainbow Factory can't be much further.'

Outside the Rainbow Factory

The road was much quieter now, the market was behind them, and they could see the tree houses on each side much clearer. Most were like the one where they had met the nosy Sorx complaining about the Sorxling. However, some were different.

One looked very important. It was painted a subtle shade of green and fitted with a sign reading:

103 SORXVILLE SUPERIOR BANK.

It had three pairs of windows, two on each floor. The ones on the lower windows were fitted with metal bars. There were no ladders or upper doors. It seemed to have only one entrance, which was at the top of a flight of smart wooden steps. These led to a Sorx-sized door painted in gold, with a splendid purple handle.

'That handle is the same shape as a Kalex,' said Jack.

Next to the bank was another tree house, again with only a single entrance door, and no ladders or upper doors. On it was a sign reading:

109 SORXVILLE FORAGING SCHOOL.

Below this was a large board with some notices pinned on. Jack and Holly walked over and read one of them:

PLEASE COME INSIDE AND ASK ABOUT FORAGING CLASSES. SORXVILLE NEEDS YOU!

and there was a picture of a Sorx in a green floppy hat with a silver 'F' badge on it, pointing directly out of the notice. Another notice read:

FORAGER'S MEETING TODAY AFTER THE MARKET CLOSES. TO BE HELD AT THE RAINBOW FACTORY.

'That apostrophe is in the wrong place,' said Holly, pointing to FORAGER'S. She was very keen on English, and had a thing about apostrophes.

'Is it?' asked Jack, who found apostrophes very confusing.

Sticking out of the top of the Foraging School was an extremely tall lookout tower, with a very long ladder, and what looked like a pole running from the top to the bottom. There seemed to be a Sorx at the top.

As they continued walking, several black shadows passed over the ground in front of them. The Cacawkers were never far away.

Further up the road on the right they found what they were searching for. There, set back a short distance, was a huge tree house. It had 2 Sorx-size doors at ground level, and no windows. Its roof was pointed like a cone, and sticking out of it were several T-shaped chimneys, and a huge pipe with a large flat V-shaped funnel on the end of it. Across the front was a large sign which read:

Underneath, a slightly smaller sign read:

We Make Happiness.

But the most noticeable thing about the tree house was that its front was covered in wobniars.

'I think this is it!' said Holly.

'I think you're right!' said Jack, laughing.

Suddenly, there was a loud whooshing sound from the roof. They looked up, and saw a wobniar being fired out of the flat V-shaped funnel high into the air. It arched across the sky, and they could see the 7 vibrant colours, all the wrong way round. It hung in the sky for a squig of time, then whooshed back into funnel.

'Wow! Did you see that?' asked Holly.

'Fantastic!' said Jack. 'I wonder what that was all about.'

They walked up to the Rainbow Factory. One of the Sorx-size doors was marked Entrance and the other Exit. Beside the exit door was a Sorx-shaped litter bin. Pinned on the entrance door was a notice, which read:

Foragers' meeting today after the market closes. Please leave your keesceptres outside to avoid affecting the rainbows.

On the ground by the side of the door was a short wooden tub with nothing in it. Written on it was:

FOR KEESCEPTRES.

They walked right round the Rainbow Factory. Only the front had wobniars on it, the rest was covered in wood like most of the other tree houses they had seen. At the very back, was a Sorx-sized door that led onto a short path. This linked to a very smart, much smaller tree house that had 2 levels of windows and one Sorx-size door. There were no ladders.

'This is very posh compared to the other tree houses we've seen,' said Holly. 'Perhaps the owner lives there.'

She noticed that just past the right-hand side of the posh tree house, was another path heading off towards a forest.

'That must lead to the Jigsaw Trail,' she said.

'Yes,' said Jack. 'That's good. We know where it is. Let's get back to the Treasure Store.'

Treacle Lake

They turned round and started walking towards the road. As they reached it, a Sorx and a Sorxling walked past them heading towards the Rainbow Factory. The Sorx was wearing a green floppy hat with a silver F on it, and was carrying a cage. This was bashed in the top corner, and a bright red handle could just be seen peeping out of the snaky hand wrapped round it. It was the same cage that they had seen earlier, and inside was a very sad looking Drongle.

'Jack!' whispered Holly. 'That's the Drongle we saw earlier!'

As it passed them the Sorx said, 'Hello!'

The Sorxling said nothing.

Jack and Holly both said, 'Hello!'

Holly slowed down and looked at the Sorx very carefully. There was something about it that she recognised. The Sorx, Sorxling and Drongle reached the Rainbow Factory and went in the entrance door.

'Come on Holly,' said Jack.

'I'm sure I've seen that Sorx before,' said Holly. 'It's a forager.'

'You probably have,' said Jack. 'We've seen lots of them today.'

They reached the road and went back the way they came. The market was still busy, and they carefully made their way through the crowds of Sorx back to the signpost at the bottom of the street.

They dadumed up to the Treasure Store, but it was still closed.

'I'd love to see the Treacle Lake,' said Holly.

'So would I,' said Jack. 'But we'll have to be quick.'

They dadumed back to the signpost, and followed the sign to the Treacle Lake. It led onto a narrow path. After a tickle of time they reached the lake, a vast expanse of treacle that spread out towards the surrounding countryside.

'Wow,' said Holly. 'That's amazing.'

'It sure is,' said Jack. 'And look at that.'

'What?' asked Holly.

Jack pointed towards the horizon where the countryside met the brownish sky.

'The land and the sky seem to be joined together,' he said.

Holly looked and sure enough they did.

'Do you think that is The Skyland Boundary?' asked Holly.

'It must be,' said Jack. 'That's the edge of Highlow, and there is no way into it except through the tunnels.'

'Or out of it,' said Holly.

They sat down by the edge of the lake and watched some Cacawkers helping themselves to a free treacle meal.

'Do you fancy something to eat?' asked Jack

'Yes. I'm starving,' said Holly. 'Why don't we have some Oodax or Yumbax?'

'I fancy a bacon sandwich with tomato sauce on it,' said Jack. 'So I think I'll have some Yumbax.' He took one out of his satchel and bit into it.

'Aaahh!' he said. 'That's so good. Just like the real thing!'

'I feel like something sweet and savoury,' said Holly. 'So I'm going to have an Oodax.' She took one out of her satchel and bit into it.

'Yes!' she exclaimed. 'That's perfect!', and quickly gobbled it up.

'And I've got a surprise for you,' said Holly. 'I bought us some drinks. I got six bottles of Burpz. We can have 2 now and keep four for later.'

She took 2 bottles out of her satchel and passed one to Jack. They unfastened the tops and took a swig. The taste was over-whelming, cold, sweet, fizzy, fantastic!

'It tastes great! Thank you!' said Jack.

'You're welcome,' said Holly. 'Burpz isn't bad at all, is it?'

She took another big swig, and burped.

Jack laughed, and burped back. This continued for several burps, with each of them trying to out-burp the other.

Just to the right of where they were sitting, the Treacle River flowed into the lake. The treacle was very thick. It moved like lava from a volcano, smothering the river bed. Mainly dark-brown with yellow and lighter brown streaks, it formed wondrous patterns on the surfaces over which it flowed. Jack and Holly were hypnotised by it.

Shapes appeared in the flow and vanished just as quickly. A dragon, a pirate ship, a dinosaur all came and went as they stared into the moving mass.

'This is amazing!' said Holly. 'Can you see all the shapes? They come and go so quickly.'

'Yes, I can,' said Jack.

'I must taste some,' said Holly.

Reaching down, she put her right hand into the flow and scooped up a gloop of treacle. She sniffed it as best she could in her Sorx costume, then put some in her mouth. It tasted so sweet. She really liked it.

'It's great Jack, try some,' she said, licking the remaining treacle from her hand.

Jack scooped up a handful of treacle. Like Holly, he first sniffed it, then ate some.

'Oh! That's very sweet!' he said.

Jack didn't usually like really sweet things, but he continued to eat it, and then licked his hand until it had all gone. He looked up the river, watching it flow under a bridge.

'That must be the road to the Nearfar Tunnel,' said Jack, remembering the bridge from the maps.

He and Holly looked at the bridge. There was a Sorxling walking along the top of the wooden barrier on the side nearest to them. Suddenly it slipped and fell straight into the river. There was a loud plop as it hit the sticky surface and was quickly carried into the lake.

'We've got to help it!' cried Holly.

'Yes we have!' said Jack.

They jumped to their feet.

The Sorxling had managed to get its head above the surface, and because of the thickness of the treacle it was able to float. It wiped treacle from its eyes and saw Jack and Holly.

'Help! Help! Help!' it shouted, bobbing up and down slowly in the treacle.

It was about 5 metres from the shore. Holly and Jack needed something long enough to reach it. Behind them was a tree house with a sign reading:

1123 SORXVILLE NUMBER FOUR SWEET SHOP.

On top of it was a very tall pointed roof, with a long flagpole.

'I wonder how they put the flag on that,' Jack thought to himself.

He ran round the back of the shop and there, lying on the ground, was one of the long ladders he'd seen on the tree houses earlier.

'Help me Holly,' he shouted.

Holly rushed over and helped him carry the ladder back to the shore. They raised the ladder up on its end next to the shoreline, and slowly lowered it across the treacle towards the Sorxling. It was just long enough.

'Grab the end of it!' Jack shouted to the Sorxling.

The Sorxling grabbed the end of the ladder. Jack and Holly pulled as hard as they could, and it began to move slowly towards them.

'Keep pulling!' shouted Holly. 'It's moving.'

Slowly, rung by rung, they hauled it in until the Sorxling was very close to the shore. Jack reached out and grabbed its hand and hauled it onto dry land. It lay there like a big stranded seal, completely covered in treacle.

'My son! My son! My son!' cried a high-pitched voice behind them.

They looked round to see a Sorx running towards them. It rushed past them to the treacle seal and fell on its knees beside it.

'Are you OK!' it shouted. 'Speak to me!'

'I'm OK Dad,' it said, rather sheepishly. 'I fell off the bridge and these Sorx saved me.'

He pointed to Jack and Holly.

The father looked over to Jack and Holly.

'Thank you! Thank you! Thank you! You saved my son's life,'

he said, as tears welled up in his eyes.

'It was nothing,' said Jack.

'It was everything,' said the Sorx.

'I'm sorry but we must go now,' said Jack. 'We've got to be somewhere urgently, and it will be opening very soon.'

'Where are you going?' asked the Sorx.

'To the Treasure Store,' said Jack. 'There may be something there that we want.'

'But I own the Treasure Store,' said the Sorx. 'And I will indeed be opening it soon. If you can let me take my son home, I'll meet you there, and you can have anything you want as a reward. Thank you again.'

He turned to the Sorxling, who was now standing up, and clipped him across one of his ears.

'You stupid boy!' he shouted. 'Wait until I get you home!'

'I'm sorry Dad,' said the Sorxling.

'You will be!' said his father.

He turned back to Jack and Holly.

'Thank you again, and I'll see you soon!' he said, very politely, before dragging the Sorxling off towards the town.

'Wow! That was an adventure,' said Jack. 'But weren't we lucky to meet the Treasure House owner. We might be able to get Podge back as a reward!'

'But only if she is there,' said Holly, anxiously.

'Well, there's only one way to find out, and at least you got to see the Treacle Lake,' said Jack.

'Yes I did', said Holly, looking over the vast lake of treacle.

Beyond it she could just make out the rising land running into The Skyland Boundary.

'That's a lot of treacle,' she said, laughing.

'It sure is,' agreed Jack. 'Now let's go back to the Treasure Store and find Podge.'

Inside the Treasure Store

When Holly and Jack reached the Treasure Store, there was a long queue of Sorx waiting for it to open. They joined the end.

'Our bandaged legs are getting a bit tatty,' said Holly. 'Yours has strips of bandages falling off it. We need to be careful.'

Jack looked down at their legs. She was right. They needed to take more care of them.

The Treasure Store owner came up the street and saw Jack and Holly. He waved at them excitedly. They waved back less excitedly. Reaching the queue he pointed to them.

'These Sorx saved my son's life,' he shouted. 'They're heroes!'

The rest of the queue applauded loudly.

Inside their costumes Jack and Holly felt very uneasy. They didn't need this attention.

'Please!' the owner said to them. 'Come into the shop first'.

He led them in through the entrance door.

The rest of the queue followed. On the wall was a big notice-board with a list of treasures, and where they could be found.

THE BOTTOMEST FLOOR	-	OUTDOOR TREASURES.
THE NEXT FLOOR	-	INDOOR TREASURES.
THE NEXTER FLOOR	-	HARD TREASURES.
THE NEXTEST FLOOR	-	SOFT TREASURES.

Holly and Jack stood beside the owner looking at the board.

'What would you like?' he asked. 'You can have anything you want.'

'Can we look at the Sorxling Treasures?' asked Holly.

'Certainly, follow me,' he replied.

They set off up a spiral staircase marked, 'UP.' Four sets of steep spirals later they arrived at The Topest Floor - Sorxling Treasures. Puffing and panting after their long climb, they gazed around the room. They couldn't believe their eyes. There were toys everywhere, all over the floor, stacked on shelves, flowing over tables, and plonked on window sills. Where to begin?

'Please look around. If you find anything you would like then let me know,' said the shopkeeper, who began to sort out a box of toys near the top of the staircase.

Jack and Holly moved round the floor quietly taking it all in. Holly lifted up a jigsaw; underneath it were toy frogs. Jack moved a bagatelle only to find a mouth organ. Holly dug into a box of soft toys but only found teddy bears. Jack pulled a bag off a shelf and got covered in toy soldiers. And so it went on. Lifting this, moving that, but with no luck. They began to slow down and lose heart.

On one window sill was a big floppy elephant, Holly's favourite animal.

'Holly, look at this,' said Jack, pointing to the window sill. 'It's an elephant!'

He was trying to cheer her up.

Holly stopped searching and came over to Jack. She picked up the elephant and gave it a hug. It had a tag on it which read:

'Hello Ellie,' she whispered in its ear. 'Please help me find Podge.'

She started to put Ellie back on the window sill and couldn't believe what she saw. For there, hidden behind where Ellie had been sitting, was Podge.

'Podge! Podge! Podge!' she shouted, unable to keep quiet. 'It's Podge!'

Jack came rushing over and saw Podge on the window sill.

'Yeesss!!!!' he said. 'We've found her!'

The sound of Holly shouting brought the shopkeeper over from his box of toys.

'Have you found something?' he asked.

'Yes,' said Jack, as calmly as he could. 'Can we have that toy please?'

He pointed to Podge.

'You most certainly can,' said the owner, reaching over to get Podge from the sill.

But before he could do so, the long snaky fingers of another hand reached out and grabbed her.

'I'll have that one!' said a voice from behind them.

They turned round to see a Sorx with a Sorxling beside it.

'I'm sorry,' said the owner. 'It's spoken for.'

'It sure is,' said the Sorx. 'It's spoken for by me. I found it, so I have the first right to it.'

Holly looked at the Sorx. It had a green floppy hat on with a silver F badge. She looked even more closely, and realised that it was the same Sorx they had seen with the Drongle in the cage. It was also the same Sorxling.

The owner looked aghast.

'Of course' he said. 'You have that right if you found it, but can you prove it?'

'This should do it,' said the Sorx.

It pulled a piece of paper out of its satchel, and handed it to the owner who began reading it.

'Wait a minute ...,' the owner began, then paused.

Holly's heart soared.

'Oh dear, that seems to be in order,' he continued, handing it back to the Sorx.

Holly's heart sank.

'Of course it is,' said the Sorx. 'And if you want further proof just look at the price tag on it, it will have my name on it, look here!'

He handed Podge back to the owner who looked at the price tag. On it was written: *29K - Foraged by 2:7:3.*

The owner looked at it, then asked, 'And you are 2:7:3?'

'Yes I am,' said the Sorx. 'Just look at my feet.'

The owner looked at its feet, and sure enough its toes were in the order 2:7:3.

When Holly heard and saw this she almost passed out inside her costume. This was the Sorx in the garden who had taken Podge from her. She couldn't believe it. Jack also realised who the Sorx was. He moved over to Holly and put his arm round her. He could feel her shaking with shock. He held onto her tightly to stop her from falling over.

'But you'll have to buy it,' said the owner, angrily. 'That will be 29 Kalex.'

'But don't forget that I get a discount as the finder,' said 2:7:3, smugly. 'It's usually down to the next prime number.'

'You're right, of course,' said the owner, trying hard not to lose his temper. 'So that will be 23 Kalex.'

2:7:3 reached into her satchel and took out a large handful of Kalex. She pushed a lot of dolls onto the floor from the top of a nearby table, and started counting out the Kalex.

'…twenty, twenty-one, twenty-two, 23!' she counted. 'There. I'll have that now please.'

She reached out towards Podge. The owner handed her over.

'Thank you!' said the Sorx, even more smugly.

She handed Podge to the Sorxling who was standing nearby.

'Here you are Sis,' she said to the Sorxling. 'I told you I'd bring you a treasure.'

The Sorxling took Podge and looked at her.

'What does it do?' she asked.

'It doesn't do anything,' said 2:7:3. 'But it's nice to hold isn't it?

'I suppose so,' said the Sorxling in a very bored voice, and rammed Podge firmly into her satchel.

Holly's heart, already very low, sank even lower.

2:7:3 turned and headed off down the spiral staircase followed by the Sorxling. The owner turned to Jack and Holly.

'I'm so sorry,' he said. 'But there's nothing I can do. It's the "Law of Foragers First Dibs" as you know. She found it, so, she was entitled to buy it first.'

Jack and Holly didn't know. But did know that Podge had now been stolen by the same Sorx 3 times!

'Is there anything else that you would like?' asked the owner.

'No thank you,' said Jack, sadly. 'We just wanted that toy.'

'I'm so sorry,' said the owner. 'It's such a shame that it was bought by that Sorx. She's a forager who brings back lots of treasures from Hubeeland. But she thinks she's much better than everyone else. The Sorxling she had with her is her sister, One:2:One, who is very spoilt.'

'Poor Podge being with her,' thought Holly, feeling very sick.

'Her father owns the Rainbow Factory,' said the owner. 'They think they own Sorxville, but most Sorx don't like them.'

'Do you think they would sell it to us,' asked Holly.

'I doubt it,' said the owner. 'But you could ask. They're probably still in the store.'

'We must try,' said Jack.

He and Holly headed downwards to the Nextest Floor where the Soft Treasures were kept. Cloth, scissors, sewing bags, needles, threads, rugs, cushions, blankets, duvets, cotton sheets and pillow cases, were neatly stacked on shelves around the room. Some cloth had fallen onto the floor and, in his rush, Jack nearly tripped over a narrow roll of white cotton. He looked at it, picked it up, and put it in his satchel.

'This might be useful,' he thought.

They checked the floor, but 2:7:3 and One:2:One weren't there.

Down the spiral staircase they went to the Nexter Floor full of Hard Treasures: pots, pans, knives, forks, spoons, jugs, mugs, plates, table mats and bread bins, waste bins, mops, dust pans and brushes. But no sign of the two thieves.

So down they went to the Next Floor. This was crammed with Indoor Treasures: pictures, mirrors, candlesticks, vases, coffee tables, nests of tables, chairs and carpets. There was even a large wooden wardrobe up against one of the walls.

'How did they get that through a tunnel?' thought Jack.

Meanwhile, Holly had searched he floor.

'They're not here,' she said.

The Bottomest Floor was Outdoor Treasures. Here, garden gnomes stretched out as far as the eye could see, carefully laid out like an army. Happy ones, sad ones, fishing ones, sleeping ones, sailing ones, running ones, footballing ones, ones holding hands and ones doing handstands.

Amongst the gnomes were rakes, hoes, spades, shovels, dibbers, brooms, buckets, statues, garden chairs, picnic tables, parasols, stepladders, hosepipes, gloves, hammers and screwdrivers.

Jack was gobsmacked.

'How did the Hubees not notice all this stuff disappearing?' he wondered.

Holly quickly scanned the floor. They weren't there.

'Let's go outside,' she shouted, and headed out of the exit door.

Jack set off after her, knocking a rake on top of the gnome army scattering it everywhere.

'I'm so sorry,' he said to the owner, who had followed them down to The Bottomest Floor.

'Don't worry,' said the owner. 'I'll sort it out.'

He picked up the head of a fishing gnome.

'Are you sure that there's nothing at all that you would like for saving my son?' he asked.

'Can I have this please?' asked Jack, digging into his satchel and pulling out the roll of narrow cotton cloth he had picked up in soft treasures.

'Yes, of course you can,' said the owner. 'With pleasure! But is that all you want?'

'Yes, that's all thank you,' said Jack. 'Guid Byo!'

He dashed out of the exit door, and immediately ran into

a Sorx coming in the wrong way, accidentally standing on the six toes on its middle foot.

'Hey! Be careful where you're going you stupid SQorxy!' shouted the Sorx, as it reached down and rubbed its toes.

'I'm sorry!' said Jack, who, thinking fast, quickly added, 'But I need a Thunderbox!'

'Oh don't worry,' said the Sorx. 'I know how you feel. Guid Lukio!'

'Thank you! Guid Byo!' said Jack, as he finally reached the road outside.

He looked around, and saw Holly in the middle of the road.

'There!' she said, pointing down the road. 'That's them!'

The wrong prime number

Sure enough, just turning into the main market street were the Sorx and her sister. The Sorx' green forager's hat gave her away. Jack and Holly followed them as best as they could through all the Sorx now strolling in the road.

They reached the entrance to the market street just in time to see them go into the Number One Sweet Shop. They walked up to the entrance and waited. They could see them inside the shop. 2:7:3 was buying some purple and green sweets for One:2:One. She paid for them, turned around, and they walked out of the shop.

'Hello! Excuse me,' said Jack.

'Hello! Didn't I see you in the Treasure Store?' snapped the Sorx.

'Yes, you did,' said Jack.

She looked Jack up and down.

'You're a bit of a SQorxy, aren't you?' she sneered. 'What do you want?

Jack bit his tongue, and ignored her rudeness.

The Sorxling opened her bag of sweets, took one out, and put it in her mouth.

'Would you be willing to sell the toy you just bought in the Treasure Store?' asked Jack. 'My friend is very fond of soft toys and she would really like that one.'

The Sorxling reached into her satchel and pulled out Podge.

'You can have it if you want,' she said. 'It doesn't do anything.'

She held Podge out to Jack.

'Not so fast!' said 2:7:3, sensing a profit. 'How much will you pay for it?'

Jack and Holly turned their backs on the Sorx and the Sorxling.

'I've got 23,' whispered Jack.

'And I've got eight,' whispered Holly.'

They turned back to 2:7:3 and One:2:One.

'We can give you 31 Kalex,' said Jack. 'That's all we have.'

A glint appeared in the Sorx' purple eye. 31 was a prime number, which she would normally have taken, but she was feeling greedy. She thought of the next prime number.

'I'll let you have it for 37 Kalex,' she said.

'But we've only got 31,' said Holly, anxiously. 'And that's a prime number.'

'Yes, but it's the wrong prime number, so you'll have to get some more, won't you?' sneered the Sorx. 'We live in the Rainbow Factory. I've got a foragers' meeting there just after the market closes. You must bring me 37 Kalex before the meeting. But remember, if you are late, the price goes up!'

She grabbed the Sorxling's hand, turned away, and walked into the market. She did this so hard, that some of the Sorxling's sweets jumped out of the bag and fell onto the road.

'Hey, my sweets!' shouted the Sorxling, trying to reach down to pick them up.

'Leave them!' shouted the Sorx back at her. 'We can get some more. There are plenty of sweet shops.'

Jack and Holly looked at each other.

'What can we do Jack?' asked Holly. 'We need to get six more Kalex before the market closes. We'll never get Podge back now.'

She sat down heavily on the kerb at the side of the road, and started to cry.

'Don't worry Holly,' said Jack, reassuringly. 'We'll think of something.'

But even he was at a loss to know what to do. He sat down on the kerb beside her, and stared blankly across the road towards the Thunder Works. He looked at the brown smoke pumping out of the dark chimneys. There was a Sorx on a ladder polishing the golden trumpet. A lightbulb came on in his head.

'Follow me!' he said.

Inside the Thunder Works

Jack stood up, closely followed by Holly, and walked over the road to the Thunder Works. The Sorx was still polishing the trumpet. Jack stopped beside the ladder.

'Hello!' said Jack, looking up at the Sorx. 'Are you open?'

'Hello!' said the Sorx. 'Yes, we are. Just go in and ring the bell.'

Jack turned the handle on one of the Sorx-size doors and pushed.

The door opened.

'What are you doing?' asked Holly, nervously.

'Just trust me Holly,' said Jack, and in he went.

Holly waited for a moment, then stepped inside after him, shutting the door behind her.

At first it looked as though they had stepped into total darkness after the brightness of the daylight outside. But slowly their eyes grew used to the gloom. Shapes and shadows began to emerge. There were several yellowy gas lamps on the walls that helped them to see.

They were in a small entrance hall. The walls and ceiling were painted light-green, and there were benches along the wall on the right. There was a window in the wall opposite the door they had come in. A small shelf under the window had a bell on it.

Jack walked over and tapped the bell, which gave off an echo-ing ting sound. Nothing happened. He tapped it again. There was the sound of something moving from behind the window. Slowly, the window slid open and a Sorx head appeared. It had a large black floppy hat with 2 ears sticking out of it. On the hat was a large silver G-shaped badge.

'Hello! What do you want it?' it snapped. 'Oh, you're a bit of a SQorxy aren't you?'

By now Jack was quite used to the rudeness of Sorx, so he ignored it.

'We've come to volunteer,' he said. 'We saw the sign outside.'

'That's news to me!' thought Holly.

'Oh you have, have you?' questioned the Sorx. 'That's brave of you.'

Jack didn't like the sound of that, and neither did Holly.

'We don't get too many volunteers, most Sorx donate via the Thunderboxes or at home,' said the Sorx, rather menacingly.

'Donate what?' thought Holly.

'Have you donated before?' asked the Sorx. 'Do you know what's involved?'

'No,' said Jack. 'But we need some money desperately. How much do you pay?'

'We pay 5 Kalex for each successful session,' said the Sorx.

'And how long is a session?' asked Jack, knowing that they had to get to the Rainbow Factory before the market closed.

'Oh, it depends on how long you take,' said the Sorx. 'But most donations are finished after only a squig of time.'

Jack turned to Holly.

'What do you think Holly?' he whispered.

'I don't know,' said Holly, hesitantly. 'We don't even know

what we are volunteering for. And what is a "successful session"? What if we are not successful?'

'But we need the Kalex,' said Jack. 'If we can get ten more, we'll have 41 and that horrible Sorx only wants 37, so we'll have enough.'

'OK then,' said Holly, reluctantly. 'Let's do it.'

Jack turned back to the Sorx behind the window.

'We'd like to volunteer now,' he said.

'That's good,' said the Sorx. 'We need as many volunteers as we can get. Please go through that door.'

It stuck its left arm out of the window and pointed to a door on the left of the entrance hall. It had a sign on it reading:

VOLUNTEERS ONLY.

'I'll meet you inside,' it said, and closed the window.

They walked over to the door, opened it, and stepped into a huge chamber full of strange noisy machinery. Up above them conveyor belts were moving from one big cylinder to another. They couldn't see what they were carrying, but whatever it was it stank.

There was an enormous dark-red balloon, running from the floor to the ceiling, swaying gently back and forth. It had a very large 3 written on it. A huge pipe ran from one of the big cylinders straight out of the side of the building. Other pipes linked into this inside the building like branches of a tree. Written on the side of the big pipe was:

CRUDAX LINE.

At ground level was a row of small rooms. The door of each room had a number on and a sign reading: SINGLE, DOUBLE or TRIPLE.

The whole place was lit by huge gas lamps dotted around the walls. These gave off strong hissing sounds, and their flames cast strange flickering shadows on the walls. There did not appear to be any windows.

It was a brooding, dingy, scary place and Jack and Holly were definitely scared. They kept close together.

The Sorx appeared out of a door from its office in the wall to their right, and walked over to them.

'OK, let me just run through what's going to happen,' it said. 'First, do you want a single or a double?'

'I'm sorry,' said Jack. 'I don't know what you mean.'

'Oh of course you don't,' said the Sorx. 'I forgot that this is your first time. What I mean is do you want to donate together or separately?'

'Together!' said Jack and Holly at the same time.

'OK, then you will have a double,' said the Sorx, nodding. 'That will be better, because you will be able to help each other. Please follow me.'

It took them across to the row of rooms and stopped at number 5, which had a sign reading: DOUBLE.

'This one will do,' he said, opening the door and stepping inside. 'Please come in.'

Jack and Holly stepped into a room with yellow walls, and a white ceiling covered in brown patches. It was lit up more than the machinery room, with four gas lamps burning away quite happily and giving off a lot of light.

Inside the room to the left of the door was a wooden seat

with a hole in the middle. Next to the seat was a big red button. The seat faced a shelf at the end of the room, with a brown deflated balloon on it. A thin tube ran from the wooden seat to the balloon.

On the wall behind the balloon was a white graduated measuring scale, like a ruler, running vertically towards the ceiling. The lines on the scale were equally spaced, and marked in black. Near the top of the scale was a heavy red line. On the ceiling above the balloon there was small golden trumpet pointing downwards.

Along the other side of the room was exactly the same arrangement. At the end of the room, between the 2 balloons, was a small shelf with a hand bell on it. Below the shelf was a wash basin with some towels and bars of soap.

'As you can see,' said the Sorx. 'This is a double. It has 2 seats, one for each of you. In a squig, I will leave you and you can then choose your seat and start. Once you're comfortably seated, you must press the red button next to your seat.'

It pointed to the red buttons.

'These will start the machinery, and you must produce as much Number 3 as you can,' it continued. 'Don't worry if you produce Number 1 or Number 2, they will be separated from the Number 3, which will pass along the tubes into the balloons and they will inflate.'

It gestured towards the end of the room.

'In order to receive your payment,' it said, firmly. 'You must inflate your balloon until the top of it reaches the red line on the scale behind. But please note that you cannot donate in each other's seat. The seat will remember your bottom. If another bottom sits on it, the machinery will stop working and you will not be able to continue. Any questions so far?'

It stopped and looked at Jack and Holly, who were looking at each other in shock.

'Er, no, I don't think so,' said Jack.

Holly just shook her head.

'Good,' said the Sorx. 'You will see that there is a golden trumpet on the ceiling above each balloon.'

It pointed to the 2 small trumpets.

'If you can inflate your balloon so that it touches your trumpet,' it continued. 'You'll be awarded a medal. But don't worry if you can't. A medal is very rarely awarded. Only the most powerful Sorx can produce that amount of Number 3. Any final questions?'

Holly and Jack looked at each other and said nothing.

'Good,' said the Sorx. 'Take as long as you like, there's no time limit. The red button will start and stop the machinery, and you can restart it if you wish. When you are done just ring that bell.'

It pointed to the hand bell on the small shelf.

'You can also ring it if you get into difficulties,' said the Sorx. 'I will then come and help you. And don't forget to wash your hands when you've finished. We must keep things hygienic in the Thunder Works.'

It started to leave the room then stopped.

'Oh yes,' it said. 'I forgot to mention that while you are donating, a spray gun will slide out from under your seat at times, and wash your bottom with warm water. We find this helps to generate Number 3, and also washes away any Number 1 and Number 2 you produce. Guid Byo!'

And with that it stepped out of the room and closed the door.

Making a donation

'Jack!' exclaimed Holly. 'What have you got us into! This place is crazy!'

'Sorry Holly,' said Jack. 'But we do need the Kalex.'

Looking round the room he noticed a bolt on the door. He quickly slotted it into place and relaxed a little.

'That should keep us safe for a while,' he said. 'Let's take our heads and hands off.'

He took off his satchel and hat, pulled off his hands, then reached up and pulled off his head. His hair was sticking up like corn in a field. Holly laughed.

'You look like a scarecrow!' she said.

'I don't mind!' said Jack, speaking in his normal voice. 'It just feels so good to take those off!'

Holly did the same. She also had scarecrow hair.

'Come on Holly, we can do this!' said Jack. 'I'll go first.'

Jack opened his flap and pulled his shorts down so that his bottom was free to donate. He sat down on the hole in the wooden seat on the left side of the room. He turned on the seat to face the shelf with the balloon on it, and pressed the red button. There was a loud whirring sound, and he could feel his bottom being sucked into the hole until that there were no gaps around the edge. He tried to fart, but nothing came out. He tried again, still nothing.

Suddenly, he felt his bottom being washed. It didn't hurt, but it did tickle. He laughed, and began to fart. Not much at first, but the more he laughed the more he farted. His farts ran through the pipe to the balloon, which began to inflate.

The water-sprayer came out again and again, each time tickling his bottom. This spurred him on and he farted more and more, squeezing as hard as possible. The balloon continued to inflate.

'This is easy!' he thought.

But he thought too soon. He farted his last fart. No matter how hard he tried, he was out of gas. The top of the balloon was nowhere near the red line on the measuring scale. He pressed the red button, and the machinery stopped.

He looked over to Holly who was sitting on the other seat.

'That was hard,' he said. 'I'm empty. Do you want to try?'

'I'll give it a go,' said Holly. 'But I think we need something to help us.'

She reached into her satchel and pulled out some Oodax.

'These should do the trick!' she cried.

'That's brilliant!' said Jack. 'I'd forgotten all about those.'

He looked into his satchel.

'I've got six,' said Jack, 'I haven't eaten any yet.'

'I've got 5,' said Holly.

'I've already filled part of the balloon, so I'll take 3, and you can have six. We'll save 2 for later,' said Jack.

He took 3 Oodax and ate them quickly.

After a trickle of time the Oodax began to work. Jack soon felt like farting. He got back on his seat and pressed the red button. His bottom was sucked into the hole. He tried to fart but nothing happened. He tried again just as the sprayer started. There was a huge explosion from his bottom, and out came one of the biggest farts he had ever done. It flowed along the pipe to the balloon which inflated rapidly, stopping just short of the red line. Jack paused and waited for the next spray. As it hit his bottom he produced another huge fart that lifted his balloon well above the red line.

'Yeesss!' he cried. He tried again, but even after several more sprays there were no more farts to be made. His balloon had not reached the trumpet. He pressed the red button and the machinery stopped.

He looked over to Holly who had been eating her Oodax very slowly while watching Jack. She was already in position on her seat.

'Good luck Holly,' he said.

She pushed her red button and her bottom was sucked into the hole.

'Ohhh!' she cried. 'That feels strange!'

The sprayer popped out and washed her bottom making her laugh. The Oodax kicked in and she began to produce the most amazing farts. Spray - fart! - spray - fart! - spray - fart! Her balloon rose rapidly. It very quickly passed the red line on the chart, and squashed into the trumpet.

'Stop it Holly!' shouted Jack. 'You're going to blow the roof off!'

Holly bashed her red button, and the machinery stopped.

'That was incredible!' said Jack.

'Yes it was, wasn't it!' said Holly, excitedly letting out another fart. 'And we've got enough Kalex for Podge. Quick, let's get them and go to the Rainbow Factory.'

'And you've won a medal!' said Jack. 'That's amazing!'

Holly didn't say anything. She wasn't bothered about a medal, all she wanted was Podge. They tidied up, and dried themselves on the towels.

Jack looked at the dirty bandages on their false legs.

'We should change these bandages,' he said. 'Some Sorx might notice how dirty they are and make comments. We don't want to draw attention to ourselves.'

'But we must get going,' said Holly. 'We have to get to the Rainbow Factory before the market closes. We haven't got time to go to the Farmer.'

'Oh, the market will be on for a long time yet,' said Jack. 'And I got this from the Treasure Store. The owner said I could have it.'

He reached into his satchel and pulled out the roll of cotton cloth.

'It'll be good for new bandages,' he said.

'Yes it will!' said Holly. 'Let's just cover the old ones up.'

They sat down on their seats and covered up each other's bandages, tying them on very tightly. Holly put her head and hands back on, and pressed the button behind her right ear. Jack put on his head and hands. They put on their satchels.

'Let's go,' said Holly.

She picked up the bell and rang it loudly. Very quickly the door opened and the Sorx entered.

'Have you finished?' it asked.

'Yes we have,' said Jack in his normal voice. He had forgotten to press the button on his head. Holly heard him and got very worried.

'Oh, what's happened to your voice?' asked the Sorx.

Jack hesitated for a moment, thinking quickly.

'I've got a sore throat,' he said. He coughed to emphasise his made-up illness.

'You sound bad,' said the Sorx. 'Just like a Hubee. You should go and see the Farmer about that.'

'Yes, I will,' said Jack. 'Thank you.'

The Sorx looked at the jars and the balloons on the shelves.

'Very good indeed!' it said. 'You have both produced a lot of Number 3, and that one has won a medal!'

It pointed to the balloon that Holly had filled.

'Whose is that?' it asked.

'Mine,' said Holly, rather quietly.

'Don't be shy!' said the Sorx. 'You have done really well. Very few Sorx win a medal. Come with me and I'll give you your Kalex and your medal.'

They put their hats on and left room 5.

'Please go back through the door you came in,' said the Sorx, walking back into its office.

'You were very lucky there,' said Holly.

'Yes I was, wasn't I?' said Jack. 'I forgot to press my button. I'd better not press it until we've left the Thunder Works.'

They walked over to the door they had come in and turned back to look into the machinery room. Holly looked at the 'Crudax Line.'

'That'll be heading for the River Crudley running under the Rodley Bottoms Tunnel' she said.

'Yes, and some of our farts are probably in there by now,' said Jack, pointing to the huge balloon. 'What a strange place this is!'

Holly and Jack left the room and walked back into the entrance hall. The head of the Sorx was sticking out of the window above the shelf.

'Here you are,' it said, counting out 2 lots of 5 Kalex on the shelf. 'Please wait there.'

Jack and Holly picked up the Kalex and put them in their satchels. The Sorx shut the window, walked out into the entrance hall, and stepped across to the exit door. Hanging just inside the door was a gold chain with a golden trumpet shaped handle on its end. The Sorx grabbed the handle and pulled the chain hard. The sound of a trumpet being blown came from the street outside.

In its hand it had a medal on a purple ribbon. It came and stood in front of Holly and showed her the medal. It was a small, very shiny, golden trumpet.

'Please take off your hat and lower your head,' it said.

Holly took of her hat and lowered her head.

'This is the "Golden Trumpet Medal", the highest honour the Thunder Works can give,' it said. 'Many congratulations!'

It placed the ribbon round Holly's neck.

'Please come back and volunteer again very soon,' said the Sorx. 'We need more volunteers like you!'

It walked over to the exit door.

'Thank you very much and Guid Byo!' it said, opening the door and waving for them to leave.

'Guid Byo!' they replied at the same time.

Holly put her hat back on and pulled her ears through the slits. She and Jack stepped out into the street.

The brightness of the sky caught them by surprise and for a moment they were blinded by the light.

'It's so bright out here,' said, Holly closing her eyes tightly.

'You'll soon get used to it,' said Jack, speaking in his Sorx voice. He had remembered to press the button on his head.

Above the door the golden trumpet was playing a loud happy tune, and they could hear high-pitched voices shouting, "Congratulations! Thank you! You're a hero! Show us your medal!"

Holly opened her eyes and saw a crowd of Sorx waving and cheering.

'What's going on Jack?' she asked.

'I think they're cheering you!' he said.

'Why me?' asked Holly.

Jack looked up at the blowing trumpet.

'They want to see your medal!' he said. 'The Sorx must have blown the trumpet when it pulled the chain by the door! Now everyone in SQorxville knows you have won a golden trumpet!'

Holly was shocked. She felt so embarrassed. She took her medal off and put it in her satchel.

'On no! Now they know how much I farted!' she said. 'Come on, let's get away from here. We've got to get to the Rainbow Factory before the foragers' meeting starts.'

She dadumed away as quickly as she could through the cheering crowds.

'Well farted! What a trumper!' shouted a group of cheeky Sorxlings as she passed them.

This made Holly even more embarrassed. But deep down she was really quite proud of herself. She'd never won a medal before.

As she dadumed, the trumpet was still playing behind her.

'They're blowing my trumpet!' she thought.

Inside the Rainbow Factory

When Holly reached the market street she got a shock. Almost all the stalls had gone and the last few were closing up. The remaining stallholders were packing their unsold goods into wooden boxes.

'What's going on?' she thought to herself. 'Where have the stalls gone and why is the market closing? Were we in the Thunder Works longer than we thought?'

She plucked up the courage to approach one of the Sorx who was putting hats into a box.

'Hello!' she said. 'Why has the market closed so early?'

'Hello!' said the Sorx. 'Oh, today it's only a morning market. There's a foragers' meeting this afternoon. The market always shuts early on foragers' meeting days. Guid Byo!'

It picked up its box and walked off up the street.

'Guid Byo!' said Holly, feeling shocked.

Jack came daduming up behind her.

'Jack!' she exclaimed. 'We've got a problem. While we've been in the Thunder Works, the market has closed. It's only on for half a day today because of the foragers' meeting. We might be too late!'

She was clearly panicking.

'Don't panic,' said Jack, reassuringly. 'It will be OK. We'll have time to get to the Rainbow Factory before the meeting.

Some stalls are still closing up, so the market isn't properly shut just yet.'

'Come on then!' cried Holly, and she set off daduming up the market street closely followed by Jack.

The street was littered with market rubbish. There were broken ice cream cones, paper bags, wobniar-coloured sweets, a few broken candles and squashed pieces of fruit and vegetables.

The Sorx-shaped litter bins were now overflowing and Cacawkers were rummaging in most of them. Other Cacawkers were hopping around on the ground, scavenging whatever food they could. They seemed to particularly enjoy some of the sweets, and fought each other over them squawking, 'Cacaw! Cacaw! Cacaw!'

Holly didn't notice any of this as she headed up the street as fast as she could. Getting Podge back was her only concern. As Jack followed Holly he noticed some purple things by the side of the road. He stopped to look at them. To his great surprise they were Kalex, 5 of them. He bent down, picked them up, and slipped them into his satchel, all the while looking round to see if he had been spotted. He stood up and started daduming after Holly.

'That's great!' he thought. 'We've now got forty-six Kalex, so we should definitely have enough even if 2:7:3 raises the price.'

He quickly dadumed past the Foraging School to the Rainbow Factory. Holly was standing not far from the entrance door. Loud whooshing sounds came from the funnel on top of roof. Another wobniar arched into the sky, paused, and then arched back into the funnel.

'I've found 5 Kalex!' he exclaimed. 'We've now got forty-six!'

Holly didn't reply. Instead she pointed to the short wooden

tub next to the entrance and said, 'Look at that!'

Jack looked and it was full of keesceptres.

'I think we are too late,' she said, very sadly, and started to cry.

'We may not be, and we have to try,' said Jack. 'We've come this far, we can't stop now!'

He grabbed Holly's left arm and pulled her closer to the entrance door. There were 2 steps up to the door, which had a sign on it. They stepped up and read:

THE MEETING HAS STARTED!
PLEASE KNOCK QUIETLY IF YOU STILL WANT TO JOIN.

'There!' sobbed Holly. 'I told you. We are too late!'

Completely ignoring her, Jack looked at the door. There was no knocker, so he knocked quietly on the door with his hand. Nothing happened. He knocked again, a little louder, but nothing happened.

'What's going on?' he said. 'I'm knocking quietly but nothing is happening.'

Holly had stopped sobbing and was watching Jack. Then she looked down at the short wooden tub.

'Perhaps you have to knock with one of those,' she said, pointing to the keesceptres.

'Yes, of course! That's brilliant Holly,' said Jack. 'It's a foragers' meeting so they will only allow foragers in!'

He grabbed a keesceptre out of the tub. Using its flat end, he knocked gently on the door. Nothing happened.

'What now?' he said.

'Wait!' said Holly. 'Remember what 2:7:3 did in our garden.

She hit the wall with her keesceptre and then said, "2, 7, 3".'

'So what should I do?' asked Jack.

'How many toes do you have on your feet from left to right?' asked Holly.

Jack looked at his feet.

'3, 2, 3,' he said.

'OK,' said Holly, who was now fully recovered from her sadness. 'Use the keesceptre and then say "3, 2, 3".'

Jack stood in front of the door and hit it gently with the flat end of the keesceptre.

Very quietly, he said, '3, 2, 3.'

There was a little creaking sound and the door swung open. He put the keesceptre back in the tub and stepped inside the Rainbow Factory, with Holly right behind him.

They found themselves in a large rectangular entrance hall. Along the left side was a window stretching the full length of the wall, overlooking a room full of machinery. In front of this window was a row of chairs. Above the window was a large sign reading:

WELCOME TO THE RAINBOW FACTORY.

On each side of this was a wobniar. Along the right side was a long counter covered in what seemed to be colourful brochures. Along the wall in front of them were 2 doors, one on the left and one on the right. Between these doors was an impressive desk. Behind the desk sat a Sorx who was concentrating on something. Jack and Holly walked over to the counter.

'Hello!' said Holly. 'We have come to see 2:7:3.'

The Sorx twitched in surprise when it heard Holly's voice

and looked up. It was doing a jigsaw puzzle.

'Oh you have, have you?' it said, sneeringly.

Holly felt a shiver down her spine. This wasn't a Sorx, it was a Sorxling and it was One:2:One.

'Yes,' said Holly, trying to sound calm. 'We've come to buy the toy. She said we could have it for 37 Kalex.'

'Oh, I remember,' said the Sorxling. 'That useless thing.'

'Yes. We've got 37 now. Can we see 2:7:3?' asked Holly, biting her tongue. 'How dare she call Podge useless!' she thought.

'You'll have to wait. She's in the foragers' meeting,' said One:2:One. 'But weren't you supposed to come before the meeting began? She won't be happy that you are late. You can sit over there.'

She pointed to the row of chairs in front of the long window, stood up, and walked out through the left-hand door.

Holly said nothing. She and Jack walked over to the chairs and sat down.

'That doesn't sound very hopeful,' said Holly, sadly. 'She'll probably raise the price.'

'Don't worry,' said Jack. 'We should still have enough. We have forty-six Kalex now and the next prime number after 37 is 41. Remember what Hornbeam said, Sorx work on prime numbers.'

Holly said nothing. She was very anxious about meeting 2:7:3 again.

Making wobniars

Jack looked through the window at the machinery. There were 7 huge cylindrical tubs each marked with a colour: Violet, Indigo, Blue, Green, Yellow, Orange and Red. On top of the tubs were walkways with Sorx on them. Each Sorx had a long pole, which they were using to stir the mixture in the tubs. A pipe ran from each tub onto a moving conveyor belt. The 7 colours streamed side-by-side hot with steam along the belt.

The other end of the conveyor belt ran into a flat-bottomed box with an open top. Above this, was a ramrod about the same width as the conveyor belt. This rammed up and down on the moving colour stream as it passed through the box. A wide flat ribbon emerged from the other end of the box onto a curved conveyor belt shaped like an arc. This stopped once the whole ribbon was on it.

The ribbon was then clamped at each end and the conveyor belt was stretched. This made the ribbon thinner and much longer. It had now formed into a very long perfect arc-shaped wobniar.

This passed onto another arc-shaped conveyor belt, which slowly became vertical and fed it into the bottom end of a slit in the ceiling. There was a loud whooshing sound as the wobniar was fired through the slit and disappeared.

'That must go out through the V-shaped funnel in the roof,' thought Jack.

After a short time, there was another whooshing sound. The wobniar reappeared and passed onto a third arc-shaped conveyor belt, which took it to the other side of the room. Here 2 Sorx rolled up the wobniar very tightly like a roll of wide ribbon, and put it in a Sorx satchel. This was then carefully stacked on a shelf beside lots of other satchels. In the meantime the whole process had been repeated, and another stream of colours was heading towards the ramrod box.

Jack was fascinated by this.

'This is how they make their wobniars,' he said to Holly. 'They test them through the funnel in the roof, before putting them into the foragers' satchels. Isn't it amazing!'

Holly was still worried about meeting 2:7:3, and had only been staring at the window looking at her own reflection.

'I suppose so,' she said, blankly.

Just then the left-hand door at the back of the room opened and the Sorxling came out.

'She'll be here in a squig,' said One:2:One.

She sat down, looked at her jigsaw puzzle, and slotted a piece into place.

The squig passed very slowly for Holly, it seemed more like a squage. She looked through the window and began to see what Jack had described. It did look amazing and she became quite absorbed in it. She particularly liked the coloured streams on the conveyor belt, and began to imagine painting with them on a big canvas.

Suddenly she was awakened from her imaginings by a loud high-pitched voice behind her. She and Jack stood up and turned round to see 2:7:3 emerging from the right-hand door.

'You're late!' she barked, as she walked over to them. 'I told you not to be late!'

Holly was shaking so much she couldn't speak.

'We're so sorry,' said Jack. 'We thought the meeting started later, we didn't know that the market closed early when there was a foragers' meeting.'

'That's no excuse,' shouted 2:7:3. 'Everyone knows that the market closes early when there is a meeting!'

'We agreed 37 Kalex,' said Jack, hopefully.

'Only if you were not late,' she shouted. 'But you were late. The price goes up when you are late.'

'We can give you thirty-nine Kalex,' said Jack, thinking that if she didn't take that she would accept 41, the next prime number.

'That's not enough,' she said. 'I want more!'

'How much do you want?' asked Jack, willing her to say 41.

2:7:3 stroked her chin and thought. The next prime number was 41. She had only paid 23, so eighteen Kalex would be a good profit. Her 2 minds were whirring.

The peaceful one said, 'Take 41 and get a good profit they may not have any more.'

The aggressive one said, 'Don't take 41, ask for more, they were late, make them suffer!'

The trouble with 2:7:3 was that she had been spoilt all her life. Her father had given her and her sister all the luxuries a Sorx could imagine. They lived in the posh tree house behind the Rainbow Factory, and wanted for nothing.

Because of this she had become greedy. It really wasn't her fault, it was her father's fault. But in the end she was greedy.

She looked at the 2 Sorx in front of her. They looked young. They would be easy pickings. The aggressive mind took over.

'Forget 41,' it said, inside her head. 'Ask for more!'

'I want 47 Kalex,' she said, triumphantly.

'But we haven't got 47,' said Jack. 'Please take 41. It's a prime number.'

'I will take a prime number,' she sneered. 'I'll take 47.'

'We've only got forty-six, but that's nearly 47,' pleaded Jack. 'Surely you will let us off one Kalex. Please!'

'No!' shouted 2:7:3, very loudly. 'I will only take 47! And I want it by this time tomorrow. And don't be late. You know what will happen if you are late. Now get out of my father's factory before I have you thrown out. I'm going to the forager's meal.'

She pointed to the exit door.

Holly suddenly spoke up, 'How do we know you won't raise the price again even if we bring you 47 Kalex? How can we trust you?'

'You don't do you? But you'll just have to won't you?' said 2:7:3, nastily. 'Now get out!'

Jack and Holly walked slowly across to the exit door, turned the handle, and left the Rainbow Factory. The door slammed shut behind them.

Spoilt sisters

Outside the Rainbow Factory, they sat down next to each other on the bottom of the exit steps next to the Sorx litter bin.

'What can we do now?' asked Holly.

'Do you still have those drinks?' asked Jack. 'I could do with one after what's just happened.'

'Yes, I have,' said Holly.

She reached into her satchel, pulled out 2 bottles of Burpz and gave one to Jack. They drank them slowly; burping quietly until they were empty, then put them in the litter bin.

'I'm afraid that we'll have to go back to the Thunder Works and get more Kalex,' said Jack.

'I don't thing I can face that again,' said Holly. 'And we've only got 2 Oodax left. We'll never be able to fill that fart balloon.'

'That's true,' said Jack.

Just then the Sorxling came out of the exit and nearly tripped over them.

'Are you still here?' she growled. 'Have you no home to go to?'

'Actually, we haven't at the moment,' thought Jack.

'We're going,' said Jack.

He and Holly stood up and started walking slowly back

towards the main road. The Sorxling turned left, and headed up the side of the Rainbow Factory towards the posh tree house behind it.

'I wonder?' said Jack.

'What?' asked Holly.

'Trust me,' said Jack. 'Let's follow her.'

Jack looked back towards the Rainbow Factory. The Sorxling had disappeared.

'Come on,' he said.

They turned round and headed back to the Rainbow Factory. They walked slowly round the side of it and saw the Sorxling walking into the posh tree house.

'What are we doing Jack?' asked Holly, who was very confused.

'Perhaps we can persuade the Sorxling to sell Podge,' said Jack. 'She doesn't like her so she might take 41 Kalex.'

'I suppose anything is worth a try,' said Holly. 'But she's as nasty as her sister.'

'Well, let's just see,' said Jack. 'You wait here. I'll knock at the door and see if I can persuade her.'

'OK,' said Holly.' But be very careful.'

Holly waited at the side of the Rainbow Factory and Jack set off towards the posh house. He had only got halfway, when the rear Sorx door to the Rainbow Factory opened, and 2:7:3 walked out. Jack dashed back to Holly.

'It's 2:7:3!' he told Holly.

They watched 2:7:3 walk towards the posh house. Just as she reached the door, the Sorxling came out.

'That wasn't a very good deal,' said the Sorxling. 'I don't think they'll come back. You should have accepted 41 Kalex.

That would have given us a good profit. You were too greedy.'

'Don't you accuse me of being greedy,' shouted 2:7:3. 'You are the greedy one. Dad and I have given you everything you have ever asked for, but you always want more. And when we give you more, you don't appreciate it. You are spoilt! I'm never going to give you anything again.'

'Don't call me spoilt!' shouted the Sorxling. 'If anyone is spoilt it's you. You think you are great. Always meeting and eating with your foraging friends, strutting around as if you are the queens and kings of SQorxville!'

'How dare you!' shouted 2:7:3. 'The foragers keep SQorxville going. If it wasn't for them, the Sorx would have nothing!'

'Don't be stupid,' said the Sorxling. 'Most Sorx hate the foragers and SQorxville could easily survive without them. In fact the place would be a lot happier. Sorx are afraid of the foragers, and I hate them. Go back to your meal with them. I hope you choke!'

'Maybe I will or maybe I won't!' shouted 2:7:3. 'But make sure you keep that Hubee toy safe or else!'

'Or else what?' screamed the Sorxling. And with that she turned round, dashed into the posh house, and slammed the door.

2:7:3 watched her go, snorted, and stormed back into the Rainbow Factory, almost breaking the door as she crashed it behind her. Jack and Holly looked at each other.

'I wasn't expecting that!' said Jack

'Neither was I,' said Holly. 'But what do we do now?'

'It's probably best to let the Sorxling calm down a bit,' said Jack, quietly. 'Then I'll go and ask her to sell Podge.'

They sat down and leant against the Rainbow Factory,

keeping an eye on the posh house. It all seemed very quiet after what had just happened.

After a tickle of time, Jack stood up and said, 'I'm going to try now.'

'Guid Lukio!' said Holly, staying sat on the ground.

Once again Jack walked towards the posh house. This time he reached the path and began to approach the door. Suddenly, above him, one of the top windows opened and he heard a voice. He recognised it as the Sorxling's.

'You have caused an awful lot of trouble!' she said, talking to someone. 'You have made me argue with my sister who is a right pain, but she is family and I do love her. And families should stick together. And you are useless. You don't do anything. I hate you, and I don't want you!'

'Who is she talking to?' thought Jack, standing on the path below the window.

'I'm going to get rid of you so that you can cause trouble to someone else,' continued the Sorxling.

Something small flew out of the window and landed at Jack's feet. He reached down and picked it up. He couldn't believe what he was holding. It was Podge!

He dashed back towards Holly and cried, 'Holly, I've got Podge!'

Holly stood up, rushed over to him, and grabbed Podge. She couldn't believe it either, and burst into tears inside her costume.

'Oh thank you, thank you, thank you!' she said, wrapping her snaky Sorx fingers round Podge so hard that she vanished into them.

'It wasn't me,' said Jack. 'The Sorxling just threw her away.'

'I knew she didn't like her,' said Holly. 'But I never thought she'd throw her away. How could anyone throw Podge away?'

She squeezed her even tighter.

'We must get away from here in case she changes her mind and comes looking for her,' she said.

'Yes,' said Jack. 'But first I need to do something. Wait here, I won't be long.'

He dadumed back to the front for the Rainbow Factory and went up to the entrance. The small wooden tub was still full of keesceptres. He reached in, took 3, put them in his satchel, and then dadumed quickly back to Holly.

'Come on!' he said. 'Let's get away from here!'

Lovesome

Holly and Jack set off up the path that ran to the right of the posh tree house. As they passed it they heard a soft gentle voice.

'I love you!' it said.

They stopped and looked around.

'I love you!' it said, again.

'That sounds like a Drongle,' said Jack. 'It seems to be coming from behind the posh tree house.'

He walked towards the sound and saw the same cage they'd seen earlier, bashed on one corner, and with a bright red handle. Inside was the same Drongle.

'I love you so much!' it said when it saw Jack. 'Please save me from this horrible place.'

By this time Holly had arrived.

'We must save it and take it with us,' she said.

'Yes,' said Jack. 'But the cage is too heavy to carry. We'll have to open it.'

He put down his satchel and looked around the back of the posh house. He found a branch and went back to the cage. Raising the branch high in the air he smashed it against the lock. The branch broke but the lock didn't.

'Try hitting the cage,' said Holly, clutching Podge tightly. 'It may be weaker than the lock.'

'Good idea,' said Jack.

He looked up the side of the path, and came back with a very thick branch.

'Move to one end of the cage,' he told the Drongle.

Jack lifted the thick branch as high above his head as he could, and smashed it onto the bashed corner of the cage. One of the bars snapped. He picked up the branch and did it again. Another bar snapped. At the third attempt, the branch went right through the cage creating a big hole in the top. Jack threw down the branch, reached into the cage, grabbed the Drongle, and carefully lifted it out.

'Oh thank you, thank you, thank you! I love you! I love you! I love you!' shouted the Drongle.

'Sshh!' said Jack 'We don't want anyone to hear us,' completely forgetting about the noise he had made hitting the cage with branches.

'Sorry,' said the Drongle. 'But I do love you!'

'That's OK,' said Jack. 'Now, quick, let's go!'

The Drongle didn't need telling twice. It ran off at high speed down the path away from the posh tree house. Holly placed Podge safely at the bottom of her satchel and set off after it.

Jack put on his satchel and tried to follow them, but realised that something was wrong. The body of his costume was badly ripped under both arms. His costume was beginning to fall apart.

'This must have happened when I was swinging those branches,' he said to himself.

He started to dadum, but it was not as easy as it had been. The springs in the costume legs were getting tangled in material. His costume body was hanging loose and getting in the way of his arms.

'If I can get onto the Jigsaw Trail I won't need my costume again,' he thought. 'I've just got to get on with it.'

The Drongle had gone off so quickly that it was way ahead of Holly and Jack. It stopped to look around to let them catch up. It didn't know where it was, it wasn't used to being on open paths. It normally lived in the deep forests, and hated the noise and bustle of SⱭorxville. But it was so pleased to be out of that cage and away from that horrible Sorxling.

'I'm feeling very frightened,' it thought to itself. 'But at least I've got 2 new friends to love. They look like Sorx, but they don't smell like Sorx. I wonder who they are. But I don't really care. I'll love them forever or as long as they love me.'

As the Drongle was thinking, Holly arrived.

'Hello!' said the Drongle. 'I love you! I remember meeting you earlier in the market.'

'Hello! And I love you too,' replied Holly. 'Have you seen my friend?'

'No,' said the Drongle. 'I got here first but I don't know where I am.'

'You're on a path that we think leads to the Jigsaw Trail,' said Holly.

'Never heard of it,' said the Drongle.

Jack still hadn't arrived. Holly was getting worried.

'Where can he be?' she said. 'We must get going.'

'Don't worry,' said the Drongle. 'I can smell him coming.'

Sure enough, Jack came daduming towards them rather slowly, with his costume in tatters.

'Jack!' cried Holly. 'What's happened?'

'My costume's falling apart,' said Jack, quite out of breath from his efforts. 'It tore while I was freeing the Drongle. Bits have fallen of it and my arms are coming away. I'm finding it hard to dadum. The springs are sticking.'

Holly looked at his costume. Some big pieces were missing.

'You can't wear that for much longer,' she said. 'You should take it off. It will slow you down.'

'I'll take it off when we find the Jigsaw Trail,' said Jack.

The Drongle walked over to Jack and looked at his costume.

'Hello!' it said. 'I love you! But what are you? You are definitely not a Sorx.' He turned towards Holly.

'And neither are you,' he said. 'You look like a Sorx but you certainly don't smell like a Sorx. You smell like rosemary. Sorx smell like Crudax.'

Holly remembered what Hornbeam had said about a Drongle's sense of smell. She looked at Jack and nodded. He nodded back. They reached up, took off their heads and looked at the Drongle.

'We are Hubees,' they said together, in their normal voices.

The Drongle didn't look surprised.

'I thought you were,' it said, and smiled at them. 'But what do we do now?'

'That's a good question,' said Jack. 'We must find the start of the Jigsaw Trail. It must be near here somewhere. Can you remember what Hornbeam said?'

'Oh, I know Hornbeam,' said the Drongle. 'He lives in The Lonely Sweet Shop. He's a friend of mine. I love him!'

'Yes, he's our friend as well,' said Holly.

'Oh, I love you even more now!' said the Drongle.

'Why?' asked Holly.

'Because the Sorx hate you and I hate the Sorx. So my enemy's enemy is my friend,' it said.

It then added, 'And the Sorx hate the Qorx and I love the Qorx so that means that I love you.'

Holly thought about this carefully.

'I think that makes sense,' she said. 'And if you are going to be our friend we should introduce ourselves. My name is Holly and this is my brother Jack.' She pointed at Jack.

'Hello!' said Jack. 'And what's your name?'

'Hello!' said the Drongle. 'I'm Lovesome.'

'What an amazing name!' said Holly. 'We're very pleased to meet you!'

'And I'm very pleased to meet you,' said Lovesome. 'Thank you for rescuing me. I love you so much!'

'You're very welcome,' said Holly.

'Do you know Affable?' asked Jack.

'Oh yes,' said Lovesome. 'She's a good friend of mine. How do you know her?'

'We met her shortly after we left Hornbeam's Lonely Sweet Shop,' said Jack. 'She warned us about some Cacawkers.'

'Oh, I hate Cacawkers,' said Lovesome. 'They're horrible. They once bit a chunk out of one of Affable's ears and it never regrew.'

'We hate them as well,' said Holly.

'But why are you dressed like Sorx?' he asked.

'Oh, Hornbeam gave us these costumes so that we could go into SQorxville and rescue Podge,' said Holly.

'Who's Podge?' asked Lovesome.

Holly reached into the satchel and pulled out Podge.

'This is Podge,' she said.

'Hello Podge!' said Lovesome. 'I love you!'

He saw Podge's torn leg.

'And I'm so sorry about your torn leg,' said Lovesome. 'I love you so much!'

'And Podge loves you too!' said Jack, getting a little exasperated with Lovesome. 'But we must find the trail. What did Hornbeam say Holly?'

She thought carefully then said, 'The starting point is marked on the ground by a tree-shaped cut in the path surface. We have to find a jigsaw piece that fits it. Then we have to find other pieces as we go along.'

'Right,' said Jack. 'Let's walk slowly along the path and see if we can find the starting point. We are looking for a tree-shaped cut in the ground. You take the left side Holly, I'll take the right side and Lovesome can go up the middle. Let's go.'

'We'd better put our heads back on!' said Holly.

'Oh yes!' said Jack. 'I'd forgotten we'd taken them off!'

They put their heads on, pushed the buttons, and set off along the path with Lovesome. After a touch of time they reached a sign fixed to a wooden post. It read:

YOU MIGHT AS WELL TURN BACK NOW.
THIS PATH GOES TO NOWHERE.

Holly saw it first and asked, 'What shall we do? We don't want to go nowhere.'

'But I think you have nowhere else to go,' said Lovesome, in his soft gentle voice. 'If Hornbeam said you had to go along this path, then that is what you must do.'

'Yes,' said Jack, laughing. 'We must go nowhere!'

'You're right,' said Holly. 'So! Nowhere it is!'

The Path to Nowhere

They started moving along the path side-by-side staring at the ground. The path entered a narrow valley and the sides of the valley grew steeper and steeper until they were almost vertical.

'Stop,' said Jack. 'We need to walk in a line. I'll go first, Lovesome second and Holly third. Keep scanning the ground.'

And off they set again.

Jack was looking at the surface of the ground very closely, glancing left and right, when he walked straight into something hard. Lovesome walked straight into him, and Holly walked straight into Lovesome. They fell in a heap on the ground.

Looking up, they realised they had walked into a huge tree, which completely blocked the valley. It was so wide there was no room to pass on either side of it, and it was far too tall to climb. They had reached a dead end. The path stopped at the tree.

Jack and the Drongle stood up and dusted themselves down. Jack's costume was looking even tattier now. Carved on the trunk of the tree was the word NOWHERE.

'We've reached Nowhere!' exclaimed Jack, in amazement. 'There really is somewhere called Nowhere!'

'Yes!' said Holly, who was still on the ground and had been looking around the base of the tree. 'And look at that!'

She pointed to where the tree met the ground. There, slightly covered in tree roots and partly hidden by grass, was a distinct shape carved in the ground surface. She brushed the grass aside and moved the tree roots out of the way. The shape was definitely that of a tree.

'This it is!' she cried. 'Just as Hornbeam said!'

'Yes!' said Jack. 'Now we need to find the jigsaw piece that fits that shape.'

Holly looked closely at the shape.

'Look at this!' she said.

Jack knelt down beside her and looked. Lovesome trotted over and looked.

2 letters had been carved in the shape. The letters I and V were written next to each other.

'What does that mean?' asked Holly. 'Is it a clue?'

'I think it is Roman for our number four,' said Jack, who had been studying Roman History at school.

'What's Roman?' asked Lovesome, who was very confused about what was going on.

'So does that mean we need to find a Roman IV or our number four?' asked Holly, completely ignoring Lovesome

'I don't know,' said Jack. 'So we'd better look for both. But where do we begin? Let's split up.'

Jack looked on the right side of the narrow trail and Holly on the left side. Lovesome just wandered around. But none of them could find anything linked to a Roman IV or a number four.

Feeling frustrated, Holly stood up and held her arms out sideways. The valley was so narrow she could easily touch both sides, which were covered in a bright green plant with small shiny triangular leaves.

'The piece must be near here,' she said.

She felt the leaves and thought. They were just like the ivy growing in their garden.

'That's it' she said. 'It's ivy!'

Jack and Lovesome heard her and came over.

'What do you mean?' asked Jack.

'The letters "I" and "V" aren't a number, they are what they sound like: "Ivy"!' said Holly. 'The piece must be hidden somewhere in the ivy on the valley walls! Help me look behind the leaves. I'll take this side, you take the other side.'

On the left side of the valley, Holly began to move the leaves apart. On the right side, Jack looked behind the leaves helped by Lovesome, who used his paws to part them. There was nothing behind them, just soil. Dust flew into the air.

'Nothing this side,' said Jack. 'How are you doing?'

'Nothing here yet,' said Holly.

Her hands were green from moving the leaves. She stopped, wiped them on her costume, turned round, and leant against the leaves. There was something hard pressing against her back. She turned round and opened the leaves. There was a distinct shape hidden behind them. She reached in, got hold of it, and pulled hard. A large jigsaw piece shaped like a tree popped out.

'I've found it!' she cried.

Holly took the jigsaw piece back to the tree and knelt down. She rotated it until it matched the hole in the ground and pushed it in. It clicked nicely into place but nothing happened.

'Take it out and try again,' said Jack, after a few moments.

Holly began to lift it. As it came out there was a deep grinding noise, and the tree with the NOWHERE sign on it began to rotate sideways to reveal a dark opening. Lovesome shot up vertically in fright, and bounced back on the ground in a heap. Just inside the entrance was another sign fastened to a wooden post. It read:

PUT THE PIECE BACK AND COVER THE HOLE,
THEN INTO NOWHERE, PLEASE GENTLY STROLL.
THE TREE WILL TURN AND BLOCK UP THE TRACK,
NO-ONE CAN FOLLOW, BUT YOU CAN'T GO BACK.

Holly put the piece back behind the ivy then carefully covered the hole. Lovesome looked at the sign.

'What's stroll?' he asked.

'It's a slow walk,' said Jack.

'So we have to slowly walk into that dark opening,' said Lovesome, who was feeling scared.

'Yes, we do,' said Jack. 'So let's do it!'

'Come on Lovesome, it's OK,' said Holly.

'If you say so,' said Lovesome, staggering to his feet. 'I love you.'

They strolled into the opening. As they did, a small piece of Jack's costume caught on a sharp piece of bark, and tore off. It fluttered down and landed on the ground just outside the opening. A touch of time later, the tree rotated in the opposite direction and the opening closed.

Anyone coming down the narrow lane towards the tree would only see the carving saying NOWHERE, and 2 sides of a steep-sided valley covered in a bright-green plant with small triangular leaves. But if they looked really carefully, they might just see a small piece of Jack's costume lying nearby.

Summoning the Cacawkers

Back at the Rainbow Factory all was not well. After their argument, 2:7:3's peaceful mind took over. It felt she had said things to her sister that she shouldn't have done. One:2:One could be a right pain, but she was family and 2:7:3 loved her. And families should stick together.

So, when the foragers' meal ended, 2:7:3 put on her satchel and went back to the posh tree house to see her sister. She went upstairs to her room and knocked on the door.

'Come in,' said her sister.

2:7:3 went in and said, 'I'm sorry Sis. I didn't mean what I said earlier. I've come to apologise.'

Her sister's peaceful mind was also in charge at that moment.

'It's me who should apologise to you,' said her sister. 'I said some horrible things to you. I don't want you to choke. I love you.'

'Well as you can see, I haven't choked, and I love you as well,' said 2:7:3, laughing.

They walked over to each other and hugged.

'I have a confession to make,' said One:2:One. 'I threw that Hubee toy away because it had made us fall out and I don't want that.'

'Don't worry,' said 2:7:3. 'We'll get it back, and I'll sell it to those Sorx for 41 Kalex.'

She was still greedy.

'Where did you throw it?' she asked.

'Out of my window,' said One:2:One. 'Let's go and see if we can find it.'

They went outside and started looking around.

'That's strange,' said the sister. 'It would have landed on the path up to the house, but it's not there.'

'Let's look around the back of the house,' said 2:7:3.

They looked. They didn't find Podge, and they didn't find the Drongle either, only a bashed cage.

'The Drongle's gone!' cried One:2:One. 'That was mine! Where is it?'

'Someone's stolen it,' said 2:7:3. 'Look how bashed the cage is. And look at this.' She pointed to the thick branch that Jack had used. 'They must have broken the cage with that and taken your Drongle.'

Just then 3 foragers dadumed swiftly up the path from the Rainbow Factory shouting and screaming, 'Someone has stolen our keesceptres! They've been taken from the tub!'

'That's a coincidence,' said One:2:One. 'To have 3 things stolen all at once: the toy, the Drongle and the keesceptres.'

'I don't believe in coincidences,' said 2:7:3. 'I think the same Sorx stole them, and I reckon it was 3;2:3 and 3:3:3. Now where could they have gone?'

She turned to the foragers and said, 'Let's split up. You go down the path to the main road and see if you can find them. We'll go this way.'

She pointed in the direction that Holly, Jack and the Drongle had gone.

'If you find anything, shout and we'll meet up,' she said.

The 2 groups set off. The foragers dadumed quickly down to the main road. 2:7:3 and her sister went back to the cage and dadumed slowly up the path looking for footprints. But the ground was hard and there didn't seem to be any.

'They didn't go this way,' said One:2:One, who was getting fed up and just wanted to go back to her lovely room.

'Keep looking,' said 2:7:3.

'Must we?' moaned One:2:One. 'I've had enough, I don't care about the toy or the Drongle anymore.'

'Yes, we must!' shouted 2:7:3.

Just then something blew across the path in front of them.

'What's that?' said 2:7:3.

She leant forward and put her left foot on it.

Reaching down she picked it up. It was a piece of cloth that looked like pretend Sorx skin. Further on she found another. They were pieces from Jack's costume.

2:7:3 shouted at the top of her voice, 'We've found something!'

The 3 foragers came daduming back up the path. She showed them the 2 pieces of cloth.

'That's very strange,' said one of the foragers. 'They look like pieces from a costume.'

'Yes, they do. Don't they?' said 2:7:3. 'Perhaps those Sorx are not Sorx at all! There's only one way to find out. We must capture them! They've gone up here!'

She pointed up the path and cried, 'Let's go!'

Before long they reached the 'YOU MIGHT AS WELL TURN BACK NOW. THIS PATH GOES TO NOWHERE.' sign and stopped.

The 3 foragers and One:2:One were alarmed by this.

'There's not much point in going to nowhere', said the sister.

The foragers nodded in agreement.

2:7:3 looked at them and said nothing for a while. She remembered that she had been up to the sign several times when practising her foraging, but she had never dared go beyond it. She didn't know who had put it up, but it had been there for a squage of time. Whenever she saw it, it made her shiver. But she was nothing if not determined, and she wanted to find out exactly who those Sorx were.

'Ignore it, someone has put it there as a joke. You can't go to nowhere, you always go to somewhere. Let's keep going,' she said, trying to put a brave face on for the others.

But the 3 foragers were not convinced and decided not to go any further. One of them spoke up.

'We'll go back to the Foraging School and call for the "Foragers' Vow",' it said. 'They will help us search for our kees-ceptres. If you find anything let us know.'

They turned round and headed back towards the Rainbow Factory.

'What's the "Foragers' Vow"?' asked her sister.

'All foragers take a vow to help their fellow foragers find stolen keesceptres, by whatever means necessary,' said 2:7:3. 'They will search SƟorxville and beyond until they are found. Whoever took them made a big mistake! Come on Sis, let's carry on!'

'Are you sure it will be OK?' said her sister. 'I don't particularly want to go nowhere either.'

'Don't worry. I've been along here before. It just leads into the forest,' lied 2:7:3, who had no idea where it led.

Reluctantly, her sister agreed to go and off they set. Soon they were in the narrow valley with the almost vertical sides, and could no longer walk side by side. Eventually, despite a lot of moaning by the sister, they reached the tree with the Nowhere sign.

'This is a dead end,' said One:2:One. 'It really is Nowhere! Let's go home.'

'I'm not so sure,' said 2:7:3. 'Look at these.'

She pointed to footprints in the soil in front of the tree. There were footprints of feet with 3 toes on them.

'Sorx feet have been here recently,' she said. 'And those 2 Sorx had 3:2:3 and 3:3:3 feet, so they could have made these footprints. And look at this.'

She bent down and picked up the small piece of Jack's costume that had torn off.

'They must have been here,' she said.

'But we can't go any further,' moaned her sister. 'I'm tired and I want to go home.'

'OK,' said 2:7:3. 'But there's something odd going on here. I think we should get some help.'

She reached into her satchel, and pulled out a long curved silver horn shaped like a corkscrew. She put it to her lips and blew. A piercing note filled the air, and grew louder and louder the more she blew. She stopped blowing and looked up at the sky above the narrow alley. Slowly but surely, black silhouettes began appearing against the brown. They danced and swopped amongst each other and then hovered above the valley. 2:7:3 put the horn back in her satchel and tilted her head upwards.

'Hunt, my friends! Hunt those creatures! Hunt!' she screamed, at the top of her voice.

The Cacawkers had been summoned!

The Nowhere Tree

Holly, Jack and Lovesome were so relieved to see the tree rotate and close the opening behind them. For the first time in a long while they felt safe. As it rotated, the space they were in became lighter as 2 windows appeared in the opposite wall. There was a door between them.

Looking around they saw that they were actually inside the tree. It was roughly circular in shape and had a wooden floor. It was enormous and could have held fifty Sorx quite comfortably. There was nothing in it apart from them. Exactly in the centre of the room, a small shape had been cut out of the floor, but they didn't see it.

All around the walls were carvings of Qorx doing all sorts of things including walking, jumping, flying, hula-hooping, juggling, pedarcing, sleeping, feeding, crying and even skiing. It was a very impressive sight. Having only ever seen one Qorx, Jack and Holly were amazed.

'Look at all those Qorx!' exclaimed Jack.

'Yes,' said Holly, looking upwards. 'There are hundreds of them going all the way up to the ceiling.'

The door between the windows was marked Exit. Jack pointed to it.

'That must lead to the Jigsaw Trail,' said Jack. 'Let's go.'

They walked over to the windows and looked out. A narrow

trail led from the door across an open field and into a thick forest. Holly grabbed the door handle and turned it. It was locked. On the door was a sign reading:

TASK ONE:

YOU ARE NOW INSIDE THE NOWHERE TREE.
FROM HERE THE JIGSAW TRAIL YOU'LL SEE.
FIND A QORX TO COMPLETE THE FLOOR.
TO JOIN THE TRAIL BY THE EXIT DOOR.

'Oh!' said Holly. 'It's a riddle!'

'Yes,' said Lovesome. 'I love riddles!'

'Do you?' asked Jack, rather surprised.

'Of course I do!' said Lovesome. 'I love everything! Except Sorx!'

'But do you know what a riddle is?' asked Holly.

'No,' said Lovesome, as he wandered around the room.

'Well, we have to complete the floor with a Qorx,' said Holly.

'But what does that mean?' asked Jack. 'How is the floor not complete?'

'There is a hole here,' said Lovesome, sniffing the cut out shape in the middle of the room.

Holly and Jack walked over to him and looked at the hole. It had the shape of a jigsaw piece.

'Of course!' said Holly. 'We need to find another jigsaw piece, then we'll be able to get onto the trail.'

'And from the riddle we need a piece shaped like a Qorx,' said Jack. 'But there are hundreds of them. Where do we begin?'

'Let's look at the shape of the hole,' said Holly, kneeling down beside the cut out.

206

It was shaped like a Qorx with its arms above its head and its feet slightly apart.

'It looks like a Qorx waving,' said Holly. 'See if we can find a carving like that.'

Holly set off in one direction looking carefully at the carvings, and Jack set off in the other direction. Lovesome went and lay down by the hole.

When they had each walked a quarter of the way round the wall they both shouted at once, 'I've found it!'

Lovesome looked at them in turn.

'How can you both have found it?' he asked.

Jack came over with his find and Holly with hers. They were both holding a jigsaw piece shaped like a Qorx waving. But they were not the same.

'Try yours Holly,' said Jack.

Holly knelt down and tried hers, but it wouldn't fit, no matter how many times she turned it and tried to push it in.

'It must be yours Jack,' said Holly.

Jack knelt down and tried his, but it didn't fit either.

'That's odd,' said Jack. 'One of them should work.'

'Only if it fits,' said Lovesome, very sensibly. 'There must be another piece that fits.'

'He's right,' said Holly. 'Let's look at that hole again.'

She knelt down, looked again and saw the same shape as before: a Qorx with its arms above its head and its feet slightly apart. She then walked round to the other side of the hole, and looked at it again very carefully.

'It's not waving!' she cried. 'It's doing a hand stand!'

Jack looked and said, 'Yes, you're right and I've seen one doing that!'

He dashed across to the wall, grabbed a shape, and rushed back.

'Here, try this,' he said, handing it to Holly.

Holly carefully turned it and pushed it in. It fitted. There was a loud clunk from behind them and the exit door swung open.

'Yeesss!' shouted Jack.

Holly lifted the piece out and handed it back to Jack.

'Quick,' she said. 'Put it back and let's get out of here!'

Jack took it and put it back. He and Lovesome dashed to the open exit door where Holly was waiting. They stepped out onto the trail and the door slammed behind them. Just to the right of the trail was a wooden post with a sign on it reading:

Task One is done. You didn't fail.
Welcome to the Jigsaw Trail.
Four more tasks you must complete.
Before you reach the Lonely Sweets.

The trail led across an open field towards the forest.

'Come on!' said Holly. 'This way to The Lonely Sweet Shop!'

Self-healing

They quickly followed the path over the open field and entered the forest. Very soon, they were deep inside, and only small parts of the sky were visible above the canopy. They were surrounded by giant trees. The trail swung sharply from left to right and back again, in order to pass around them . It was so narrow that they had to walk in line with Lovesome in front, Holly in the middle, and Jack at the back.

While they followed the twisting trail, 13 Cacawkers in SQorxville heard the corkscrew horn and flew towards its sound. They gathered above the Nowhere Tree and listened to 2:7:3 urging them on from the narrow valley below. They circled, grouped into a V-formation, and flew over the Jigsaw Trail towards the forest. As they approached the dense forest canopy, four of them split off in different directions to search separately, while nine stayed in the V-formation.

As Jack walked, his costume got tattier and tattier. It was hanging off him like rags. He stopped on the path.

'This is useless,' he said to Holly. 'I'm going to get rid of it!'

Holly stopped and waited for him. Lovesome kept on walking.

Jack took off his satchel, pulled off his hands and head, and tore the remnants of his body off. It felt great to be just in his T-shirt and shorts but he looked at his bare feet.

'I think I'd better keep 2 of the Sorx feet,' he said.

Reaching down he picked up what was left of the body and found the 2 good feet. He tore them away from the legs and put them on. Stepping off the path he hurled what remained of his costume into the undergrowth.

'Thank you and goodbye! I don't need you now!' he shouted at the top of his voice.

Overhead a Cacawker heard Jack's shout. It stopped in its flight and started hovering. It tipped its head downwards and scanned the forest canopy below, stopping at a small gap. Focussing its incredible eyesight on the ground below the gap, it could clearly see a Drongle.

'Food!' it thought.

Jack walked up to where Holly was waiting.

'It feels so good without my costume on,' he said. 'You should take yours off.'

'I think I'll keep it on for the moment,' said Holly. 'It may come in useful.'

The trail continued to snake around the trees. After a while they realised that there was no sign of Lovesome.

'Where's he gone?' asked Holly.

'Don't worry,' said Jack. 'He'll be up ahead. He'll stop and wait for us to catch up.'

The trail turned sharply to the right and passed narrowly between 2 of the giant trees. Beyond was a small clearing. In the middle of the clearing was a Cacawker face-to-face with Lovesome. It hadn't yet seen Jack and Holly. They quickly hid behind the 2 giant trees and watched.

Lovesome kept jumping up on his hind legs, raising his front legs at the Cacawker, trying to fend it off. The Cacawker had its wings fully extended and was thrusting its red beak towards him. They danced around each other, alternatively moving forwards and backwards.

Suddenly the Cacawker charged at Lovesome and stuck its beak into his side. Lovesome gave a sharp cry of pain and fell over. The Cacawker pulled its beak out, shook its head, and spat something onto the ground. It then turned away, ran swiftly on its claws, and launched itself into the air at high speed. As Jack and Holly watched, it rapidly turned into a tiny dot in the sky. They rushed over to Lovesome who was lying on the ground moaning gently. Nearby was a piece of his skin.

'Are you alright?' asked Holly, in a panic.

She could see yellow liquid coming out of a hole in Lovesome's side, where the Cacawker's beak had penetrated.

'What's that yellow liquid?' she asked, anxiously.

'Oh, that's my blood, but don't worry, I'll be OK in a short while,' said Lovesome. 'It's only a flesh wound. The Cacawker tore off a piece of my skin and spat it out.'

'Why did it do that?' asked Jack.

'Well,' said Lovesome, between his moans. 'Cacawkers are stupid birds who have very short memories. All they want to do is to eat. They see Drongles and they think of food. So they attack them and peck chunks out of them. But, thankfully, they can't stand their taste, so they spit the chunks out. They then fly away and leave them alone, as you just saw.'

'I suppose that's good,' said Holly, trying to be sympathetic.

'Yes, it is, and that's the reason why we've survived in Highlow,' moaned Lovesome. 'But after they have attacked us, they soon forget that they don't like our taste. So the next time they see us they attack us again! It's very annoying!'

'But are you hurt?' asked Jack. 'You seem to be bleeding a lot. Is there anything we can do?'

'No,' said the Drongle. 'I really will be fine very soon. Because they peck us so often, our bodies have developed very good self-healing systems. My wound will heal up very soon, and my body will regenerate the blood I have lost.'

'That's amazing!' said Jack.

'Yes it is, but we'd better keep moving,' said Lovesome, trying to stand up. 'The Cacawker knows I'm here, but it hasn't seen you. If it had it would've alerted the Sorx, and they would be hunting for you now. I'm glad I ran ahead of you, otherwise the Cacawker would have seen you when you came into this clearing. Let's get back onto the path, it's heading back into the forest.'

'It's so good of you to protect us,' said Holly. 'Thank you Lovesome.'

'You are most welcome,' said Lovesome, who had managed to get up onto his four paws. 'After all isn't that what friends are for? But I think you will need more friends than me.'

'What do you mean?' asked Holly.

'Just wait and see!' said the Drongle, laughing mysteriously. 'I'm just going over to that tree. Please wait here.'

Lovesome hobbled over to one of the giant trees and went behind it. Very soon there was the sound of drumming, very faintly at first but then growing louder and louder.

First, in an irregular time: drum - drum, drum - drum, drum- drum -drum, drum, drum - drum, drum - drum - drum - drum - drum.

Then, in a waltz time: drum - drum - drum, drum - drum - drum, drum - drum - drum.

And finally, in a marching time: drum - drum - drum - drum, drum - drum - drum - drum, drum - drum - drum - drum.

'What's that sound?' asked Jack.

'I don't know,' said Holly. 'But Lovesome's making it behind that tree.'

She pointed to the giant tree. The drumming continued for a while, then stopped. Lovesome emerged from behind the tree.

'OK,' he said. 'Let's go!'

'But what was that drumming?' asked Holly.

'Oh, you'll find out soon,' said the Drongle, who was feeling much better.

His body was quickly healing, and he scampered ahead of them along the path, away from the clearing and into the forest.

'We'd better not let him get too far ahead this time,' said Jack.

'You're right,' said Holly. 'Let's go after him!'

Chasing his tail

They set off along the trail after Lovesome, making sure that they kept him in sight. They soon caught up to him. He was standing on a wooden arch bridge, which crossed a stream. He was looking at something on the decking of the bridge.

'Look! It's me!' he cried, happily.

Holly and Jack reached the bridge and joined him. He was looking at a carving. It was a circular shape, which showed a Drongle chasing its tail.

'Yes! It is!' laughed Jack.

'I can do that!' said Lovesome.

He immediately began to chase his tail like the Drongle in the carving. He spun round and round and round. After a while he stopped and started to stagger all over the place.

'Are you OK Lovesome?' asked Holly.

'I'm feeling dizzy,' he said, as he staggered straight into a huge tree and fell over. He stood up, wobbled across the path, and walked into another tree. He fell over again, and lay still on the ground.

Holly and Jack rushed over and knelt down beside him.

'Lovesome, Lovesome, speak to me!' said Holly.

'Love I you. I you love. Really love I you,' said Lovesome, very softly. 'Head my hurts.'

'He's mixing up his words,' said Jack. 'He's bumped his head.'

'I'll give him some Burpz,' said Holly.

She reached into her satchel, pulled out a bottle of Burpz, and held it to Lovesome's lips. He took a big swig.

'You thank. I you love. You really love I,' he said.

He finished the bottle and gave an enormous burp that echoed through the trees.

'Oh thank you! That tastes great. I love you. I really love you,' he said. 'My head hurts, but I'm OK.'

He jumped up, scampered off along the trail, and disappeared round a sharp bend to the right.

'Well he seems to be alright,' said Jack.

'Yes, he does,' said Holly, thankfully. 'But come on, we need to keep him in sight.'

'Easier said than done!' said Jack, laughing.

They followed the trail round the sharp bend and saw Lovesome moving ahead of them. As they walked along, Holly sensed that they were being watched. She looked to the left of the trail and some of the ferns were moving. She looked to the right, and saw more moving ferns.

'Jack!' she said, anxiously. 'I think we are being watched. The ferns are moving on either side of the trail. Something must be moving them.'

Jack looked and saw the ferns moving gently back and forth. Then they stopped.

'It's just the wind,' he said, trying to reassure her. 'Don't worry.'

But Holly was worried. There didn't seem to be any wind. However, she said no more about it, and they walked along in silence, which was soon broken by Lovesome's voice.

'I've found one!' he cried.

He was standing by a sign. Jack and Holly walked up to him

and stopped by the sign, it read:

Task 2:

Here's the second clue on the trail:
Find a friend, one with a tail.
Who fits inside this circle bold.
And whose species is partly gold.

In the middle of the trail near to the sign was a beautifully formed circular hole.

'We must be looking for a circular jigsaw piece,' said Lovesome.

'Yes,' said Holly. 'And I think it must show a picture of a friend with a tail.'

'And who belongs to a species, which is partly gold,' said Jack.

'What does that mean?' asked Lovesome. 'What is a species?'

'A species in the name for a group of animals that are the same or very similar, like Hubees, Sorx, Qorx, Cacawkers and Drongles,' said Holly. 'You are a member of the Drongle species.'

'Thank you,' said Lovesome, very pleased that he was a member of the Drongle species!

Jack kept reading the sign.

'A friend whose species is partly gold. A friend whose species is partly gold,' he repeated over and over to himself. Then he stopped.

'I think it means you Lovesome!' he cried.

'Me?' asked Lovesome. 'What do you mean?'

'Well,' said Jack. 'You're a friend, you've got a tail, and you're a member of the Drongle species.'

'Yes,' said Lovesome. 'But what about partly gold?'

'The word "gold" can be made from some of the letters in the word "Drongle",' said Jack, triumphantly. 'So the name of your species is partly gold!'

'That's clever!' said Lovesome, even more pleased now that he had gold in his species name!

'But how does that help us?' asked Holly.

'Don't you remember the bridge Holly?' asked Jack.

'Yes!' said Holly. 'Of course I do. I remember Lovesome getting dizzy!'

'No,' said Jack. 'Not that part. I mean the carving on the decking. It was a Drongle in a circular shape. It must be the jigsaw piece that fits in here!'

'Yes, of course!' said Holly.

'I'll go and get it,' said Jack. 'You stay here and keep an eye on Lovesome. Make sure he doesn't wander off.'

With that he turned and ran back to the bridge.

'He looks very odd with those Sorx feet on,' Holly thought to herself, as she watched him go.

He came quickly back with the circular piece and slotted it into the circular hole in the trail. It fitted perfectly.

They walked over it and shouted for Lovesome to follow them. He did, but stopped to look at the carving of a Drongle chasing its tail.

'Don't copy it!' shouted Jack and Holly together, remembering what happened last time.

'I don't know what you mean,' said Lovesome, as he walked deliberately slowly over the piece and off down the trail.

'You get going Holly,' said Jack. 'I'll put the piece back and catch you up.'

Not holes

The trail snaked left then left again. Holly kept looking to either side. The ferns were moving. It wasn't the wind, because there wasn't any wind. There was definitely something in the undergrowth.

'Jack, the ferns are moving again,' she said. 'I'm sure they are.'

Jack looked, and they were definitely moving.

'Yes, they are,' he said. 'Let's go and look.'

'I don't know,' said Holly. 'I'm scared. It might be Cacawkers.'

'I think if it was they'd be making a lot of noise,' said Jack. 'Keep close together.'

They stepped off the trail and walked towards the ferns on the left side. The ferns stopped moving as they approached. They reached them and looked around, but they could see nothing unusual. They did the same with the ferns on the right side of the trail. Again they found nothing. They returned to the trail.

'Whatever is moving the ferns is being very careful,' said Jack. 'Come on, all we can do is to keep going.'

They set off towards Lovesome who, for once, had been waiting for them. The trail continued its twists and turns and they began to think that it was never ending. They had only completed 2 tasks and there were still 3 to go; they were getting tired.

But the third one was just around the next bend and, as they went round it, there was one of the biggest trees they had ever seen. Even by the size of some of the huge trees in the forest, it was vast.

'Look at that!' cried Jack. 'What a tree!'

Lovesome was standing beside it. He looked like a mouse compared to it. But this tree presented a great problem. It had fallen right across the trail and there seemed to be no way around. They walked up to Lovesome. He was standing by another wooden post with a sign on it. This one read:

TASK 3:

THIS ONE IS AN OPPOSITE TASK.
IMAGINE YOU ARE MAKING A MASK.
REMOVE 2 PIECES, FORM 2 HOLES.
THROUGH THE TUNNEL YOU MUST STROLL.'

'What does this one mean?' asked Lovesome, sitting down by the wooden post.

Holly read it carefully before answering.

'I think it means that we have to take out 2 pieces to make a tunnel,' she said.

'But I thought you had to put pieces in to make a jigsaw,' said Lovesome.

'Yes you do,' said Holly.

'So how can we take pieces out, if we have to put them in?' asked Lovesome.

'I don't know,' said Holly. 'But it says we have to take out 2 pieces to make a tunnel to stroll through.'

'So, we have to slowly walk through this great big tree?' asked Lovesome.

'Yes,' said Jack. 'I think so.'

'You're making my head hurt again,' said Lovesome, who wandered away to have a lie down.

Holly turned to Jack.

'So, I suppose we will have to make a tunnel through this enormous tree,' she said. 'But where do we begin. Surely we will need 2 big holes, one on each side, if we are to be able to stroll through it.'

'I think we should look for a very large piece that we can remove to form the first hole. Perhaps it will have some sort of handle on it.' said Jack.

They walked up to the fallen tree. Like many of the huge trees in the forest it had a very rough bark in amongst which were lots of knots.

Lovesome's head had stopped hurting, so he stood up and wandered back to join them.

'Can you see all these knots, Lovesome?' asked Holly, pointing to the tree trunk.

'What are knots?' asked Lovesome.

'Knots are small pieces of wood. Usually they have a round shape,' said Holly. 'If you can take them out they form knot holes. Here are some knot holes.'

She pointed to some holes that knots had fallen out of.

'Those holes?' asked Lovesome.

'Yes, those holes. They're knot holes,' said Holly.

'But you said that they are holes,' replied Lovesome.

'Yes, they are holes,' said Holly. 'Knot holes.'

'How can they be holes if they are not holes?' asked Lovesome. His head was starting to hurt again.

'Because they are!' said Holly, laughing. 'And in any case we

220

aren't looking for holes, we are looking for no holes.'

'So you're looking for no holes?' asked Lovesome.

'Yes,' said Holly.

'Why do you want no holes?' asked Lovesome.

'So that we can turn them into holes and they become knot holes,' said Holly.

'Let's see,' said Lovesome. 'You want no holes so that you can make them not holes?'

'Well you've found some! Because they are not holes!' exclaimed Lovesome triumphantly, as he wandered across to the sign and sat down.

'That went well!' said Jack, laughing.

'Yes!' laughed Holly. 'But now we must find our no holes! You start at one end and I'll start at the other.'

They split up, moved to opposite ends of the tree, and slowly started to work their way towards each other, examining the trunk very carefully. When they met they still hadn't found anything.

'We must be missing something,' said Jack.

They walked up and down the side of the tree looking at the knots on the trunk. Most of them were randomly dotted around as would be expected, but in one area they formed a very large circle.

'Of course!' said Jack. 'These knots form a circle so they must mark the opening.'

He pushed each knot in turn with his fingers. The knots fell inside the tree leaving a big circle of knot holes.

'Yeesss!' exclaimed Jack.

He stepped back and kicked the centre of the big circle. Nothing happened. He leant against it and pushed hard. Nothing happened. Holly joined him and they pushed together as hard as they could. Still nothing happened.

'Why won't it open?' asked Jack, getting annoyed.

'Well, we've kicked it and pushed it,' said Holly. 'There isn't a handle to pull it out, so what's left?'

Jack looked at the circle.

'Perhaps we have to twist it,' he said.

He pushed his fingers and thumbs into some of the knot holes and turned them to the left. At first nothing happened, but as he turned harder the whole circle of knot holes moved. He kept turning, and a large thin circular piece of the trunk unscrewed to reveal a wide tunnel running through the tree.

'It's the tunnel!' cried Holly.

She strolled through the tunnel and found another circle of knots at the far end. She took her costume hands off and pushed the knots out leaving another big circle of knot holes. She put her fingers and thumbs in some of them and turned. A second large thin circular piece of the trunk unscrewed to reveal the trail heading off into the distance. She stepped out onto the trail.

'Yes! We've done it!' she cried. 'Get Lovesome and let's go!'

'Come on Lovesome!' called Jack.

Lovesome bounded over to him. He and Jack entered the tunnel and Jack replaced the piece from the inside, screwing it into position. They then strolled through the tunnel onto the trail. Holly waited for them to leave, then replaced the piece from the outside, screwing it into position.

'There!' she said, putting her costume hands back on. '3 down and only 2 to go!'

'Yes,' said Jack, pointing along the trail. 'And I think the next one is just up ahead.'

The rainbow wall

The trail straightened out and was about to enter a clearing. On the other side was a large wall. It was too high to climb, and stretched far into the distance on either side. It was built of rough stone, and most of it was that brown-black colour that old walls have. However, where the trail ran straight into it, a section of the wall had been painted with beautiful rainbows, real ones, not wobniars. Cut out of the rainbows were 7 star-shaped holes.

Nearby was a wooden post with a sign attached. They walked over and read it:

TASK FOUR:
THIS PIECE IS GIVEN FROM THE START.
JUST FIND A HOLE TO FIT THE PART.
PUT IT IN AND TWIST IT RIGHT.
THE LONELY SWEETS WILL BE IN SIGHT.

Lying at the bottom of the post was a star-shaped jigsaw piece with rainbow colours on it.

'This one looks quite easy!' said Lovesome, who was beginning to understand how the clues worked. 'All we have to do is to fit the star into one of those holes!'

'Yes, you're right, and if we twist it to the right the wall will open,' said Holly, reaching down to pick up the star.

Just then a large black shadow crossed the clearing. They looked up and knew immediately that they were in trouble. Nine Cacawkers were overhead, moving in a V-formation.

'Quick Jack!' said Holly, pleased she had kept her Sorx costume on. 'Hide! They may not have seen you. They might think I'm a Sorx. Lovesome, you'd better hide as well. I don't want them to attack you.'

Up above her, the Cacawkers had indeed spotted their prey. After their four companions had peeled off to search separately, they had stayed together since being summoned by 2:7:3, and had been scanning the tree canopy all the while.

They had seen fragments of the trail through gaps but hadn't had any definite sightings until now. A Hubee, a Drongle and a Sorx all spotted at once. It was just what they had been hoping for. They locked onto them with their bright blue eyes. The V-formation stayed together and swooped down into the clearing.

Jack and Lovesome dashed back towards the fallen tree not realising that they too had been spotted, while Holly stepped out into the clearing.

The V-formation swooped lower and lower, landing a short distance in front of her. The 5 in the front of the V hopped forward, their blue eyes and red beaks shining in the light of the clearing. They stopped and formed a line in front of her, opening and closing their beaks like scissors, making a terrible Click-Clack sound.

The other four took to the air and swooped backwards and forwards over her, occasionally touching her with their sharp claws. She was being inspected. She stood firm and didn't move.

Her heart pounded in her chest.

The four inspectors returned to the others, and they all formed into a closed circle with their heads inwards.

'This is what they did on the road to SQorxville,' thought Holly, trying not to shake.

The sound of beaks Click-Clacking echoed through the clearing as the circle of Cacawkers slowly rotated.

'Will I get away with it?' thought Holly. 'Will they do their "Cacawker Ceremony" and let me go?'

She very soon had her answer when the sound instantly changed to the cacophonous noise of the Cacawker Call.

Cacaw! Cacaw! Cacaw! Cacaw! Cacaw! Cacaw! Cacaw! Cacaw! Cacaw!, screamed through the clearing, as each Cacawker let rip with a piercing shriek. This was repeated over and over until the whole forest seemed to be echoing the sound. It was caught by the wind, and it blew towards SQorxville.

'Oh no!' thought Holly. 'They're making the "Cacawker Call"! They're summoning the Sorx!'

3:Four:Four

In the lookout tower on top of the Foraging School, 3:Four:Four was leaning on the protective fence. He had been there all solar and was very bored. His replacement would be coming in a squig of time, and he was looking forward to going home and putting his feet up.

He had been on duty every solar for a quarter of a continuum, and was sick of climbing the 97 steps on the ladder to get to the top. However, he did enjoy going down the forager's pole. He was there so that he could summon the foragers quickly in the event of trouble.

Fixed to the wall beside him was an enormous shiny silver bell with a big F stamped on it. Inside the bell was a big clanger. Fastened to the clanger was a thick piece of rope with a knot in its end.

This was the alarm bell. He had only rung it once, and that was by mistake when he thought he had heard the Cacawker Call. But it was actually some Sorxlings mucking about.

It had happened very early one morning and he had woken up the whole town. He had got in terrible trouble for that and was now scared to ring it. Fortunately, he hadn't had to do so since then.

'Nothing ever happens up here,' he said to himself. 'I don't know why we bother keeping watch.'

He stood up straight and stretched his arms above his head. He put his hands on his green forager's hat, pulled it tight on his head, played with the silver F badge, twiddled his ears, and stared over the town.

'I'm so bored,' he thought. 'I wish something would happen.'

Then something did.

Through the air came the distinctive call the forager had been trained to detect: Cacaw! Cacaw! Cacaw! Cacaw! Cacaw! Cacaw! Cacaw! Cacaw! Cacaw!

He leant forward and listened.

'It's the "Cacawker Call"! It's coming from the direction of the Rodley Bottoms Tunnel,' he cried. 'They've found a creature that isn't a Sorx!'

He panicked.

'What shall I do? What shall I do?' he shouted to himself. 'What if it's a false alarm? What shall I do?'

Fortunately, he'd been retrained after ringing the bell by mistake.

'Listen!' his trainer had said. 'Listen! If it is the "Cacawker Call" it will start echoing all around the town. Sorxlings voices don't echo!'

So 3:Four:Four listened and listened.

Cacaw! Cacaw! Cacaw! Cacaw! Cacaw! Cacaw! Cacaw! Cacaw! Cacaw! came wafting through the air followed by a quieter, Cacaw! Cacaw! Cacaw! Cacaw! Cacaw! Cacaw! Cacaw! Cacaw! Cacaw! And then by an even quieter, Cacaw! Cacaw! Cacaw! Cacaw! Cacaw! Cacaw! Cacaw! Cacaw! Cacaw!

'Yes,' he said to himself. 'That is definitely echoing!'

His retraining kicked in. Overcoming his fear, he grabbed the rope and banged the clanger backwards and forwards against the bell as hard as he could. Its sound crashed over SQorxville, summoning the foragers from their tree houses.

The sound also crashed round and round in his head. He let go of the rope and collapsed on the floor.

'My ears! My ears!' he shouted. 'I can't hear anything!'

This was true. He couldn't even hear himself shouting.

'But I must go down the pole,' he thought.

He stood up quickly, felt dizzy, and fell over again right next to the pole. He reached out and locked his fingers round it. Pulling himself forward, he wrapped his 3 legs on it, and then relaxed his fingers. He began to move down the pole.

'That's better!' he said, but he still couldn't hear himself. As he picked up speed, he realised that something was wrong.

'Oh no!' he shouted. 'I'm upside-down!'

Now he really panicked. The ground below was approaching rapidly, and he was dropping like a stone towards it head first. He froze on the pole forgetting to tighten his fingers and legs. His floppy hat slipped down his ears and fell off.

'Help! Help! Look out below!' he bellowed at the top of his voice. His hearing returned.

At the bottom of the pole, the forager-in-chief had heard the alarm bell and had come out to see if it was a false alarm. She didn't trust 3:Four:Four after what had happened last time. Hearing his bellows, she looked upwards to see him hurtling towards her. She stepped back, just before his head hit his floppy green hat lying on the ground. He landed in a crumpled heap beside her.

'Are you OK?' she asked, reaching down to help him up.

He groaned and staggered to his feet holding his hat in his hand.

'Yes, I think so,' he said. 'I came down upside-down by mistake.'

The chief didn't bother to ask him why, she knew that he was accident prone. She was more concerned about the alarm call.

'Did you hear the echo?' she asked.

'Yes,' said 3:Four:Four. 'There were 2 echoes.'

'Good!' she said. 'Let's go and get ready for the foragers arriving.'

She looked at him.

'What have you done to your face?' she asked.

'What do you mean?' he replied, rubbing a hand over his face. He felt something on his right cheek.

'There's a big letter "F" on your cheek!' she said, laughing.

Sure enough, pressed into this right cheek was the print of his forager's badge. When he had landed on his hat, the badge had put a big dent in his cheek.

When his fellow foragers saw it they nicknamed him 3:Four:Four:F, but he didn't mind. It felt like a badge of honour, and he considered himself to be a real forager. Eventually the F disappeared from his cheek, but forever afterwards, even when he grew some more toes, he always put F after his name.

The Drongle Drums

As soon as the Cacawkers started screaming, Holly turned and started running back towards the forest to warn Jack and Lovesome. She had only gone a few steps when she felt something on her back. She turned to see a Cacawker tearing at her costume with its claws. 2 others came at her from each side and jabbed her arms with their sharp beaks, pulling at her costume. 2 more came out of the sky in front of her and flew straight towards her.

She stopped. She was petrified, and could do nothing as they flew right into her with their claws extended. They knocked her to the ground and tore off large chunks of her costume. As she fell, she saw four Cacawkers heading into the forest in the direction of the fallen tree.

'Jack!' she screamed at the top of her voice. 'Run!'

The Cacawkers were all over her. She thrashed at them with her arms and legs, but the more she did so the more they jabbed and scratched her. She was in big trouble and she knew it. He costume was being ripped to shreds.

'This is it,' she thought to herself. 'I can't do anything to stop them.'

She clutched her satchel tightly to her, protecting Podge inside it.

'Help me! Please help me! Somebody please help me!' she

shouted at the top of her voice as the Cacawkers continued their attack.

Then, through the chaos she heard something she had heard before.

First, in an irregular time: drum - drum, drum - drum, drum- drum -drum, drum, drum - drum, drum - drum - drum - drum - drum.

Then, in a waltz time: drum - drum - drum, drum - drum - drum, drum - drum - drum.

And finally, in a marching time: drum - drum - drum - drum, drum - drum - drum - drum, drum - drum - drum - drum.

It got louder and louder, and nearer and nearer. The Cacawkers stopped attacking her and looked round to see where the sound was coming from. Bruised and dazed, she managed to lift her head from the ground and look in the direction of the drumming.

To her amazement, there were four rows of Drongles marching towards the Cacawkers. There were at least ten Drongles in each row, all making the sound with their feet that she had heard when Lovesome had hidden himself behind a tree in the forest.

'He must have called the Drongles,' she thought, hardly able to believe that the Cacawkers had left her alone.

She tried to stand up but found it very difficult. Her arms and legs hurt and what was left of her costume was tripping her up. She tore it away, keeping the feet on like Jack had done. Pushing hard on the ground, she raised herself upright and looked towards the advancing Drongles. They were now close to the Cacawkers, who had formed a line across the clearing. The four other Cacawkers joined them from the forest. The

Drongles stopped marching and the 2 sets of enemies eyed each other up.

To the Cacawkers it looked like a feast had arrived for them to devour. Their first thought was always food, and now in front of them was a banquet! They raised their wings sideways, and started advancing towards the first row of Drongles. As they got nearer they started their Cacaw! Cacaw! Cacaw! shriek, but the Drongle row stood firm. The Cacawkers surged forward with their beaks extended, and drove towards the Drongles.

Just as they reached the front row, it dropped to the ground, and the second row leapt over it right on top of the advancing Cacawkers, clawing and pawing at them in a frenzied attack. Caught off-guard, the Cacawkers stopped and tried to defend themselves. They flapped their wings furiously and stuck their red beaks into the Drongles. They tasted terrible. Spitting out pieces of Drongle, the Cacawkers started to retreat.

The first row of Drongles now stood up, leapt over their fallen friends, and attacked the retreating Cacawkers. As they fell, they were replaced by the third row, which was replaced by the fourth row. Then the second row regrouped and took over from them. And so it continued, with each row replacing the previous one and piling on top of the Cacawkers. The Drongles attack plan was working perfectly. The Cacawkers were being overwhelmed. Each one was being pawed and clawed by at least 3 Drongles. They could not fly because of the sheer weight of Drongles on top of them.

Holly couldn't believe what she was seeing. The Drongles had not only saved her, but also were beating the Cacawkers. It was amazing, and she stood transfixed by the battle raging before her. The ground was a seething mass of Cacawkers and Drongles.

'Holly! Holly! Are you alright!' cried a voice behind her.

Jolted from her trance, she turned to see Jack and Lovesome emerging from the forest.

'I don't know,' she said, as they rushed over to her. 'I think so.'

She looked down at herself. There were scratches on her arms and legs. Her back hurt and she felt dizzy. Jack examined her all over. Her T-shirt and shorts seemed OK.

'I don't think there is anything serious,' he said. 'But you need to clean up some of those cuts.'

'What happened to you in the forest?' asked Holly.

'Oh, we ran back to the fallen tree and got back in the tunnel,' said Jack. 'We hid there looking through the knot holes to see what was happening. Four Cacawkers appeared and started swooping round the tree, picking at the bark. Then suddenly they flew back to the clearing. We waited a while then came back here. That's when we saw you staring at the battle.'

'Oh that's good,' said Holly. 'I'm glad you didn't get hurt.'

Meanwhile, the battle was raging near them. The Drongles were definitely on top, but the Cacawkers were inflicting some severe wounds. Several Drongles lay on the ground, obviously in pain. Suddenly, another V-formation of Cacawkers swept out of the sky.

'You've got to get away from here!' interrupted Lovesome. 'My friends can hold off these Cacawkers for a while, but others will be on their way. They will have heard their shrieks and will soon come to their aid.'

He paused, and then continued, 'And so will the foragers. I must stay here and help my friends, but you must go!'

Holly looked at Lovesome.

'Did you summon the Drongles?' she asked.

'Yes, I did,' said Lovesome. 'I summoned them when we were in the forest. They have been following us ever since.'

'So was that the drumming noise you made?' asked Holly.

'Yes,' said Lovesome. 'That's the "Drongle Drums", and we use it when we need help. I called them as protection in case we got into difficulties. That's why you saw ferns moving. The Drongles were always there.'

'Thank you so much,' said Jack. 'It's a good job they were.'

'But why are they willing to fight for us?' asked Holly.

'Because I love you, they love you, and they will do anything to protect you,' said Lovesome, very gently.

'That's incredible,' said Holly. 'They are so brave.'

'Yes, they are,' said Lovesome. 'But they will heal and all their pain will go. Our bodies are very good at healing. By the end of this solar they will be back to normal.'

'Please thank them for us,' said Holly.

'I will,' said Lovesome. 'But you must go, and I must help my friends. Go and finish the jigsaw tasks.'

'Will we see you again?' asked Jack.

'Who knows?' said Lovesome. 'But never say never! And always remember that I love you!'

And with that he turned and ran into the battle, jumping on the first Cacawker that he saw.

'Oh! I will miss him,' said Holly, sadly.

'Me too,' said Jack.

The star and the stripes

With the battle raging behind them they ran up to the rainbow wall. Holly picked up the star-shaped jigsaw piece. She looked at the 7 star-shaped holes on the wall and looked at the star. They all seemed to be the same size.

Rotating the star, she tried to match up its rainbow with the rainbows on the wall. Again they all looked the same.

'We'll just have to try each hole in turn,' said Jack. 'Put it in this one.'

He pointed to one of the holes in the middle.

Holly pushed the star in, but it didn't quite fit. The rainbow didn't match, and there was no way it would fit exactly in the hole.

'Now this one,' said Jack, pointing to the hole next to it.

Holly took the star from the first hole and pushed it into the second hole. It fitted exactly.

'Yeesss!' exclaimed Jack. 'Turn it to the right!'

Holly placed both her palms on the star, pushed hard, and tried to turn it to the right. It wouldn't move. She tried again. Nothing happened.

'Oh come on!' she shouted at the jigsaw piece. 'Please turn. Why won't you turn?'

'Stand back Holly,' said Jack.

Holly stepped back from the wall. Jack looked at the piece

Holly had put in. It did fit perfectly, but its rainbow didn't quite match the rainbows on the wall.

'The rainbow doesn't match,' said Jack. 'Try the next hole.'

Holly prised the piece out with her fingernails and tried putting it into the next hole. It didn't fit.

From behind them they heard, Cacaw! Cacaw! Cacaw!, and turned to see a third V-formation of Cacawkers landing in the clearing. As soon as they touched down, they joined the battle and charged into a group of Drongles. Cries of pain filled the air.

'We've got to get out of here!' said Jack. 'Keep going!'

Hole four was too small, and hole 5 was too big.

The battle behind them grew louder. Holly lifted the piece towards hole six. As she did so, she felt something on her back. She turned to see a Cacawker, with its claws fully open, reach for her satchel strap. She dropped the jigsaw piece and screamed, but the Cacawker didn't move. It closed its claws around the strap and started to pull the satchel from her shoulder. Holly clutched the satchel tightly, as the strap began to stretch. The Cacawker leant forward and stabbed its red beak into her arm. The pain was intense. She let out another scream and let go of the satchel.

The Cacawker flapped its wings, took off, and landed on the ground in front of her. It dropped the satchel and began rummaging inside it with its beak. It pulled out Holly's medal and dropped it on the ground. It stuck its head in again and suddenly Podge appeared in its mouth. The Cacawker tried to eat her then spat her out. It went back into the satchel and pulled out a Yumbax. It put one of its claws on Podge. It put its other claw on the Yumbax and started to eat it. Holly's heart sank. She dropped to the ground staring at Podge in the Cacawker's claw.

Jack bravely moved towards the Cacawker. It saw him, picked up the remains of the Yumbax in one claw, closed its other claw around Podge, and turned to fly away. Just as it turned, a black and yellow mass came crashing out of the undergrowth and landed on top of it, knocking it over. The Cacawker dropped Podge and the Yumbax and turned to face the Drongle.

Holly noticed that the Drongle had a chunk out of one of its ears. It was Affable!

Affable turned towards Holly.

'I always knew you weren't Sorx!' she said. 'I love you! Guid Lukio!'

With that she rushed forward, clawing and scratching at the Cacawker.

'Grab Podge!' shouted Holly, who was still stranded on the ground.

Jack grabbed Podge and Holly's medal, put them in his satchel, and picked up the jigsaw piece. He turned to the wall and tried hole six. The piece fitted perfectly, and the rainbow matched. He put his palms against it, pushed hard, and tried to turn it to the right. Nothing happened. He tried again, pushing and twisting his hands even harder. Suddenly, the piece turned. There was a loud creaking noise, and a rainbow-coloured door in the wall swung inwards.

'Yeesss!' he shouted. 'Come on Holly!'

Holly forced herself from the ground and turned to see Affable still battling with the Cacawker.

'And we will always love you too,' she said, quietly. But Affable didn't hear her.

237

She ran towards Jack who was waiting by the door.

'You go in,' he said to her. 'I'll put the piece back.'

Holly rushed through the opening. Jack took the piece out of the sixth hole and dropped it beside the wooden post. The opening began to close. He dived in, just in time, as it slammed shut behind him.

Outside in the clearing, the tide of the battle had turned. The Drongles had been winning due to their larger numbers. But with the arrival of more and more Cacawkers, their resistance had weakened. They didn't have the same weapons as the Cacawkers. No sharp red beaks, no huge black claws, just padded feet with a few stumpy paws.

Many Drongles lay moaning on the ground, with yellow streaks of blood coming from rips in their sides where the Cacawkers had stabbed them. Some Drongles kept on fighting, but there were fewer of them who could do so. They had nothing left to give. Their strength lay in their numbers, in their ability to swamp their attackers, but they just couldn't do it anymore.

Eventually, all the Drongles lay wounded, and the Cacawkers regrouped. Most of them had feathers missing, or gashes in their sides, but none was seriously injured. They would heal and they could still fly and that's exactly what they did. They lined up at the edge of the battlefield in a series of V- formations and took off in unison, flying back to roost in the top branches of the forest. They had done their job. They had found the Hubees for 2:7:3, and the Drongles had been defeated. As they flew away, they still remembered that they didn't like their taste, but that memory would soon fade and they would once again try to eat any Drongle they saw.

Back on the ground, the Drongles were scattered like autumn leaves. But they too were all alive, and slowly their self-healing systems began to work. After a while they began to stand up and walk, unsteadily at first, but then less so. Eventually they were all on their feet and moving normally. They headed back into the forest undergrowth where they lived. They too had done their job. They had protected their friends.

A close call

On the other side of the wall, Holly was shattered. Her body ached, and she was covered in cuts and bruises. She sat down and leant against the closed door. Jack stood beside her leaning against the wall.

'We made it through the wall Holly, and we have Podge!' he exclaimed.

He reached into his satchel, pulled out Podge, and waved her above his head. She looked rather bedraggled having recently been in a Cacawkers mouth and claw. He placed her very carefully back in his satchel.

'Yes, we have,' said Holly, softly. 'But I'm so sore and achy. Are we nearly at The Lonely Sweet Shop?'

Jack looked around. The trail came out of the wall and led off ahead of them. They were in a very narrow valley. He could see the sky clearly above them. The trail ran straight towards a dark shape.

'I can't see much from here,' he said. 'The trail is very narrow. Are you able to keep going?'

'Oh yes!' said Holly. 'We can't be far away now; I just want to see Hornbeam again.'

She pushed herself off the ground and stood up.

'Let's go!' she said.

They began walking along the trail towards the dark shape

that Jack had seen. As they got nearer, they could see that it was a tunnel entrance. It ran under what appeared to be a road. On the other side of the road they could see a tree house with a T-shaped chimney sticking out of its roof.

'Look!' cried Jack. 'It's The Lonely Sweet Shop!'

Holly looked and sure enough it was; she could just make out the old sign hanging at a crazy angle. Her heart lifted.

'The tunnel must lead to the spiral staircase that goes up into the tree house,' said Jack, excitedly. 'Come on, we're almost there.'

They picked up their pace and walked towards the tunnel entrance. As they did so they heard a high-pitched Sorx voice say, 'We'd better not tell 2:7:3 what just happened.'

Jack and Holly looked at each other. They were too far from the tunnel entrance to make a run for it, and there was nowhere to hide on the trail. They pushed themselves hard against the steep valley walls and made the Sshh sign to each other.

2 other Sorx voices spoke, but it wasn't clear what they said. They echoed off the sides of the narrow valley and in and out of the tunnel. It was impossible to say where they were coming from. Then the voices stopped and the sound of daduming started: da-da-da-dum, da-da-da-dum, da-da-da-dum.

Holly and Jack looked towards The Lonely Sweet Shop and saw 3 Sorx moving quickly away from it. But not out of the tunnel; they were on the road above. Their green hats identified them as foragers, although there didn't seem to be any keesceptres sticking out of their satchels. They were heading in the direction of the Rodley Bottoms Tunnel.

As they dadumed, the 3 foragers kept their eyes firmly on the road ahead, and didn't look down into the valley on their left, where Holly and Jack were forcing themselves against the walls. The sound of their dadums faded and eventually disappeared.

Holly and Jack breathed huge sighs of relief.

'That was close,' said Jack. 'They must be foragers hunting for us.'

'Yes,' said Holly. 'I thought they were coming out of the tunnel.'

'Well, I think we should go into the tunnel and try to find Hornbeam,' said Jack.

The foragers' plan

2:7:3 was very unhappy. She had lost her Hubee toy, her sister's Drongle and, worst of all, 3 keesceptres had been stolen.

To lose one keesceptre was an extremely serious offence, but to lose 3 was unheard of. She was in great danger of being drummed out of the foragers. She wasn't too concerned about the Drongle, she could easily get another one, although she was annoyed that it had been stolen. But she had to get those keesceptres back at any cost, and also the toy. That toy was her treasure. She owned it!

After she had summoned the Cacawkers at the Nowhere Tree, she and her sister returned to the Rainbow Factory. Her sister went to have a lie down, but 2:7:3 had no plans to do the same.

The 3 foragers whose keesceptres had been stolen had already gone to the Foraging School to summon help. They told the foragers about the stolen keesceptres, and the Foragers' Vow came into force.

2:7:3 dadumed down to the School just as a large group of foragers emerged onto the road. The forager-in-chief was with them. She looked very serious.

'Ah! There you are 2:7:3,' said the chief, very sharply. 'Where have you been? We've been waiting for you. Have you any news?'

243

'Sorry chief, it took me a while to get back from the Nowhere Path. I think that 2 Hubees are disguised as Sorx, and they have taken a Drongle with them,' she said, nervously. 'But I've summoned the Cacawkers and they are already hunting them in the forest.'

'Yes, our lookout has just heard the Cacawker Call from the direction of the Rodley Bottoms Tunnel. Hopefully we can catch them there,' said the chief. 'But this is a bad business, very bad indeed. 3 keesceptres stolen! I've never heard of such a thing! Why did you tell the foragers to leave them in a tub outside the Rainbow Factory? They should have been kept indoors.'

2:7:3 felt very ashamed.

'Keesceptres can interfere with the rainbow production,' she said, trying to justify what she had done.

'Couldn't you just have shut the production down while the foragers were there, or held the meeting somewhere else?' ask the chief, angrily.

'Yes, I suppose I could have,' said 2:7:3, meekly.

'Well, we can investigate what happened later,' said the chief. 'What we have to do now is to get those keesceptres back. Gather round everyone!'

The chief went into the Foraging School while a group of twenty-one foragers gathered on the road outside. She emerged with a megaphone in her hand and stood in the doorway.

She put the megaphone to her mouth and began to speak into it.

'The fugitives were last seen on the Path to Nowhere, and have been seen by the Cacawkers somewhere in the direction of the Rodley Bottoms Tunnel,' she bellowed. 'We think they are 2 young Hubees disguised as Sorx who are accompanied by a Drongle.'

Her voice boomed out of the megaphone and bounced off the outside wall of the Foraging School. The foragers put their fingers in their ears. She saw them, stopped talking and turned the megaphone down, but only a bit.

She then continued, '2:7:3 will take the foragers' A team along the road to the Rodley Bottoms Tunnel and reinforce the entrance to prevent them getting in.'

The foragers kept their fingers in their ears.

'They will try to escape through the tunnel,' bellowed the chief. 'So we must get there before they do. I have already sent 3 foragers to guard the entrance. I've also sent four to guard the Woodpecker Woods Tunnel just in case.'

She coughed into the megaphone.

Everyone jumped.

'I will take the foragers' B team along the road to search the trees and undergrowth to see if they are hiding there, before joining the A team at the tunnel,' she bellowed on, completely unaware of how loud she sounded. 'Remember to listen out for the Cacawker Call in case they see the fugitives again. Any questions?'

She put her megaphone down.

The foragers took their fingers out of their ears.

A forager spoke up, 'If they are disguised as Sorx. Where did they get their costumes from?'

A murmur ran through the group.

'I reckon it was that Qorx at The Lonely Sweet Shop,' said another. 'He must have helped them.'

'That's a good point,' shouted the chief. 'Some of the A team

245

must go to The Lonely Sweet Shop and interrogate him. Any further questions?'

There were no more questions.

'Right!' said the chief. 'Split into your 2 teams.'

The group lined up into 2 teams. The chief walked to the front of team B. 2:7:3 rather sheepishly walked to the front of team A.

'OK!' shouted the chief. 'Put your hats on and let's go!'

2:7:3 led team A down the road towards the signpost, and then along the road to the Rodley Bottoms Tunnel. In her team were the 3 foragers whose keesceptres had been stolen. The chief followed with the B team, who began searching the undergrowth and trees next to the road.

While team B moved slowly along the road, team A made good progress. They had passed through the Check Point, waking up a very grumpy guard, and were heading towards The Lonely Sweet Shop. As they approached it they could see smoke coming out of its T-shaped chimney. The team stopped on the road outside.

'You 3!' shouted 2:7:3, pointing to the 3 foragers whose keesceptres had been stolen. 'Go in there and interrogate the Qorx. Find out if he has been helping the Hubees and if he knows where they are. And see if he knows about the Hubee toy. We will go to the tunnel. When you have finished you should join us there.'

The interrogation

The 3 foragers walked over to The Lonely Sweet Shop. They reached the small door and saw that it was locked. A new lock had been put on quite recently, it was still shining. One of them put its thumb and the prime number fingers of its right hand into the 5 key holes, and it opened. It unhooked the lock, and dropped it on the ground. Grabbing the door handle, it turned to his 2 companions.

'When I say "Go" we rush in. OK?' he said.

His 2 companions nodded.

'Ready! Steady! Go!' he said.

On Go, he pushed the handle on the door, the door swung open, and they found themselves inside The Lonely Sweet Shop.

In front of them, and towering over them, was Hornbeam.

'Hello! What can I do for you?' he asked, in his big booming voice.

The foragers had not seen a Qorx for some time and the sight of Hornbeam scared them. But they had a job to do, and they were foragers, so they stood as tall as they could and started to interrogate him.

'Have you been hiding 2 young Hubees?' asked the first.

'Did you provide them with Sorx costumes?' asked the second.

'Do you know where they are?' asked the third.

Hornbeam said nothing.

'They have stolen a treasure from 2:7:3 and 3 keesceptres,' said the first.

'We are here to search your house,' said the second.

'Let us pass!' shouted the third.

'Be my guest,' said Hornbeam, stepping to one side.

The foragers spilt up, and started to search all the nooks and crannies on the ground floor, including Hornbeam's cage. Several times, they walked over an old carpet on the floor near to the bottom of the staircase. Had they lifted it, they would have found the trapdoor. But they didn't.

'Should we go upstairs?' asked the first.

The second and third ones looked at the vast spiral staircase with its very high steps, and then looked at each other.

'No. I don't think we need to. The young Hubees are too small to climb up those steps,' said the second, who was quite a lazy Sorx.

'OK,' said the third, who was just as lazy.

'I agree,' said the first, the laziest of them all.

Not having found anything, they began to taunt Hornbeam.

'What's it like being the only Qorx in Highlow?' asked the third.

'Aren't you lonely?' asked the second.

'Don't you wish you could leave this horrible old tree house?' asked the first.

Hornbeam said nothing.

'Why are you so ugly?' asked the first.

'Why have you only got 2 legs, like Hubees?' asked the second.

'Why do have you an extra arm?' mocked the third, laughing.

By now Hornbeam was getting annoyed with these stupid Sorx. He leant down and reached towards them with his 3 arms then, in his deepest loudest voice possible, he bellowed, 'So that I can do this!'

He thrust his 3 hands forward, flipped off their hats with his first fingers, and grabbed each Sorx by one of its ears using his first fingers and thumbs. Jerking his hands upwards, he lifted them off the ground.

'Leave me alone!' he thundered; his voice echoing round the room. 'Get out of my house or else I will pull your ears off!'

The 3 foragers hanging from his fingers were scared, very scared. They kicked and wriggled, but Hornbeam held on tightly.

He looked at them and, one-by-one, he let go. As they fell towards the floor, he kicked out with this left foot and booted them towards the open door. Soon there were 3 foragers with very sore bottoms. They stood up and looked at Hornbeam, and then at each other. They knew instinctively what to do. They turned and ran as fast as they could out of the open door.

Hornbeam picked up their hats, and hurled them out of the opening.

'And take these silly hats with you!' he bellowed.

Hornbeam laughed his foghorn laugh, and slammed the door.

'Stupid Sorx!' he muttered to himself, as he went up the spiral staircase to his bedroom.

Outside, the foragers picked up their hats from where Hornbeam had thrown them.

'We'd better not tell 2:7:3 what just happened,' said the first.

'No, we'd better not. We should just say that we interrogated the Qorx,' said the second.

'Yes, and that he didn't know anything,' said the third.

They all nodded in agreement, put on their floppy hats, and waggled their ears through the slits. They checked their satchels were comfortable, then dadumed away towards the Rodley Bottoms Tunnel. Hornbeam watched them go from an upstairs window.

Had the lazy foragers been more observant, they would have seen Jack and Holly hiding in the steep-sided narrow valley on the left side of the road.

Round the twist

After their close call with the foragers, Holly and Jack set off walking towards the tunnel. Just inside the entrance was a wooden post with a sign on it. It read:

TASK 5:

SOON YOU'LL REACH YOUR LONELY SWEETS
BUT NOW THEY'RE JUST BEYOND YOUR REACH
GO ROUND THE TWIST, UNBOLT, PUSH HARD
THROUGH THE FLOOR, AND THERE THEY ARE!

Holly read it carefully.

'It's telling us what we have to do,' she said. 'The twist must be the spiral staircase. We have to go up it, unbolt the trapdoor, and push it up to get into the tree house.'

'Yes!' said Jack. 'All we have to do is to find the bottom of the spiral staircase. It must be somewhere in the tunnel. You take the left side and I'll take the right.'

They moved into position and slowly set off into the tunnel, running their hands along the sides as they went. The further they got in, the darker it became, until it was completely black and they could not see a thing.

The tunnel seemed to curve and to be made out of stone. They could feel the individual pieces and the mortar holding them together. It was very regular and had been made well. Holly got into quite a rhythm as she felt it: stone, mortar, stone, mortar, stone, mortar.

She chanted this to herself as she moved along the tunnel, 'Stone - mortar - stone - mortar - stone - mortar - stone - mortar - stone - mortar - stone - mortar - stone - mortar - stone - mortar - stone - gap.'

'Gap!' she cried. 'Jack! I've found a gap!'

She kept feeling with her hand, but there was nothing to feel. The gap was getting wider.

Jack, on the other side of the tunnel, stopped running his hand along it. He turned, and walked very slowly and carefully across the tunnel.

'I'm coming over to you,' he said. 'Say something so I can find you.'

'I'm here!' cried Holly. 'Try to find my voice. I'm here! I'm here! I'm heee …'

At that moment Jack bumped into her, and she fell backwards into the gap in the wall. She landed on a wooden step and felt it with her hands. Reaching up, she found another step and another and another, until she couldn't reach any more. The steps were curving round. It was the spiral staircase.

'I've found the staircase Jack!' she cried.

Jack was still disorientated, and had set off down the tunnel again after bumping into Holly. When he heard her cry, he turned and walked back in the other direction running his hand along the wall. He found the gap, went into it, and immediately fell on top of Holly.

'Ow!' she said. 'Watch out, I'm already covered in cuts and bruises!'

'I'm sorry Holly,' said Jack. 'It's just so dark down here.'

'It's OK,' said Holly. 'Just reach out and find my hand.'

She held her hand out into the darkness, and waved it about slowly. Jack did the same, their fingers touched, and they grasped each other's hand firmly.

'That's great!' said Holly. 'Now let's try to go up the staircase. It's probably best if we go up on our hands and knees.'

'Good idea,' said Jack. 'You start and I'll follow.'

Holly set off one step at a time. Hands then knees, hands then knees. Jack followed. As they climbed they could feel the spiral in the staircase.

'Hands then knees, hands then knees,' recited Holly. 'Hands then knees, hands then Ooowww!!!' she cried, as she banged her head on a wooden ceiling. 'I've reached the top!'

'Good,' said Jack, 2 steps below. 'Now see if you can find the bolt.'

Holly reached up to the ceiling and ran her hands slowly in all directions. She felt a solid metal tube. It had a handle on it. She pulled, and the tube moved. There was a clicking noise, and the trapdoor opened slightly. She pushed, and it moved slightly. She pushed harder, and it opened a little more. She pushed a third time, and it didn't move at all. It was stuck.

'Come and help me!' she called to Jack. 'Put your hands on the trapdoor!'

Jack moved up a step and put his hands on the trapdoor.

'OK,' said Holly. 'Push!'

They pushed together. Slowly, the trapdoor opened higher and higher until it was vertical. With one final push, it went right over and crashed on the floor. Light and dust poured in. They were inside The Lonely Sweet Shop.

'We've done it Jack!' shouted Holly. 'We are home!' forgetting that this was not really her home.

She climbed out onto the floor on her hands and knees, and looked back to the trapdoor. It had been covered by an old carpet, which was now scrunched up underneath it.

'Yeesss!' cried Jack in relief, as he followed her through the open trapdoor.

He took off his satchel and joined Holly on the floor.

A deep voice that they hadn't heard for some time called from the floor above, 'Welcome back!'

It was Hornbeam, who came rushing down the other spiral staircase to greet them.

'Holly!' he cried, reaching down to pick her up. He gave her a big hug. Her cuts hurt as he did so, but she didn't mind. He put her down gently on the floor.

'Jack!' he cried, reaching down to pick Jack up. He squeezed him hard, before carefully putting him back on the floor.

'You've made it! Fantastic! But look at the state of you,' he said, looking them up and down. 'Where are your Sorx costumes? You've only got one satchel, and you are filthy. And Holly, you are covered in cuts and bruises! Are you alright?'

'We are fine,' said Holly. 'We've just had an unusual day!'

'We sure have!' agreed Jack.

'You must have had. You've now got Sorx feet!' laughed Hornbeam, pointing to the last remaining parts of their costumes.

'But did you get Podge?' he asked, anxiously.

'Yes. We did!' said Jack, triumphantly.

He reached into his satchel, and gently took Podge out. She was battered and soggy, but still defiant, still Holly's Podge! He handed her to Hornbeam.

'Hello Podge!' said Hornbeam, holding Podge very gently. 'It's good to meet you at last!'

He laughed his foghorn laugh, and handed Podge to Holly.

'It's been quite an adventure rescuing her,' said Holly.

'Well you must tell me all about it,' he said. 'But first let's get you both cleaned up. You wait here. I'll just close the trapdoor, and then I'll be back.'

He walked over to the opening in the floor, lifted the trapdoor, and dropped it back into position. He grabbed the old carpet, and dragged it back over the trapdoor.

'There! That's better!' he said.

Hornbeam disappeared behind the stove, and returned with 2 large bowls of hot soapy water and 2 huge green towels. A bright-blue sponge shaped like a Qorx floated on top of each bowl.

Right,' he said. 'Take off your Sorx feet and start washing yourselves. Come upstairs when you're ready.'

With that he turned and walked back up the spiral staircase. Jack and Holly washed and dried themselves, and began to feel better. Holly noticed that she didn't seem to hurt quite so much, as she slowly climbed up the staircase wrapped in her enormous towel. Jack picked up his satchel and followed her, wrapped in his. They were both glad to be back with Hornbeam.

Hornbeam met them at the top of the staircase. He gave them each a pair of yellow socks, lifted them gently onto his huge bed, and leant them against the vast pillows. The socks were far too big and they laughed when they put them on.

'You look as though you've got enormous bananas on your feet!' said Jack.

'So do you,' laughed Holly. 'But they're so comfortable aren't they?'

'They sure are,' said Jack, waggling his toes inside them.

For the first time since heading off to SQorxville they felt warm and safe. Hornbeam brought a chair near the bed and sat down.

'Right,' he said. 'Before you tell me what happened I have something to tell you. Not long before you came through the trapdoor, 3 foragers burst into my house, and started to ask me questions.'

'They must have been the ones we saw on the road before we went into the tunnel,' said Holly.

'They wanted to know if I had seen 2 young Hubees,' continued Hornbeam. 'They got aggressive and accused me of harbouring you, and providing Sorx costumes for you to disguise yourselves. They searched downstairs, poking into all the nooks and crannies, but didn't find anything. Fortunately, I'd covered the trapdoor with an old carpet, and they didn't look underneath it. And they were too lazy to go upstairs.'

He paused.

'They were rather annoying. I told them nothing, and I persuaded them to leave,' he said, mysteriously. 'I don't think they will be back!'

'That's good,' said Holly.

'They also said that you had stolen a treasure from 2:7:3,' said Hornbeam.

'How dare they! Podge is my treasure!' said Holly, keeping a tight hold on a now much cleaner Podge.

'I saw them leaving along the road to the Rodley Bottoms Tunnel. They have probably gone there to look for you,' said

Hornbeam.

'Did they hurt you?' asked Holly, who was now hurting more herself.

'No,' said Hornbeam. 'They didn't have any keesceptres, so all they could do was to shout at me. They said you had stolen them.'

'Do you mean these ones?' asked Jack, reaching into his satchel and pulling out 3 keesceptres.'

'Incredible!' cried Hornbeam. 'You've got their keesceptres!'

'Yes,' said Jack. 'I took them from a tub outside the Rainbow Factory when they were having a meeting.'

Holly suddenly spoke.

'I'm sorry to be a nuisance,' she said. 'I know we've got so much to talk about. But I'm afraid my cuts and bruises are really painful. Do you have anything you can put on them please?'

'Oh, I'm so sorry Holly,' said Hornbeam. 'I'm so wrapped up with the foragers that I forgot about your injuries. Yes, I do have something that might help.'

He stood up from his chair and walked over to the wall. He pressed a knot and a drawer slid out. He reached in, pulled out a piece of white cloth, and a small wooden bowl with a lid on. He pushed the drawer back in, returned to his chair, and sat down. He put the cloth on the bed, and took the lid off the bowl.

'Put this on your cuts and bruises,' he said.

Drointment

Holly shuffled across the bed with Podge, wincing in pain as she moved. She took the cloth, and looked in the bowl. In it was a pale-yellow cream.

She smeared it on the cuts on her legs and forearms. It felt so soothing.

'Oh!' said Holly. 'That feels so good!'

'But what is this stuff?' she asked, as she smeared on the cream.

'It's called "Drointment",' said Hornbeam. 'It's made from a mixture of Drongle blood, Drongle sweat and a small amount of tree sap to bind it together.'

Holly stopped applying the Drointment.

'Ugh! That's disgusting!' she cried, throwing the cloth onto the bed.

'Yes,' said Hornbeam. 'It may sound disgusting, but I'm told it definitely works, and there don't seem to be any side effects.'

'What do you mean by "don't seem"?' asked Holly, nervously.

'Well,' said Hornbeam. 'I haven't used it very much, but all the Drongles I meet tell me that it works. It's supposed to have the same effect as their self-healing system.'

'How often have you used it?' asked Holly.

'Actually, you're the first one I've tried it on,' he said. 'I don't need it you see because I'm mainly made of wood, and that heals itself with its own sap.'

'So you're experimenting on me?' asked Holly, who was now getting quite worried.

'Yes, I am,' said Hornbeam. 'Because I believe the Drongles who gave it to me.'

'I hope you're right,' said Holly, sharply, although secretly she was already starting to feel better, and the pain was definitely going away.

'Don't worry,' said Jack, trying to reassure her. 'You'll be fine. I trust the Drongles as well. Remember what they did for us in the battle.'

Holly thought about this.

'Yes. You're right,' she said, picking up the cloth and putting more Drointment onto her cuts, slapping it on rather too generously.

'What battle was that?' asked Hornbeam, keen to change the subject and also eager to find out what they had done in SQorxville.

'Oh,' said Jack. 'That happened towards the end.'

'Well perhaps you can start at the beginning and tell me everything,' said Hornbeam.

'OK. I will,' said Jack.

He snuggled his back into his pillow and made himself comfortable. By now, Holly had used up all the Drointment and was feeling warm and cosy. She snuggled her back into her pillow. Hornbeam made himself comfortable in his chair, and leant forward.

'I'm ready,' he said. His six leaf ears swivelled forwards.

And so Jack told Hornbeam about everything that had happened since they had left The Lonely Sweet Shop.

When he had finished Hornbeam clapped his 3 hands together, very cleverly.

'What a journey you've had!' he cried. 'And you got Podge back! And you met Affable and Lovesome. And Holly won a medal! And you got 3 keesceptres! Can I see them please?'

Jack handed them to Hornbeam, who took hold of them very carefully as if they were precious pieces of art.

'This is unbelievable!' he said. 'I never thought I'd be holding 3 keesceptres.'

He held one in each of his 3 hands and waved them in the air liked swords. It was an impressive sight.

'That looks good'!' said Jack, watching the keesceptres sweep through the air.

'I love you!' said a Drongle voice from the bed.

It was Holly.

Jack turned on the bed and looked at her.

'Was that you Holly?' he asked.

'Yes,' said the Drongle voice. 'I love you!'

It was coming out of Holly's mouth. Jack looked at Hornbeam and laughed.

'What's happening to her?' he asked.

'Oh, I hoped this wouldn't happen,' said Hornbeam. 'The Drongles warned me about it. It seems that if you give Drointment to non-Drongles it can affect them oddly for a while. Most times they just fall asleep, but sometimes their voices change to Drongle voices, and they keep saying, "I love you". This appears to have happened to Holly, but it usually wears off after a touch of time.'

'So there are side effects,' said Jack.

'Well I didn't know for certain, because I've never seen them,' said Hornbeam.

'I love you!' said Holly, smiling.

'It's very funny,' said Jack, trying hard not to laugh.

'I love you!' said Holly. 'I really love you!'

'Perhaps she should wipe some of the Drointment off,' said Hornbeam. 'She has put rather a lot on.'

He put the keesceptres on the bed and went across to the wall. He pressed the same knot and the same drawer slid out. He took out a clean cloth and pressed the knot again. The drawer closed.

'Here Holly,' he said. 'Why don't you wipe some Drointment off? You don't need that much.'

Holly took the cloth and began wiping off some big dollops of cream. When she had finished, Jack and Hornbeam looked at her for a touch of time. They noticed that most of her cuts and bruises had disappeared. While they were looking at her, she looked back at them, continuing to smile and say, 'I love you!' over and over again.

Then she suddenly coughed, sat up straight, and said, 'I love you! I love Yumbax! I'd love a Yumbax! Can I have a Yumbax please?'

'Are you OK Holly?' asked Jack, anxiously.

'Yes, of course I am!' said Holly, who did feel very well. 'Why shouldn't I be?'

'You kept saying, "I love you!", over and over again,' said Jack. 'Can't you remember?'

'Don't be silly Jack,' she said. 'You're making it up. Why would I do that?'

She had absolutely no idea what Jack was talking about.

Jack was just about to tell her about the side effects of

Drointment when Hornbeam spoke up.

'Holly's quite right Jack, stop teasing her!' he said. 'She was just asking for a Yumbax. I'll get her one. Would you like one as well?'

He reached over, gave Jack's arm a gentle squeeze, and looked him straight in the eyes. Jack looked back. He got the message, and knew not to say any more about Drointment. All that mattered was that it had worked. Holly's cuts and bruises had all disappeared. The side effect secret was safe between him and Hornbeam.

'Yes please,' said Jack, smiling.

Hornbeam went to the wall and took out 2 Yumbax from a drawer. He came back and gave them one each. They devoured them very quickly. Jack tasted cheese on toast. Holly tasted a big bowl of mushroom soup.

Hornbeam's Escape Plan

Hornbeam picked up the 3 keesceptres from the bed, sat down on his huge chair, and leant back.

'Those foragers will be very angry that you stole their keesceptres,' he said to Jack. 'You've no idea what you have done.'

He sounded frightened.

'What do you mean?' asked Jack

'Well,' said Hornbeam. 'The wood from the Super Bremmin Hoose is running out. So keesceptres are highly prized by the foragers, who are very protective of them. Anyone stealing a keesceptre is in serious trouble if they get caught. Foragers take a vow, the "Forager's Vow", to help their fellow foragers find stolen keesceptres, by whatever means necessary. They usually do, and all the foragers will now be looking for them. So if they catch you ...'

He looked at Jack.

'... you will be in big trouble!' he continued.

'So I'd better not let them catch me, had I!' said Jack, boldly.

'Easier said than done,' replied Hornbeam. 'As you know, they're already out there looking for you.'

He nodded downstairs towards the door.

'They don't give up easily,' he continued. 'So the sooner we go, the better it will be. But don't worry, I have an Escape Plan.'

Hornbeam put the keesceptres on the bed. Grabbing Jack

in his right hand and Holly in his middle hand, he lifted them into the air and put them down gently on top of the table. Holly held tight onto Podge.

'I'm going to get the maps,' he said, walking over to the wall.

He returned with the large sheet with the 2 maps on, that he'd shown them before they set off to SQorxville. He laid it out beside them on the table.

'You are familiar Map 2,' he said, waving his middle hand over Map 2.

'Yes we are,' said Jack.

'Apart from that wavy dotted line,' said Holly, pointing to the dotted line at the bottom of Map 2.

'Ah yes, the dotted line,' said Hornbeam. 'I'll come to that later. But first let me tell you my plan.'

He pulled one of his huge chairs up to the table, and sat down.

'We know that the foragers are searching for you,' he said. 'And they are expecting you to try to escape through the Rodley Bottoms Tunnel.'

'Yes,' said Holly. 'That's our only way out. The way we came in.'

'But that's not true,' said Hornbeam. 'There's also the Woodpecker Woods Tunnel. If you could escape through that, you would get back not very far from Rodley Bottoms. When I did it as a Qorxling it was only about two hundred and fifty pedarcs.'

'Where does that tunnel come out?' asked Holly.

'Near a bridge over the canal that the cows use,' said Hornbeam.

'Oh,' exclaimed Holly. 'The Cow Bridge! We know exactly where that is!'

'Yes,' said Jack. 'It's very close to the rhubarb fields.'

'The rhubarb fields?' asked Hornbeam, in astonishment.

'Oh, it's not real rhubarb,' said Jack. 'It's just fields of wild plants with big leaves that look like rhubarb leaves. We cycle along the towpath to see them sometimes. It's just a name we made up for them. They're not very far from our house.'

'And a splendid name it is too,' said Hornbeam. 'But let's get back to the matter in hand. You know where the bridge is, and it's not far from your house. So if you can get there you can walk home.'

'But how can we do that?' asked Jack. 'There will be Sorx everywhere.'

'That's true up to a point,' said Hornbeam. 'There'll certainly be many foragers along the road outside, and around the Rodley Bottoms Tunnel, but there may not be too many guarding the Woodpecker Woods Tunnel.'

'Why not?' asked Holly.

'The Woodpecker Woods Tunnel has not been used since the Qorx left, and they will never come back while the Sorx are still here.' said Hornbeam. 'The Sorx know that, and they also know that I am the only Qorx still living in Highlow. They think they have me permanently locked up. They don't know that I can come and go as I please.'

'So they're not expecting anyone to use the Woodpecker Woods Tunnel?' asked Jack.

'Exactly!' said Hornbeam. 'I suspect that they don't guard it very well.'

'So, we may be able to get through it without being seen?' asked Holly.

'Exactly!' said Hornbeam again, getting quite excited. 'I'm sure you can!'

'That sounds good,' said Jack. 'But how do we get from here to the Woodpecker Woods Tunnel without getting caught?'

'That brings me to my plan, and the dotted line on Map 2,' said Hornbeam, pointing to the dotted line. 'This line runs from The Lonely Sweet Shop to the Woodpecker Woods Tunnel.'

He ran the first finger of his right hand along the dotted line.

'It isn't a proper trail,' he went on. 'But it's part of the route I took when I tried to escape. I think we should be able to go along it without being seen. We will have to cross some roads, but if we are careful we should make it.'

'We?' asked Holly. 'Are you going to escape as well?'

'On no!' said Hornbeam. 'I'm too big to escape. I'm bound to get caught. But I'll help you to get safely to the tunnel entrance. If necessary, I can act as a decoy to distract any guards. If they catch me, all they'll do is to bring me back here.'

'That's so kind of you,' said Holly. 'Thank you!'

She reached over the map and squeezed his right hand.

'You are most welcome,' he said, slightly embarrassed.

He did like these young Hubees.

'When are we going to do this?' asked Jack.

'Not just yet,' said Hornbeam. 'There will be too many foragers on the road at the moment. We should wait until things calm down. I think we should stay here for a tickle of time, and then set off really early while it's still dark. You need some rest.'

Jack and Holly were very pleased to hear that. They were very tired after their unbelievable day, and the thought of sleeping in Hornbeam's very comfy bed was very appealing.

'I don't think any foragers will come here again,' said Hornbeam. 'They've already searched The Lonely Sweet Shop.

They'll be more concerned about finding you.'

He tweaked the little branch on his nose thoughtfully.

'But perhaps you can look out of the windows, and see what is happening on the road just in case,' he continued. 'You should get a good view from up here. I'll start getting things together for the morning.'

The 2 upstairs windows gave an excellent view of the road. Holly took one and Jack took the other. Kneeling down so that they wouldn't be seen, they looked outside. After a while, a large group of foragers slowly came past, searching the undergrowth and looking between the trees. It was getting dark, and they were using their teeth to help them search. After a tickle of time, they moved up the road, and the light from their teeth faded away.

While Holly and Jack kept watch, Hornbeam opened several drawers in his wall, pressing different knots in the wood.

From one, he took 2 new satchels. From another, he took some Oodax and Yumbax. From a third, he took their wellies, and from a fourth, he took 2 small wooden bottles of Perx. He shared all these out between the satchels, and he put Holly's medal into her satchel.

'They need something better than wellies for their escape,' he thought to himself.

He walked over to the dressing up box, opened its lid, and started rummaging around. Pieces of costume flew into the air, as he searched for something.

'Yes!' he said, after most of the contents had been thrown out.

He pulled out a big Drongle costume, which had detachable feet. He took them off, and put 2 of them in each satchel.

Picking up the satchels, he walked over to the bed and put them down beside the keesceptres.

'Are there any foragers on the road?' he called out to Jack and Holly, who were still looking out of the upstairs windows.

It was much darker outside, and they hadn't seen any glowing teeth for some time.

'No,' said Holly. 'There haven't been any for a while.'

'Good,' said Hornbeam. 'Let's finalise our plan. Come over to the bed.'

Jack and Holly stood up and walked over to the bed. Hornbeam lifted them up gently and lowered them down beside the pillows. Holly stopped clutching Podge, and put her down on her pillow.

'These are for you,' he said, pointing to the satchels lying beside the keesceptres. 'In there are some Oodax, Yumbax, bottles of Perx and the wellies you came in. I've also put these in for you.'

With his left and right hands he reached into the satchels and pulled out the four Drongle feet. Holly burst out laughing.

'Wow!' said Jack, also laughing. 'That must have been a big Drongle!'

'Yes!' said Hornbeam. 'It was, but now it's four feet shorter!' He laughed his foghorn laugh.

'These came from a fancy dress Drongle,' he said, as he passed the feet to them. 'They will be better than your wellies when we walk the dotted line route.'

Holly took off her yellow socks and put the Drongle feet on. She stood up rather shakily on the bed.

'Oh, these are comfy!' she said, stepping forwards and backwards to try them out.

Jack did the same, and was equally impressed.

'You look very good in those!' said Hornbeam. 'They fit you well, and will keep your feet safe on the journey. They're waterproof, just like real Drongle feet.'

'I wish Lovesome could see us now,' said Holly, sadly. 'Do you think we'll ever see him again?'

'I do hope so,' said Jack, sitting down on the bed and taking his feet off. He put his yellow socks back on.

Holly kept her feet on a little longer before she changed into her yellow socks. She was still thinking about Lovesome.

'Right!' exclaimed Hornbeam. 'You need to eat something and then it will be time to have a short sleep. What would you like?'

'Can I have a Yumbax and a couple of Oodax please?' asked Holly, perking up at the thought of food.

'And the same for me please,' said Jack.

'Would you like anything to drink?' asked Hornbeam.

'Can I have some Perx please?' asked Holly and Jack at the same time.

'OK,' said Hornbeam. He walked over to his wall and came back with 2 Yumbax, four Oodax and 2 small wooden bottles of Perx.

'Here you are. I'm going downstairs to feed. I'll wake you soon, well before Enzor rises,' he said. 'Eat and drink well, and sleep well.'

He turned, crossed the floor, and set off down the spiral staircase.

Jack and Holly were very hungry. They devoured the Yumbax and Oodax. Holly tasted a big cheese and tomato pizza. Jack's taste buds went for spaghetti Bolognese. They washed this down with the Perx, draining their bottles. The Oodax were as good as ever, and soon little farts began to be emitted. They snuggled into the comfy bed. Holly hugged Podge, Jack turned on his side, and in a tickle of time they were fast asleep amongst the huge pillows and four Drongle feet.

Goodbye Lonely Sweet Shop

Hornbeam walked up the spiral staircase and went over to the bed.

'Come on you 3! Wakey! Wakey!' he shouted, in his booming voice.

Jack and Holly stirred in bed, Holly still hugging Podge. It was very dark and it would be some time before Enzor rose. Holly turned over and almost disappeared into her pillow. Jack opened an eye and looked out. He could hardly see Hornbeam through the gloom.

'What time is it?' he asked, forgetting that Qorx have no concept of Hubee time.

'It's time to go!' boomed Hornbeam.

Holly stirred again.

'What do you mean, you 3?' asked Jack very sleepily. He still only had one eye open.

'I mean you, Holly and Podge!' laughed Hornbeam. 'Now come on, get up. I've brought you a couple of Yumbax for breakfast. Here you are.'

He threw 2 onto the bed beside them.

At the mention of Yumbax, Holly sat up quickly and grabbed one. She really fancied a lovely warm bowl of porridge. She bit into it. She wasn't disappointed. The Yumbax passed over her taste buds, and warm porridge flowed into her tummy.

'Oh! That's so good!' she said.

Jack opened both eyes and sat up slowly, snuggling his back against this pillow. His eyes were getting more used to the gloom. He took the other Yumbax, and bit into it. He hadn't thought about breakfast, so he was not expecting any particular taste. What he got amazed him, hot pancakes with maple syrup. It was wonderful!

Hornbeam watched them as they finished their porridge and pancakes.

'Right!' he said. 'Put your Drongle feet on.'

They took off their huge yellow socks and put on the Drongle feet.

'These are great aren't they!' said Holly, showing her brown and black fluffy claws to Podge.

'Grab your satchels and come over to me. Yours has got your Golden Trumpet Medal in it Holly,' said Hornbeam, picking up the 3 keesceptres from the bed.

They grabbed their satchels and shuffled to the edge of the bed. Hornbeam gently lifted them down to the floor.

'Follow me!' he shouted, as he headed off down the spiral staircase carrying the 3 keesceptres. When they reached the bottom step, he asked them to sit down on it. He sat down on the floor beside them and began to speak, holding the keesceptres in his left hand.

'What we're about to do could be very dangerous for all of us,' he said, firmly. 'We must be extremely careful at all times. Do you understand?'

Jack and Holly nodded but said nothing.

'Good!' said Hornbeam. 'We are going to follow the dotted line that we looked at on the map. But it isn't a proper trail.

We'll have to make our own path as we go. Hopefully, we'll be able to, but we may have to change it depending on what we find along the way.'

'We understand,' said Jack. 'But we're willing to do anything to get back home.'

'That's good,' said Hornbeam. 'We'll be passing close to the Rodley Bottoms Tunnel. There'll be lots of Sorx guarding it, and many others searching the countryside for you. Fortunately, they won't be expecting me, so we may be able to turn that to our advantage.'

'Thank you for coming with us,' said Holly. 'We're very grateful.'

'You are very welcome,' said Hornbeam. 'But I'm looking forward to it. I'm excited, it's a long time since I've had an adventure, and I do enjoy them!'

He laughed his foghorn laugh.

'I only hope that they believe you'll be trying to get to the Rodley Bottoms Tunnel, and not the Woodpecker Woods Tunnel,' said Hornbeam.

'Will this help?' asked Jack. He reached into his back pocket, and pulled out the finger key for the lock on the portcullis at the Rodley Bottoms Tunnel. Hornbeam looked at it in amazement.

'You've got the finger key!' he shouted. 'That's great! When they find that it's missing, they will be convinced that you are going to use it to get back to Rodley Bottoms that way! Excellent! But why did you keep it?'

'I just thought it might be useful,' said Jack, putting the key back in his pocket.

'Well it certainly will be,' said Hornbeam. 'But possibly not

273

in the way you imagined. You're not actually going to use it, but they think you will! Amazing!'

He laughed his foghorn laugh again.

'Now just a couple of other things,' he continued. 'First, if we get separated we must try and meet at the Woodpecker Woods Tunnel. OK?'

Jack and Holly nodded.

'Second, if I get caught and you don't, you must continue on your own. You must not think of trying to rescue me. I will try to distract them, so you must make your own way. OK?'

Jack and Holly nodded again.

'Finally, take care of these,' he said.

He handed each of them a keesceptre and kept one for himself.

'They can help you if you get into difficulties,' he continued. 'Remember that they can open doors in walls if you hit them with the flat end, and shout out your Sorx name. Do you know what your Sorx names are?'

'Don't they depend on how many toes we have on our feet?' asked Holly.

'Yes,' said Hornbeam. 'Look at your feet. How many toes do you have on your feet?'

They looked at their Drongle feet, and counted the toes on their paws.

'I have 7 on each paw,' said Holly.

'And so do I,' said Jack.

'Good,' said Hornbeam. 'So your Sorx names are the same. They are "7:Zero:7".'

'Surely they are "7:7",' said Jack.

'No,' said Hornbeam. 'Sorx have 3 feet, a left, a middle and a right. But you only have 2 feet, a left and a right, not a middle. The keesceptre will expect 3 numbers so you must say zero for your middle foot. Hence, "7:Zero:7".'

'Ah!' said Jack. 'I see!'

Hornbeam tapped his keesceptre on the floor.

'These will also help us if we meet any foragers with keesceptres,' said Hornbeam. 'Keesceptres are very loyal to whoever is holding them and they will defend them from attack. If we get into a fight, our keesceptres will fight their keesceptres. But remember to be firm with them. Don't let your keesceptre be the boss!'

He swished his keesceptre in the air.

'Are you ready?' asked Hornbeam.

'Yes!' said Jack.

'I am!' said Holly, carefully snuggling Podge into the bottom of her satchel. She looked around the room.

'Goodbye Lonely Sweet Shop,' she said. 'And thank you.'

OK! Let's go!' boomed Hornbeam.

He stood up, picked up his satchel, and walked towards the door, holding his keesceptre in his left hand.

Jack and Holly stood up, checked their satchels, grabbed their keesceptres, and followed him.

Hornbeam stopped in front of the huge door. He grabbed its handle with his middle hand and pulled hard. It creaked open to reveal a dark sky, with the ground being illuminated by a fascinating pale-blue and pink light.

'After you,' said Hornbeam, waving them towards the door with his right hand.

Jack and Holly stepped out and Hornbeam closed the door. He turned sharply to the right and disappeared up the side of

The Lonely Sweet Shop, following his dotted line route. Jack and Holly gasped in amazement at how quickly he moved.

'Come on,' said Hornbeam, in a loud whisper from behind the tree house. 'Let's go!'

Setting the trap

2:7:3 was very keen to make amends for losing the keescep-tres. After leaving the 3 foragers to interrogate Hornbeam, she made her team dadum as fast as possible. Very soon, they arrived at the Rodley Bottoms Tunnel. Near the signpost, 3 Sorx were on guard sitting inside the small guardhouse. They came rushing out when the foragers arrived.

'Is everything OK?' asked one of them.

'That's what we have come to ask you,' said 2:7:3. 'Have you seen the 2 young Hubees?'

'No,' said another guard. 'No Hubees have been here while we've been on guard. But we have only been here for a squig of time. The chief sent us here as soon as the lookout told her about the Cacawkers' Call.'

2:7:3 looked around. Everything seemed to be in order. The portcullis was locked, and there were no footprints in the soft ground near the entrance. She walked over to the gate and inspected the lock. Something seemed to be wrong. The bottom of the lock was sticking out. She reached down and felt inside the lock. There was nothing there.

'The emergency key is missing!' she said to herself. 'The Hubees must have taken it when they entered Highlow! That means they will try to use it to escape!'

She called to her foragers, 'OK Team! Please gather round!'

The foragers grouped together in front of her.

'The chief is right!' she shouted. 'The Hubees will try to escape through this tunnel. They took the emergency key when they entered Highlow, and they will try to use it to escape. We need to guard the entrance, so that they do not see us and we can surprise them.'

'Should we hide?' asked one of the foragers.

'Yes! Split into pairs,' shouted 2:7:3. 'Then conceal yourselves very close to the entrance. Some in the bushes, some in the undergrowth, and some behind the trees. Leave the guardhouse empty so that they think that it's deserted. Turn your hats inside out, and remember to keep silent! If the fugitives come, I will give the signal to attack them.'

The foragers split into pairs and hid themselves as close to the portcullis as they could. They then settled down and waited.

Nothing happened and they started to get bored.

They began to talk to each other. The sound of their high voices drifted through the air.

'Stop talking!' bellowed 2:7:3, who was hiding behind some tall grasses near the portcullis. 'You'll give yourselves away to the enemy! Remember your training!'

The voices stopped drifting through the air and silence prevailed. But it didn't last long. The familiar da-da-da-dum sound began in the distance, and grew louder and louder. It was the foragers who had been interrogating Hornbeam. They stopped at the guardhouse and looked around. They couldn't see anyone.

'Team A should be here,' said the first.

'Yes they should,' said the second.

'Perhaps they've gone into the tunnel,' said the third.

They walked up to the portcullis and looked into the tunnel. 2:7:3 crept from behind her grasses and tiptoed up behind them.

'Boo!' she shouted, in a loud voice.

The 3 foragers jumped in the air in shock. When they landed, they turned in all directions and bumped into each other, falling to the ground.

'Get up!' shouted 2:7:3.

They untangled themselves and stood up. They saw 2:7:3 standing nearby.

'Come here and tell me what you found out,' said 2:7:3.

They walked over to her.

'We interrogated the Qorx really firmly,' lied the first.

'Yes, he was crying in pain,' lied the second.

'At first, he said he knew nothing about the Hubees,' lied the third.

The other 2 looked at him in surprise. This was not what they had agreed.

'But the more we hit him,' continued the third. 'The more he talked.'

'And what did he say?' asked 2:7:3, hopefully.

'He kept saying, "I know nothing, I know nothing, I know nothing",' lied the third.

'That's right,' lied the first, hoping that the third would stop talking. 'He burst into tears and said he could not tell us what he didn't know. Eventually he was so beaten, he just lay on the floor sobbing.'

'Then we left him and headed for the tunnel,' said the second.

2:7:3 looked at them suspiciously. She wondered how a Qorx could be beaten to the ground by only 3 Sorx without their keesceptres. It sounded very unlikely.

'Are you sure about this?' she asked.

'Oh yes,' lied the first. 'We were extremely thorough with our interrogation. We know he was telling us the truth.'

'So you are absolutely sure he doesn't know where the Hubees are, and he hasn't been helping them?' asked 2:7:3.

'Absolutely,' lied the second. 'We are sure he knows nothing.'

'Did you ask about the keesceptres and the treasure?' asked 2:7:3.

'Yes,' said the third. 'He didn't know what we were talking about.'

2:7:3 looked at them. She was disappointed by their news. She had hoped that the Qorx would have provided some useful information.

'OK,' she said. 'You'd better find somewhere to hide. Remember to turn your hats inside out and keep silent. I will give the signal when it's time to attack.'

The 3 foragers wandered around for a while, then hid behind some bushes on the other side of the portcullis. Silence descended again. Turq and Cora were high in the sky, shining their blue and pink rays. Their combined effect was mesmerising, lighting up the landscape in a purple sheen that shone through the branches of the trees.

Apart from the occasional soft farts and gentle snores, it was a very tranquil scene, and it was hard to realise that 13 foragers were hidden not far from the tunnel entrance. Then the silence was broken in the same way as before. Da-da-da-dum, came echoing through the air, growing louder and louder.

All of a sudden, the chief arrived with her B team. They had found nothing. She looked around and checked inside the guardhouse, but couldn't see anyone. She walked over to the portcullis, and immediately saw that the bottom of the lock was sticking out. Leaning forward she felt inside the lock and couldn't find the emergency key.

'Hello chief!' bellowed a voice behind her. She jumped in the air and landed hard on the ground. Scrambling up and nearly falling over again, she turned round quickly and saw 2:7:3.

'Oh! 2:7:3!' shouted the chief, trying to sound unflustered. 'You startled me! Do you know that the emergency key is missing?'

'Yes chief and that means that you were right. The Hubees will try to escape through this tunnel using the key,' said 2:7:3, trying to get back in the chief's good books.

'Where are your team?' asked the chief.

'They're all hidden nearby ready to surprise the Hubees,' said 2:7:3.

'That's a good strategy,' said the chief. 'Order them to reveal themselves.'

'Stand up Team A!' shouted 2:7:3.

Pairs of foragers appeared out of the undergrowth, and from behind bushes and trees.

'That's a good spread,' said the chief. 'But there are some gaps. I'll fill them in with my foragers to form a complete circle. The fugitives will never get through that without being caught!'

The chief looked up to the sky and the 2 moons.

'We will have a clear night to help us,' she said. 'Cora and Turq will light us on our way to catching the fugitives.'

She turned to her foragers and cried, 'Team B! Split into pairs and fill in the gaps in team A!'

Her foragers did as they were told, and soon there was an

almost complete circle of Sorx guarding the tunnel entrance. The only gaps were where the roads from the signpost headed off into the darkness.

'You know how cunning Hubees can be. Do you think we have enough foragers?' asked 2:7:3.

'Probably,' said the chief, who was always very cautious. 'But perhaps we should call in the others. I left 2 back on guard at the Foraging School, and there are four guarding the Woodpecker Woods Tunnel.'

'I think the fugitives will be here soon,' said 2:7:3. 'It's probably too far for the foragers to come from the school, but you could call in some of those guarding the Woodpecker Woods Tunnel. It's not too far away.'

The chief thought for a while then spoke, 'You are right 2:7:3. Let's recall half the Woodpecker Woods Tunnel guards. Send your fastest forager.'

'Yes, Ma'am,' said 2:7:3.

She turned towards the circle of Sorx, all of whom were still standing in their positions.

'Four:5:3!' she called.

An unusually tall Sorx walked over to her.

'You're the fastest forager I know,' she said. 'Go to the Woodpecker Woods Tunnel and bring back 2 guards to help us.'

'Yes, Ma'am,' said Four:5:3, who then turned and started daduming incredibly swiftly along the road towards the Woodpecker Woods Tunnel.

'OK foragers!' bellowed the chief. 'Hide yourselves, turn your hats inside out, and remember to maintain absolute silence. When the fugitives arrive, I'll give you the order to

282

charge. There'll be big rewards for the foragers who catch them.'

The circle of foragers vanished into the undergrowth, and behind the bushes and trees. Silence fell, and the tunnel, signpost and forest appeared to be absolutely deserted. The light of the moons illuminated the foragers upturned hats. They looked like the tops of large mushrooms lying in the undergrowth.

Walking the dotted line

Holly and Jack had trouble keeping up with Hornbeam. After passing through a dense forest, his dotted line route had entered a clearing and he was pedarcing quickly. They could see him in the pale night light, but they could never catch him.

'Slow down Hornbeam!' called Jack. 'We can't keep up!'

Hornbeam didn't hear him.

Holly picked up a stick and threw it towards the disappearing Hornbeam. It hit a tree with a loud crack. Hornbeam heard the sound and turned to look.

'Hornbeam! Hornbeam!' shouted Holly. 'Please wait for us!'

Hornbeam stopped and waited while they ran up to him.

'I'm so sorry,' he said. 'I forgot how quickly I can move. It's just so good to get out and stretch my legs like this. I'll walk more slowly from now on.'

'Thank you,' said Jack, who was quite out of breath. 'Can we just rest for a touch of time please?'

'Alright,' said Hornbeam. 'But not for too long.'

'Thank you,' said Jack, as he lay down on the grass. He looked up at the sky and for the first time saw the 2 moons.

'Look!' he cried. 'It's Cora and Turq!'

Cora's pink light was mixing with Turq's blue light.

'I wondered where that purple light was coming from,' said Jack.

Holly looked up and saw them.

'They look beautiful,' she said.

'Yes, they do,' said Hornbeam. 'Turq and Cora have helped me over the continuums to forage in the forest during the night, when the Sorx are sleeping. I think of them as my friends.'

'Well if they're your friends,' said Holly, looking at the moons. 'They're our friends. Hello Turq and Cora!'

'That's kind of you,' said Hornbeam. 'But we must get going. Are you ready Jack?'

Jack stood up.

'Yes I am,' he said.

'And you Holly?' asked Hornbeam.

'Yes me too,' said Holly, laughing. 'But please don't start pedarcing away!'

'I won't,' said Hornbeam, who set off walking normally out of the clearing into the forest.

Soon they reached a stream. It was the same one where Jack had washed his face after being splattered by the young Cacawker. Hornbeam stepped over it very easily. They had to paddle through, but the Drongle feet did their job and kept them warm and dry.

'Come on you 2,' said Hornbeam, from up ahead. 'Keep going. We'll soon be crossing the SƟorxville road.'

Hornbeam stopped just before the road and waited for Jack and Holly to join him.

'Holly,' he said. 'Can you see if it's safe to cross please?'

Holly nodded and crept towards the SƟorxville road through some long grass. As she got nearer she heard some scuffling to her left. She stopped dead and looked towards the sound. The blades of the grass were definitely moving, and they were tall enough for a Sorx to hide behind. She froze unsure of what to do. As the blades of grass parted she feared the worst.

'Hello! I think I love you but I'd better ask my Mum first,' said a soft little voice.

It was a baby Drongle. Like Lovesome it was mainly light-brown with four large floppy feet covered in black fur. But because it was a baby, its large black feet and ears were enormous compared to its body and its head.

It's yellow tail was quite stubby and had not yet begun to spiral. Underneath its ears on its bright-yellow head were 2 enormous brown eyes above a tiny black button nose and a gently curving mouth. It was one of the cutest things that Holly had ever seen. She sighed with relief that it was not a Sorx.

'Hello!' whispered Holly.

'Hello!' said a second soft voice.

It was another baby, just as cute as the first.

'Hello!' said Holly, quietly. 'And who are you?'

'My name is Nice,' said the first baby.

'And I'm Gentle,' said the second.

'I'm Holly,' said Holly. 'I'm very pleased to meet you,'

'Hello Holly!' said the 2 babies at the same time. 'We are very pleased to meet you too. We love you.'

'Our Mum tells us not to talk to strangers,' said Nice. 'But I really love you.'

'And I really love you too,' said Gentle.

Just then Mum arrived in a bit of a panic.

'Oh, there you are!' she cried. 'I've told you not to wander off! You can get lost in the long grass!'

'They are so cute!' said Holly to their Mum. 'I love them!'

'I love you too!' said Nice and Gentle at the same time.

'Hello! I love you!' said Mum. 'Oh yes, they may look cute, but they're always getting into trouble. I thought they'd got lost. I was getting very worried.'

'Sorry Mum,' said Gentle. 'It's just that we love having adventures.'

'They're just like me and Jack,' thought Holly. 'We are always having adventures and getting into trouble.'

Nice looked at Holly's feet.

'Why have you got feet like Mum's?' it asked. 'Is part of you a Drongle?'

'Oh no,' laughed Holly. These are pretend Drongle feet. We have put them on to keep our real feet dry.'

'We?' asked Gentle.

'Yes,' said Holly. 'Me and my brother Jack.'

'Are you on an adventure?' asked Nice.

'Oh yes,' said Holly. 'We really are on an adventure!'

'Oh can we come with you, we love adventures?' asked Nice.

'Oh yes please. Please say, "yes"! I love you!' cried Gentle.

'I don't think that would be a good idea,' said Holly, laughing.

'It certainly wouldn't!' said their Mum, sternly. 'Now come on you 2, it's time to go home, and don't get lost again.'

'But we weren't lost Mum,' said Gentle.

'We were just having an adventure,' said Nice.

'Well, your adventure in over,' said Mum

'I hope you enjoy your adventure,' said Mum to Holly. 'But I must get these 2 home in case any Cacawkers see them. They are too young to be pecked. I love you!'

She rounded up Nice and Gentle, and the 3 of them headed off through the grass, leaving a trail of waving blades in their wake.

'We love you!' called Nice and Gentle as they disappeared.

'I love you too!' whispered Holly, as she watched them go.

She crept up to the edge of the road and looked both ways. It was clear. She turned and beckoned Hornbeam and Jack to join him. They crept towards her and stopped at the edge. Hornbeam looked both ways and then pedarced across in one enormous stride. Jack and Holly ran after him and soon they were all safety on the other side.

'I'm sorry I took my time calling you,' said Holly. 'But I met a Drongle with her 2 babies called Nice and Gentle; they were so cute.'

'Oh, I wish that I'd seen them,' said Jack.

'Never mind Jack,' said Hornbeam. 'The important thing is that we have just 2 more roads to cross. Keep going!'

They headed into the woods once again.

'Do you think we will manage to escape?' asked Holly.

'So far, so good!' said Hornbeam.

In a touch of time they reached a second road.

'This is the road to the old Sorxville,' said Hornbeam.

As before, Holly inspected it first. There were no Drongles this time, and no Sorx. Satisfied that all was clear, they quickly crossed it and headed into the undergrowth on the other side. They reached the road to the Farsley Tunnel very quickly.

'We're over halfway now,' said Hornbeam. 'Please go and check it out Jack.'

Jack crept up to the edge of the road and looked to the left. It was clear. He looked to the right. Again it was clear and he could see the signpost not far from the Rodley Bottoms Tunnel. It looked mysterious in the purple light of the moons. He was about to beckon Holly and Hornbeam to join him, when he noticed what looked like the tops of large mushrooms, illuminated on the undergrowth on either side of the road not far from the signpost. As he looked at them they seemed to be moving gently up and down.

2 of them were not far from him, so he very slowly and quietly crept closer to them. As he got nearer he stopped and looked again. They were definitely moving, and they also seemed to be making a sound. He crept 2 steps closer and listened. It sounded like snoring.

Then one of them farted.

As the combined purple moonlight flickered on the mushroom tops, he realised that they were not mushrooms but hats, foragers' hats. The mushrooms were foragers asleep in the undergrowth.

'They must have turned them inside out to stop their badges shining,' he thought to himself. 'That's very clever!'

Walking backwards very carefully, all the while looking at the mushrooms, he withdrew to a safe distance, then turned around and crept back to Hornbeam and Holly.

'The road is clear,' he said, quietly. 'But there are foragers hidden in the undergrowth not far for the signpost. I saw their floppy hats, and heard them snoring and farting.'

'Ah!' said Hornbeam. 'They must have reinforced the tunnel entrance area with foragers, and set a trap for us to fall into.'

'So they're expecting us to try to escape through the Rodley Bottoms Tunnel,' said Holly. 'Isn't that a good thing?'

'Indeed it is Holly,' said Hornbeam, very positively. 'They're playing right into our hands. Once we cross this road, our route will take us away from the Rodley Bottoms Tunnel. Please check the road again Jack.'

Jack crept up to the edge of the road and looked up and down. It was clear. He beckoned to Hornbeam and Holly. They joined him. On the other side there were a lot more trees.

'There's a small forest between here and the Woodpecker Woods Tunnel,' said Hornbeam. 'We'll be well hidden in there. Let's go.'

Hornbeam pedarced across the road and disappeared into the forest. Jack and Holly followed him but, once again, he was getting well ahead of them. After a while they lost him.

'Where's he gone now?' asked Holly.

'I don't know,' said Jack. 'He keeps forgetting that he's much quicker than us.'

They looked into the forest. They had no idea in which direction the dotted line route went.

'Shall we call him?' asked Jack. 'We better had,' said Holly. 'Ready? One ! 2! 3!'

'Hornbeam! Hornbeam! Hornbeam!' they called, as loudly as they dared.

Deeper in the woods, Hornbeam stopped. He heard his name drifting quietly through the air. He looked round, but couldn't see Jack and Holly.

'Oh no!' he said to himself. 'I've done it again.' He turned and started walking back. After a tickle of time he reached Jack and Holly.

'I'm so sorry.' he said. 'I keep forgetting. I promise I'll go slower from now on.'

'Thank you,' said Holly. 'That would be good!'

Hornbeam turned and headed back into the forest at a slower pace, followed by Holly and Jack.

Four:5:3

Four:5:3 was making good progress. She was the fastest of the foragers by far. Daduming was her hobby, and she was very good at it. She was delighted to have been chosen for this task by 2:7:3. All her life she had never been chosen for anything.

Because she was unusually tall for a Sorx, she had been bullied when she was a Sorxling. She had been laughed at and mocked because of her height, and even now she was often called a SQorxy. She hated it, but there was nothing she could do about it.

She had no friends, and had spent her time alone learning how to dadum fast. And she could dadum very fast indeed. Because of it, she had managed to gain a place in the Foraging School. She had felt very proud when she graduated as a forager, and she hoped the other foragers would accept her as a friend. But only a few had. Many of the foragers were bullies.

But she wasn't bothered any more. She now knew that she could achieve anything. Being chosen for this task was just the beginning. She even let herself dream that one day she would be forager-in-chief.

'Come on feet and hands!' she said to herself, as she dadumed quickly along. 'We'll be there in no time!'

Just then a name came drifting through the air. A voice was

calling, 'Hornbeam! Hornbeam! Hornbeam!'

Four:5:3 stopped in her tracks.

'What was that?' she said to herself.

She stood up, walked to the edge of the road, and listened. She heard nothing. She listened harder, and heard the sound of something moving very slowly in the undergrowth. She reached into her satchel and pulled out her keesceptre.

'Who's there' she called bravely.

There was no reply.

'Come out!' she called, waving her keesceptre above her head. 'I'm a forager! Show yourself!'

After a long pause, the undergrowth opened, and out walked a Drongle.

'Hornbeam! Hornbeam! Hornbeam!' called out the Drongle.

'Oh hello!' it said, on seeing Four:5:3.

'Oh, it's a Drongle,' said Four:5:3. 'I might have guessed.'

She put the keesceptre back into her satchel and looked at the Drongle.

'Who is Hornbeam?' she asked.

'Oh, that's a friend of mine who I love,' said the Drongle, in its soft gentle voice. 'I was just thinking of him and decided to call his name.'

'I thought Drongles loved everyone,' said Four:5:3.

'Yes, that's true,' said the Drongle, then paused.

'Well, nearly true,' it said. 'We love everyone except Sorx!'

It laughed, turned quickly, and vanished into the undergrowth.

'Stupid Drongle!' said Four:5:3, as she watched it disappear. She turned and began daduming quickly up the road.

The Drongle watched her go, and then headed back into

the woods carefully following Hornbeam, Holly and Jack at a distance.

'No, she's wrong,' it thought to itself. 'You are not stupid, you are a very clever Drongle, aren't you Lovesome!'

The fight for the portcullis

While Lovesome was distracting Four:5:3, Hornbeam, Holly and Jack reached the last 3 trees in the forest and hid behind them. Close ahead they could see an enormous portcullis.

'That's the entrance to the Woodpecker Woods Tunnel,' whispered Hornbeam. 'Impressive isn't it! Easily big enough for a Qorx to go through!'

Peeping out from behind their trees, they had a clear view of the tunnel in the moonlight, and could see a small tree house just in front of the portcullis.

'That must be a guardhouse,' whispered Holly.

Inside the guardhouse were 2 Sorx. They were sitting on 2 chairs with their feet up on a table. One of them seemed to be asleep, and the other was leaning back with its hands behind its head. Behind them, the enormous portcullis seemed to be slightly open. There was a gap underneath it, and they could hear 2 more Sorx standing just inside the tunnel entrance. They seemed to be checking the portcullis mechanism.

'I hope we can catch those 2 young Hubees,' said one. 'How dare they steal keesceptres!'

'I know,' said the other. 'They should be locked up, and the key thrown away! I hate Hubees!'

'Yes!' said the first one. 'So do I! I'd love to be the one to catch them!'

'Me too!' said the other one.

Just then a forager dadumed swiftly up the road and stopped near the portcullis.

'The chief needs help!' she shouted. 'The Hubees are heading for the Rodley Bottoms Tunnel. She wants 2 of you to come with me.'

The sleeping Sorx kept on sleeping. The other one at the table rocked back in his chair and fell over. The 2 in the tunnel heard the cry, ducked under the partly open portcullis, and came running out of the tunnel. This was their chance to catch a Hubee!

'We'll come! We'll come!' they shouted, daduming over to the messenger.

'Oh! It's you SQorxy!' said one of them to her.

'Don't call me that!' said Four:5:3. 'I don't like it!'

'Sorry,' said the Sorx. 'I didn't mean any harm. It's just a bit of fun.'

'Well, I don't find it funny OK!' said Four:5:3, very sternly. 'Now follow me, we must get to Rodley Bottoms Tunnel as soon as possible.'

She dadumed away as fast as she could. The 2 foragers watched her go.

'That's impressive!' said one of them. 'She sure can dadum!'

They headed after her, with no hope at all of catching her up.

The sleeping Sorx kept on sleeping. The one who had fallen off its chair stood up, dusted itself down, and resumed its position on the chair, putting its feet back on the table. It looked at the sleeping Sorx.

'No point in waking her up,' it said to itself. 'No Hubees will be coming here tonight.'

It rocked back on its chair and put its hands behind its head. Soon its eyes closed and it started gently snoring.

Behind their trees, Jack, Holly and Hornbeam turned to each other.

'That was lucky,' said Hornbeam. 'If you're very careful, I think you should be able to get into the tunnel and lock the gate behind you. Come on, follow me.'

They moved stealthily across the road towards the guard-house with its 2 sleeping Sorx. Slowly, silently, they sneaked past them to the portcullis. It was only slightly raised off the ground, but high enough for Jack and Holly to slip in.

'In you go,' said Hornbeam.

Jack and Holly ducked under the portcullis into the tunnel.

'If you close the gate behind you, it will take them at least a tickle of time to open it, and you should be able to get well ahead of them,' said Hornbeam. 'Just keep next to the tunnel wall and you should be OK. There is a bridge towards the end of the tunnel, so be careful when you get to that. If the guards wake up, I will deal with them. Goodbye and good luck my friends. I've enjoyed your company.'

Holly looked at Hornbeam and her eyes filled with tears. She really didn't want to leave him.

'Can't we stay with you?' she asked.

'No you can't' said Hornbeam. 'You must go. You belong in Hubeeland!'

Holly felt very sad, but she knew he was right.

'Thank you for everything you've done for us,' she said. 'We'll never forget you.'

'We certainly won't,' said Jack. 'Thank you so much.'

He held out his hand and touched Hornbeam's knee trying not to cry.

Behind them one of the guards stirred. Then Holly had a thought.

'Why don't you come with us?' she asked. 'You can escape as well. You've done all the hard work. You've reached the tunnel and the gate's open. All you have to do is to get through the tunnel and you can be with your friends in Woodpecker Woods! Isn't that what you want?'

'Yes it is,' said Hornbeam. 'But I never thought we'd get this far. It never entered my head that I could escape as well. However, I did bring my most important things with me, just in case.'

He smiled and patted his satchel.

'That's fantastic!' said Holly. 'Come on, let's go before the guards wake up and sound the alarm!'

She lifted the gate from the inside and it moved slightly. But as it rose its chains and pulleys creaked. The guards stirred again but didn't wake up.

'Careful Holly!' said Hornbeam. 'It hasn't been opened wide for a tumble of time. Its chains and pulleys are probably rusty and won't move. Those 2 Sorx must have been trying to free them. Let me try.'

He reached up, grabbed one of the bars of the gate in his middle hand, and pushed upwards. The gate rose a little, but the creaking got louder. One of the Sorx snorted and grunted. Hornbeam stopped pushing. The Sorx settled down and started snoring again. The gate was not yet open enough for Hornbeam to get underneath.

'Let me try,' said Jack.

He lay on his back underneath the gate, put his Drongle Feet on either side of one of the portcullis spikes, and pushed them upwards as hard as he cold. The gate lifted a fraction and the creaking was quieter. Hornbeam tried to squeeze himself through, but couldn't quite manage it. Jack pushed again, but the gate didn't move at all. Holly got underneath the gate and helped him. It didn't budge. It was stuck.

Outside, Hornbeam was getting very anxious. The 2 Sorx could wake up at any time. He grabbed the gate with all 3 of his hands, and pulled upwards as hard as he could. With a loud crack the mechanism freed. The portcullis shot upwards, and he was thrown backwards by its force. He landed on the table where the 2 Sorx were sleeping, and knocked them to the ground. They woke up instantly and saw the Qorx. Hornbeam dragged himself from the ground and stood up.

'It's a Qorx! It's a Qorx!' one of them cried in alarm.

'It's a Qorx! It's a Qorx!' shouted the other one at the same time.

They pulled themselves off the ground, looked at each other, and then at Hornbeam who was towering over them.

'What can we do?' one asked.

'You grab one of its feet to slow it down, and I'll get my keesceptre,' said the other.

Hornbeam tried to move out of the way, but the first Sorx threw itself forwards and latched onto his left foot. He tried to walk towards the portcullis, but the Sorx was slowing him down.

Meanwhile, the other Sorx had grabbed its keesceptre from its satchel and was running towards Hornbeam. It reached him and poked him in the back of his right leg with the pointed end.

Hornbeam felt an agonising pain, and began to feel weak. The power of the keesceptre was beginning to drain his strength.

He kept moving towards the gate, but he was slowing down. The Sorx poked him again. The pain was much worse this time; it seemed to be building in his body like a poison running through his sap. Almost at the gate, he fell to his knees. He knew that he couldn't go on.

He looked towards the open portcullis and shouted to Jack and Holly, 'I don't think I can make it. You must go on without me!'

'No way!' said Jack, reaching into this satchel and pulling out his keesceptre.

'Come on Holly, grab your keesceptre,' he shouted. 'Let's see if they work!'

Holly grabbed her keesceptre. They took off their satchels, and dashed out of the tunnel into attack. Holly prodded the pointed end of her keesceptre into the bottom of the forager holding onto Hornbeam's foot. She felt a rush of power run along her arm, and out through the keesceptre into the Sorx. The Sorx screamed in agony, and let go.

Jack ran behind the forager who was prodding Hornbeam's leg. Holding his keesceptre in front of him like a sword, he stabbed him in the back, holding the flat end of the keesceptre against him. He remembered what Hornbeam had said about taking control. He held tightly onto the keesceptre. Its power surged into the Sorx, who shrieked in pain and fell to the ground.

Hornbeam sighed in relief, and tried to stand up. He had great difficulty, but managed to stagger to his feet. His body ached from the power of the forager's keesceptre.

Jack saw him stand up and shouted to him, 'Get into the tunnel Hornbeam. We'll deal with the Sorx.'

Hornbeam limped slowly through the entrance. He took off his satchel and sat down, leaning against the tunnel wall.

'Engage!' he cried.

His roots emerged from his feet, and began to burrow into the ground. Just then the portcullis started to rattle. It should have closed very soon after it had opened, and it was trying to do so now; but it was faulty. The rattling got louder and louder. Suddenly, the portcullis dropped quickly towards the ground, and creaked to a halt where it had been stuck before. The mechanism was still clogged up with rust. The gap at the bottom was big enough for a Sorx or a Hubee, but not for a Qorx. Hornbeam was trapped inside the tunnel.

The Sorx who had been hanging onto Hornbeam's leg had recovered from Holly's attack. It grabbed its keesceptre from its satchel, and ran towards Holly with its keesceptre raised above its head.

As it ran towards her it shouted, 'I hate Hubees! I hate Hubees!'

It reached her and lunged forward with its keesceptre. Holly swung her keesceptre and batted it out of the way. She lunged at the Sorx, and its keesceptre batted hers away. This went on for some time. The 2 keesceptres now seemed to take on a power of their own. Holly and the Sorx were holding them, but it was the keesceptres that were running the fight. One swung to the left and was defended; the other swung to the right and was defended. Holly felt she had no control over her keesceptre and it looked as though the Sorx had no control over its keesceptre. The power she had felt surge through her had disappeared. She felt that if they both let go, the keesceptres would continue to fight without them.

'This is no good,' she said to herself. 'They are just going to defend against each other all the time. I need to attack. But how?'

Then she remembered what Hornbeam had said, "Don't let your keesceptre be the boss!"

She tightened her grip on her keesceptre, and felt the power surge back into her body. She was in control again. The Sorx' keesceptre was just waving about defending against hers. She controlled hers, and lunged downwards towards the Sorx' tummy. The pointed end of her keesceptre pushed right into its flesh and its power surged into it. The Sorx let out a high-pitched scream, fell to the floor, and dropped its keesceptre. Holly picked it up and ran back into the tunnel, ducking under the bottom of the portcullis.

Jack had been having more luck fighting the other forager. His first attack had severely weakened his opponent, and he was definitely on top, as their keesceptres crashed against each other. The Sorx seemed to be getting weaker and weaker, and lost ground as Jack attacked. All of a sudden, the Sorx tripped on a rock and fell backwards. Jack lunged at him, and the pointed end of his keesceptre pierced the Sorx right shoulder. It screamed in pain, and dropped its keesceptre. Jack picked it up and ran back towards the tunnel.

Holly saw him coming.

'Quick Jack, run fast, you're almost there!' she shouted.

The 2 Sorx saw him go. They stood up and tried to follow him. But they were too weak. They had lost their keesceptres, and they knew that they were beaten. They collapsed onto the ground just as Jack scrambled under the portcullis. He grabbed the portcullis from the inside and pushed down. It moved a little then stuck again.

'Help me Holly!' shouted Jack.

Holly dashed over and together they pushed down of the bars of the portcullis with all their might. All of sudden, the mechanism freed again and the spikes on the end of the portcullis slammed into the ground. Its lock emitted a loud click. It was closed and they were safely inside.

'Get the finger key Jack!' shouted Holly. 'If we can get it they can't use it.'

Jack looked at the lock. It was the same type as the one on the Rodley Bottoms Tunnel. Grasping the top of the lock in one hand and the bottom of the lock in the other, he pulled them in the opposite directions. The bottom of the lock slid open, and a finger key fell out.

'I've got it,' said Jack.

He threw it deep into the tunnel.

'Good!' said Holly.

'And we've got their keesceptres,' said Jack. 'They won't be able to use them against us!'

Hornbeam was still sat on the ground leaning against the tunnel wall. He looked very weak. They had never seen him like this before, and never imagined that they would. He had always seemed so strong and tough.

'Are you OK Hornbeam?' asked Holly.

'I'll be alright soon,' he said, faintly. 'Just let my body do its work. Those keesceptres sapped me of my strength, and I need my sap to build up again. Let me feed for just a tickle of time longer.'

Jack and Holly put their satchels over their shoulders and

sat down beside him. They took out their bottles of Perx and had a swig. They burped gently and said nothing for a while. Then Hornbeam spoke.

'You've done so well,' he said. 'I can't believe we are in the tunnel and the portcullis is locked. But those 2 foragers will raise the alarm. Soon, others will be coming for us from Rodley Bottoms Tunnel. They'll be able to operate the lock with their fingers. Hopefully the mechanism will still be stuck, but we must get going.'

'Are you sure that you are able to?' asked Jack, anxiously.

'Yes! I am!' said Hornbeam. 'I can feel my sap rising. I will be fine in a touch.'

Sure enough, a touch of time later he shouted, 'Retract!'

His roots pulled themselves out of the ground and disappeared back into his feet.

'I'm ready!' he said, picking up his satchel.

'Let's get going then!' shouted Holly.

Outside the tunnel, the 2 wounded Sorx managed to stagger over to the locked portcullis. Looking through its bars, they saw the Qorx and the Hubees disappearing into the darkness. One of them dadumed very slowly back to the guardhouse and grabbed a megaphone from a cupboard. It turned it on, put it to its lips, and shouted, 'Qorx! Qorx! Hubees! Hubees! There are Qorx and Hubees in the tunnel!'

It repeated this over and over at the top of its squeaky voice, until it was hoarse.

Nearby, at the edge of the trees, a gentle voice said to itself, 'Well done my friends. Have a safe journey and remember that I will always love you.'

And with that, Lovesome padded softly back into the forest.

The Deesceptre

Hornbeam was right. The foragers were soon on their way. Not long after Four:5:3 had arrived with the 2 reinforcements, the chief heard the cry of, 'Qorx! Qorx! Hubees! Hubees!', echoing through the night air.

She immediately ordered Four:5:3 to gather together some of the faster foragers, and return to the Woodpecker Woods Tunnel. The rest of the troop, including 2:7:3 and the chief, followed on at a slower pace.

Four:5:3 had been the first to arrive with the fast group. They had found their 2 injured companions and tended to their wounds. Four:5:3 had dadumed over to the closed portcullis and tried to open it with her fingers in the lock. But nothing had happened. The 2 reinforcement foragers followed her to the gate. They told her that the mechanism was stuck, and they had been trying to fix it when she called them to go to the Rodley Bottoms Tunnel.

The chief and 2:7:3 soon arrived with the slower group. The chief walked up to the portcullis and took charge.

'2:7:3,' she said. 'Take your team and get that portcullis open by any means. I will speak to the 2 wounded foragers.'

She walked over to them.

'Tell me exactly what happened,' she said, sternly.

They told her what had happened, or rather what they

wanted her to know had happened. They said they had fought hard, which was true. They said that they had been outnumbered, which was also true. They said they had severely injured the Qorx and the 2 Hubees, which was only a little bit true. They said that they had been alert and on guard at all times, which was not true at all. And they didn't tell her that their keesceptres had been stolen.

'That's good!' said the chief, believing their tale. 'You clearly did your best against superior numbers. I must take some of the blame. Had I not taken 2 of your companions away, you would probably have been able to catch the fugitives. And you've severely injured them, which will slow them down. We need to get into the tunnel as soon as possible.'

She set off towards the portcullis.

At the portcullis, 2:7:3 was not having much luck. She had looked for the finger lock but it was missing. She had lined up her team in front of the gate, ordered them to grab the bars, and to lift as hard as they could. The gate hadn't budged.

'Why is this gate not open!' shouted the chief, as she reached the portcullis.

'It's stuck,' said 2:7:3. We can't open it.'

'Move aside!' ordered the chief.

2:7:3's team moved away from the portcullis. The chief reached into her satchel, and pulled out a very different keesceptre. One end had 2 points and the other had 3 points. It was not twisted. The grain of the wood ran evenly from one end to the other, and it shone like a mirror. As she pulled it out, the pale blue and pink moonlight reflected off it and danced across the sky. It looked magical and 2:7:3 was almost hypnotised at the sight of it.

'That's amazing!' she cried. 'I've never seen one like that before!'

'There is only one like this,' said the chief. 'This is the "Deesceptre", the first keesceptre ever made from the wood of the Super Bremmin Hoose. It has been handed down from chief to chief over the continuums, and I will pass it on to my successor. It holds deeper secrets than the keesceptres, and has very special powers, some of which have yet to be discovered. Watch!'

The chief walked up to the gate and grasped the deesceptre firmly in her right hand. She touched the finger lock with its 2-pointed end. Her arm began to tremble, and a pulse of energy flew along the deesceptre and crashed into the lock. There was a blinding flash and the portcullis shot upwards. 2:7:3 and the foragers made to run into the tunnel.

'Wait!' said the chief. 'We don't want it to come down on top of us.'

She turned the deesceptre around and held the 3-pointed end against one of the chains that moved the portcullis up and down. There was another surge of power, and the chain melted into a solid column. She moved to the other chain and did the same.

'There!' she said. 'That should keep the portcullis out of the way. We can fit new chains later, but now we have fugitives to catch!'

She put the deesceptre back in her satchel and entered the tunnel. 'Follow me!' she cried, and twenty-eight foragers dadumed after her.

Verdax

Up ahead, Holly, Jack and Hornbeam worked their way slowly along the tunnel. The darkness was enveloping them. Jack and Holly kept close to the tunnel wall, feeling its stones and mortar as they moved forward. Hornbeam walked behind them, holding 2 of his hands above his head and feeling the tunnel roof.

'Don't worry,' said Hornbeam. 'I've been through this tunnel many times. It's very well built. The walls and roof are strong and the ground is dry. Just stay together and walk slowly beside the tunnel wall.'

'I'm glad you are with us Hornbeam,' said Jack.

'Yes. So am I,' said Holly.

'Thank you,' said Hornbeam. 'But it is you who deserve the thanks. Without your help, I would now be being interrogated in the Jail House.'

He shivered at the thought.

As they walked along, the floor of the tunnel became softer, and their Drongle feet made a gentle crunching sound. They were walking through what felt like plants growing on the floor.

'Can you feel plants?' Jack asked.

'Yes, I can,' said Holly. 'I can feel their leaves.'

'They will be the Verdax,' said Hornbeam. 'They are very unusual plants, with furry leaves. They only grow deep inside the tunnel. Because it's so dark in here, their leaves grow longer trying to find light. But because there is no light, they fall off and they try again by growing new leaves. The fallen leaves land on the tunnel floor, making it soft to walk on.'

'But how can they grow in the dark?' asked Holly. 'Don't they need light and water?'

'That's generally true,' said Hornbeam. 'But the Verdax can manage without light. They get water from the tunnel floor by burrowing their roots into the soil.'

'I think we have at least one plant that can grow in the dark,' said Jack. 'Rhubarb.'

'Rhubarb!' exclaimed Hornbeam. 'You've mentioned rhubarb before.'

'No, I mean proper rhubarb,' laughed Jack.

His laugh echoed through the tunnel.

'Proper rhubarb is grown in sheds in the dark,' he said. 'This forces it to grow quicker. In Hubeeland there is an area known as "The Rhubarb Triangle" where a lot of rhubarb is grown.'

'Incredible!' said Hornbeam. 'Hubees never cease to amaze me. Triangular rhubarb!'

He shouted this at the top of his voice, and laughed his foghorn laugh. It sounded as though a train was passing through the tunnel.

'No, it's not triangular rhubarb!' laughed Jack. 'The area that it grows in is roughly triangular in shape!'

Holly had been listening to the conversation as she was working her way slowly along the tunnel wall.

'If you ask me,' she said, laughing. 'You are both talking a load of rhubarb!'

They all laughed at this, and their combined laughs filled the tunnel.

Holly and Jack were getting used to the darkness, and were feeling less anxious. Hornbeam felt quite at home. He spent a lot of his time in darkness, sitting in his chair feeding. He found it comforting. It enveloped him like a warm blanket, but he knew that Jack and Holly were not used to the overwhelming blackness.

'Are you 2 OK?' he asked, after they had been walking during a period of silence.

'Yes!' said Holly, trying to keep her spirits up.

'Me too!' said Jack, in the darkness. 'What about you?'

'Oh! I'm fine!' said Hornbeam. 'I am used to darkness. In The Lonely Sweet Shop it helped me to sleep.'

'Well please don't fall asleep now!' said Holly, laughing.

'I'll try not to!' said Hornbeam.

As they shuffled along the side of the tunnel, the Verdax became denser and the leaves became longer. It was getting harder to walk through them. They were wrapping round their Drongle feet, and almost tripping them up.

'It's getting harder to walk through these Verdax,' said Holly.

'Yes, it is,' agreed Jack.

That's very odd,' said Hornbeam. 'Their leaves are getting longer instead of falling off. It's almost as if they are sensing light.'

Hornbeam, with his very long legs and greater strength did not have any problem, he could easily brush them aside, but he realised that he, quite literally, had a big advantage.

'Trying stepping along,' he said. 'Raise your feet higher.'

Jack and Holly tried stepping. This worked for a while, but

309

the Verdax leaves were getting even longer and denser. Passing through them was becoming extremely difficult, like walking through a field of fully grown wheat.

'Stepping doesn't seem to help,' said Jack, almost falling to the ground as a Verdax leaf wrapped itself completely round his left Drongle foot.

'I'm getting tangled up,' said Holly, trying to kick off a group of leaves that had wrapped themselves around her waist.

'OK,' said Hornbeam. 'Let's swap places. I'll walk ahead, and you follow me. I will step on the leaves and flatten them for you.'

After some bumping and laughing they managed to swap places.

'Right! Follow me,' said Hornbeam, feeling the ceiling with his left hand and the wall with his middle hand.

'Please go slowly!' said Holly, coming behind him.

'And don't forget me,' said Jack, bringing up the rear.

Then Hornbeam had an idea.

'Why don't you hold onto my left hand Holly, and Jack can hold onto your satchel,' he said.

'That's a good idea,' said Jack from the back, not wanting to be left behind.

'OK,' said Holly.

Hornbeam and Holly reached for each other, and their hands touched in the darkness. Hornbeam's fingers wrapped round Holly's.

Jack reached forward and touched Holly on the shoulder. He found her satchel strap and held onto it.

'Are we all ready?' asked Hornbeam.

'Yes,' said Jack and Holly at the same time.

'OK,' said Hornbeam. 'Let's move forward slowly.'

He felt the wall and started walking, stamping down the Verdax leaves as he went. Holly and Jack followed on, finding it much easier to walk.

The sound of rhubarb

The foragers in the tunnel had one huge advantage over Hornbeam, Holly and Jack: their teeth. As soon as they entered the tunnel they began to smile, and the tunnel walls, ceiling and floor were illuminated by 29 beams of light. As they dadumed along, the beams flickered and danced like moonbeams creating a white kaleidoscope of patterns, bouncing off the mortar gaps between the stones.

The chief had moved to the front with 2:7:3 and Four:5:3. Although they were making progress, the chief was anxious not to dadum too quickly. She had never been into the Woodpecker Woods Tunnel, and as far as she knew neither had any of her foragers. There were many strange tales about the tunnel, so she set a medium pace, which the foragers seemed happy to follow.

All, that is, apart from 2:7:3 who was very anxious to catch the Hubees and regain the stolen keesceptres. She kept moving ahead of the group, so much so that there was often darkness between her beam of light and the kaleidoscope being generated by the others behind her.

The chief had to keep sending Four:5:3 to tell her to slow down. 2:7:3 did this reluctantly, then started getting ahead of the group again. The chief was just about to send Four:5:3 to tell her to slow down once more, when 2:7:3's beam stopped moving. She had stopped. Something had happened.

'Halt!' shouted the chief.

The foragers stopped daduming.

Up ahead, 2:7:3 couldn't believe what she had just heard. Out of the darkness in front of her came the sound of a voice shouting, 'triangular rhubarb!' It shot past her and was quickly followed by 3 voices laughing loudly. A tickle of time later the chief, Four:5:3 and the rest of the foragers also heard, 'triangular rhubarb!' and 3 laughing voices fly past. 2:7:3 dadumed back to the group.

'Did you hear that?' she asked.

'Yes,' said the chief. 'What is triangular rhubarb?'

'I've no idea,' said 2:7:3. 'But it was definitely a Qorx voice!'

'You are right!' said the chief. 'And the laughter sounded Hubeeish. The fugitives can't be too far ahead. Let's go! And please stay with the group 2:7:3!'

The Scarlet Crunchers

The Verdax leaves were getting longer, and even Hornbeam was having difficulty trampling them down. Every now and then he had to stop to unwrap them from around his legs.

'Did the leaves cause so much trouble last time you came through this tunnel?' asked Holly.

'No,' said Hornbeam. 'There seem to be so many more of them than I remember. Let's just stop for a tickle.'

Jack and Holly were glad to do so. They stood next to each other and reached into their satchels. They felt for the Perx bottles, took them out, and had a drink. Jack took out a couple of Oodax, and Holly felt for a Yumbax.

'Would you like an Oodax, Hornbeam?' asked Jack.

'Or a Yumbax or some Perx?' asked Holly.

'No thank you. I'm just going to feed,' said Hornbeam. 'Engage!'

Holly bit into her Yumbax and enjoyed a cheeseburger. Jack gobbled down his Oodax and was soon gently farting. The Perx quenched their thirst. Hornbeam sucked up goodness from the soil below the floor.

As they stood there, the Verdax leaves started to grow even longer, and began to turn back down the tunnel. From the other direction came the sound of running water.

'Can you hear that?' asked Holly. 'It sounds like running water!'

'Yes! I can!' said Jack. 'Can you Hornbeam?'

'Yes!' exclaimed Hornbeam. 'We must be near the bridge! Retract! Let's go!'

They tried to go but they couldn't. There was a rustling sound, which grew louder and louder, and they were pushed back against the tunnel wall. A huge mass of growing leaves crashed past them and headed back down the tunnel. The swirling leaves brushed heavily against them. They pressed themselves harder against the wall to avoid being swept along. The sound became deafening.

'What's happening!' shouted Jack, at the top of his voice.

'I'm not sure!' bellowed Hornbeam. 'They seem to be growing and heading back down the tunnel. They must have sensed light, and are growing towards it.'

'But we can't see any light,' said Holly.

'No, but they have very finely tuned light sensors that can see tiny amounts,' said Hornbeam. 'Somewhere back down the tunnel there must be a source of light. I have heard of this happening in the past, but I have never seen it before.'

'It's amazing,' said Jack. 'The whole tunnel feels as though it's filled with leaves, and even the roots are moving under my feet.'

'Stay calm,' said Hornbeam. 'If I am right, they will all be gone soon.'

They pushed themselves harder against the wall and stood firm. Leaves rushed past their bodies, and roots tore past their feet. Then suddenly they were gone. The plants disappeared down the tunnel taking their sound with them. All that remained was the sound of running water.

'What just happened?' asked Holly. 'Where have they gone? How did you know that they would go?'

'If I'm right then something bad is about to happen,' said Hornbeam, very gravely.

'What do you mean,' asked Holly.

'What's going to happen,' asked Jack.

'In the darkness of the tunnel the Verdax are harmless,' said Hornbeam. 'They grow their leaves, they can't find any light, so the leaves drop off and the plants try again. But when they sense light they change. The leaves don't drop off. They get longer and longer and grow towards the light. They also develop flowers. But not normal ones.'

'What sort of flowers?' asked Jack.

'Nasty red ones,' said Hornbeam. 'Carnivorous ones!'

'You mean ones that eat meat!' exclaimed Holly.

'Yes,' said Hornbeam. 'They eat meat, and they have incredible appetites. The flowers have a lot of teeth that they would love to sink into a Sorx or a Hubee. We call them "Scarlet Crunchers" because of their colour and the way they eat.'

'Oh, I'm glad they have gone the other way,' said Jack. 'I don't fancy being eaten by a Scarlet Cruncher.'

'Unfortunately, I think that something will be,' said Hornbeam. 'Crunchers grow incredibly quickly once they have sensed light. By the time they get to the source of the light, there will be tangles of them on the ends of the leaves looking for a meal.'

'That's horrible,' said Holly.

'It is,' said Hornbeam. 'But there's nothing we can do about it. Come on. Let's head towards the bridge and see what state it's in. When I was being tortured, the Sorx told me it had collapsed under the weight of all the Qorx fleeing from Highlow.'

They resumed their positions and set off again. Holly and Jack felt very worried about what Hornbeam had just told them.

The Crunchers attack

Having heard the laughter passing through the tunnel, the chief became bold. She picked up the pace, and the group moved forward at speed. Even 2:7:3 stayed with them, unable to dadum any quicker.

After a time, their dancing kaleidoscope illuminated something green in the far distance. In fact, it illuminated lots of green things that were heading straight towards them. The whole tunnel was filled with long swirling leaves. On the ends of the leaves were red bulbs which appeared to be multiplying.

'Halt!' shouted the chief.

The foragers stopped and regrouped behind her. She and 2:7:3 walked forward a few steps, and shone their teeth towards the advancing plants.

Sensing their beams, the Scarlet Crunchers opened, exposing rows of jagged teeth, which shone back to them with intense red beams. The Verdax flowers were reacting to the Sorx teeth. But unlike Hubees, who went into a trace at the sight of Sorx teeth, the teeth of the Scarlet Crunchers became excited and hungry. They started opening and closing rapidly, shining a bright-red kaleidoscope toward the foragers.

'What are these?' asked the chief.

'I don't know,' said 2:7:3.

She leant forward and shone her teeth further into the tunnel. The leaves advanced even quicker, and their teeth opened and closed more rapidly.

'But whatever they are there are squalls of them, and they are heading straight for us!' she screamed.

'Let's get out of here!' shouted the chief.

2:7:3 and the chief turned and dadumed back down the tunnel as fast as they could, straight past the regrouped foragers who were waiting patiently for instructions, completely unaware of what was about to happen.

Safely past them, the chief turned and shouted back up the tunnel, 'Follow me foragers!'

But by then it was too late for many of them to escape. The Verdax leaves and bulbs had found the light. It was what they existed for, and they had never sensed any until this moment. The crunching teeth flew along the tunnel towards the retreating foragers.

The tunnel filled from floor to ceiling with Verdax advancing rapidly towards the dancing white kaleidoscope. The foragers ran for their lives, lighting up the tunnel with their teeth as they went. This only encouraged the Verdax. The slower foragers were overwhelmed and sucked into the advancing tide of leaves and bulbs. Some disappeared under the jaws of the crunchers. Others were wrapped up in cocoons by the advancing wall of leaves, and dumped at the side of the tunnel for later. The faster foragers kept ahead of the green and red mass for as long as they could, but most of them were engulfed. A horrendous crunching sound echoed through the tunnel.

Only the chief, 2:7:3 and Four:5:3 made it back to the portcullis safely. The chief and 2:7:3 because they were cowards who had deserted their foragers, and Four:5:3 because she was the fastest of them all.

The leaves with their Scarlet Crunchers poured out of the tunnel, and spread into the undergrowth up to the edge of the Woodpecker Woods Road. But their progress was slowed by the lack of light. Turq and Cora were still shining and their blue and pink light was much dimmer than the Sorx teeth. The Verdax stopped advancing, their leaves shortened, and their crunchers fell off scattering the ground in a carpet of red bulbs.

In the morning, as Enzor rose, the Verdax were flooded with so much light that their genetic make-up changed instantly. After that, in the open air their leaves never grew more than a metre high, and they didn't produce any more Scarlet Crunchers.

In a tumble of time, they spread slowly through Highlow to open areas such as clearings in the woods, and by the sides of streams, but kept away from forests and woods where it was too dark for them to flourish. They made excellent cover for the Drongles to hide from Sorx and Cacawkers.

The Drongles loved to eat their leaves, but the Verdax didn't mind. They could easily grow new leaves and they liked to feel the Drongles wandering through them.

The morning after the Verdax had poured out of the Woodpecker Woods Tunnel, dazed and disoriented foragers began to emerge through the portcullis. Many had Verdax leaves wrapped round them, and all had wounds inflicted from being dragged along the tunnel floor, and crashed against the tunnel walls by the advancing Verdax. They were all covered in bites from the Scarlet Crunchers but these could be treated.

And they had all survived.

The new chief

A few solars later, a formal meeting was held in the Police Station to carry out an inquiry into what had happened in the tunnel. Present at the meeting were some of the less injured foragers who had taken part in the battle. Evidence was presented to the chief-of-police, and decisions were made.

The forager-in-chief and 2:7:3 were sentenced to a squage of time in the Jail House for running away and deserting their teams. They were also banned from ever being foragers again, and told that when they were eventually freed they would have to work in the smelliest part of the Thunder Works.

Four:7:3 was promoted to forager-in-chief and given the deesceptre, which she greatly treasured. She was so proud. She finally believed in herself, and realised that with hard work and dedication it was possible for even the most ambitious dream to come true. No-one ever called her a SQorxy again.

All the other foragers were given special medals to commemorate their participation in what became known as, The Battle of Woodpecker Woods Tunnel. Stories began to spread about what it had been like to be there. Legends were created. As with most legends, they had an element of truth, but with the passage of time, they became more and more exaggerated. However, no-one minded, especially not the Sorxlings who pestered their parents and grandparents to tell them the story over and over again.

The Circular Hall

While the crunchers were attacking the foragers, Hornbeam, Jack and Holly moved slowly along the tunnel wall, as the sound of running water grew louder.

'Stop!' shouted Hornbeam. 'We are there!'

'We are where?' asked Holly, from the darkness.

'We have reached the Circular Hall,' said Hornbeam. 'The wall is starting to curve outwards. Just stay where you are. I'm going to find the light pipe.'

'What's a light pipe?' asked Jack.

'I'll explain when I get back,' said Hornbeam, who had begun to walk down and across the tunnel feeling the roof with his hands.

He moved his fingers across the surface searching for something.

'Yes!' he exclaimed, as his fingers touched a handle in the roof.

He pulled it hard downwards. There was a big plopping sound, and a piece of the roof came away. Light flooded into the tunnel, closely followed by a torrent of water, most of which cascaded over Hornbeam.

'Ugh!' he cried. 'I'd forgotten it would be full of water!'

Back by the wall, Holly and Jack gasped at the sudden appearance of light. They blinked, and shielded their eyes, not used to its brightness. Peeping through their fingers, they could see Hornbeam with water dripping from him and holding something in his hand. They walked over to him. He was standing in a small pool.

'What have you done?' asked Holly, anxiously.

'I've opened a light pipe,' said the dripping Hornbeam. 'But I forgot that it would be full of water from the surface. I knew there was a plug at the bottom of the pipe, and I managed to find it and pull it out.'

He showed them the plug. It was a thin circular piece of wood with a handle on one side.

'What's a light pipe?' asked Jack again.

'It's a hollow vertical tube put into the tunnel roof that runs up to the surface to let light in.' said Hornbeam. 'There are 2 of them, one on each side of the bridge. It is the only tunnel that has them. The plugs were put in to stop light attracting the Verdax. The Qorx take them out so that they can see to cross the bridge, and then put them back when they have crossed safely.'

'Why did they put them in?' asked Holly.

'This tunnel has a wide river crossing it at this point and a bridge was needed,' said Hornbeam. 'The pipes were fitted to provide light to illuminate the bridge construction. When it was finished, they were left in to enable the bridge to be seen, to avoid anyone falling into the fast-flowing river.'

'That's clever,' said Jack.

'Yes, light pipes are very simple, but work very well,' said Hornbeam.

Light was now pouring through the pipe, and they could see the inside of the tunnel clearly. The straight tunnel walls had opened out to form a large circular room. Directly ahead was a long arch bridge. On the opposite side, the walls curved back to form a straight tunnel again. Hornbeam put down plug.

'This is known as the Circular Hall,' said Hornbeam. '2 tunnels meet here. The river flows through one tunnel, and the Woodpecker Woods Tunnel passes over it using this bridge.'

He pointed to the bridge in the middle of the Circular Hall.

'Let's see what state it's in,' he said.

The bridge had wooden handrails on either side of it. As they walked towards it they could hear the sound of the river whooshing underneath. It was flowing very fast out of a tunnel to their right into a tunnel to their left. Hornbeam looked at the bridge.

'It looks safe to me,' he said. 'The Sorx in the Jail House must have been lying.'

He looked across to the other side where it was darker. The light from the pipe didn't travel that far, but he could just make out the second plug in the roof.

'If I could unplug the second light pipe, I will be able to see if the bridge is damaged, but to do that I will have to walk over it first,' said Hornbeam. 'I will take it slowly.'

He stepped onto the bridge.

'No,' said Holly. 'Step back! If it's weak you might fall in and you said yourself that Qorx can't swim. Even if you can float, this river would sweep you away. I'm the lightest; I'll go over and see if there is anything wrong with it.'

'Are you sure?' asked Hornbeam.

'Yes, I am!' shouted Holly, very firmly.

'Thank you,' he said, gently. 'But please be careful.'

Very slowly, Holly started to walk over the bridge, holding tightly onto the handrail. The light pipe illuminated the handrails and the bridge deck on the rising side of the arch quite clearly. Using its light, she inspected them both carefully. There was no sign of damage.

As she started to go down the other side, the light weakened and Jack and Hornbeam lost sight of her. Using her hands as well as her eyes she continued checking. Again everything seemed to be in order. She reached the other side, turned round, and slowly walked back across the bridge, checking again. Hornbeam and Jack were waiting for her.

'I can't see any damage,' she said. 'It looks alright to me.'

'That was very brave Holly,' said Hornbeam. 'Let's cross one at a time. You go first.'

Very carefully and slowly Holly retraced her steps, and reached the other side of the bridge safely.

'Right Jack,' said Hornbeam. 'It's your turn.'

'But what if I get across and you don't?' asked Jack.

'Then you and Holly must go on without me,' said Hornbeam. 'It's not far to the wall at the end of the tunnel and you know how to use your keesceptre to open it. You will then be near Woodpecker Woods.'

'Do you have to use the bridge?' asked Jack. 'Is there any other way?'

'No,' said Hornbeam. 'This is the only crossing and the river is too wide for me to cross in one pedarc. Don't worry, I'll get across. You can't get rid of me that easily! Off you go!'

Jack stepped onto the arch and crept over it one Drongle foot at a time. As he reached the top, the bridge shook and creaked. He panicked and ran down the other side as quickly as he could, shooting past Holly who was waiting for him. The bridge was still shaking and creaking.

'Are you alright Jack?' asked Holly, anxiously.

'Yes, but did you hear the bridge creak?' he asked.

'Yes,' she said. 'And it's still shaking.'

'Do you think it'll be safe for Hornbeam to cross?' asked Jack. 'Should we shout and warn him?'

'I don't think that'll work,' said Holly. 'The river's too noisy. He'll never hear us.'

On the other side Hornbeam looked at the bridge carefully.

'It looks about 2 pedarcs,' he thought to himself. 'Perhaps I can make one pedarc onto the top of the arch, and a second pedarc onto the other side.'

He stood at the edge of the bridge and made one of his giant pedarcs. His right foot swept into the air and curved upwards towards the roof, and then descended slowly to touch the centre of the arch. All his weight was on his left foot.

'Here goes!' he said, as he transferred his weight and forced his right foot down onto the highest point of the bridge.

There was loud creaking sound. He swung his left foot upwards and put it beside this right foot. The creaking continued. He was now standing upright on the top of the arch.

On the other side, Jack and Holly suddenly saw a huge Qorx-shape appear in the middle of the bridge, silhouetted against the light pipe behind it.

'He's coming!' said Holly.

'Come on Hornbeam!' shouted Jack.

Hornbeam saw them, and raised his 3 arms above his head to wave at them in triumph.

But he had forgotten that the roof was much nearer now that

he was at the top of the arch. As he raised his arms, his hands crashed into it, and he lost his balance. He clawed at the roof, but there was nothing to grip onto. He stepped sideways to try to regain his balance and smashed into the handrail, which immediately shattered under his weight.

In slow motion, he toppled sideways from the top of the bridge, and disappeared head first into the raging torrent. Jack and Holly looked on in horror. He bobbed up to the surface, his arms waving in panic, and was swept into the mouth of the tunnel on their right.

'Oh no!' screamed Holly, collapsing to the floor. 'Hornbeam! Do something Jack!'

She sobbed uncontrollably. Jack was too shocked to answer. He collapsed beside her and burst into tears. Hornbeam, their first and best friend in Highlow, had been swept away by the river.

Indoor rain

Jack and Holly lay on the ground in the Circular Hall for some time. They felt wretched. Hornbeam had gone. It was Jack who spoke first.

'We've got to keep going Holly,' he said. 'It's what Hornbeam wanted. Before I crossed the bridge, he said that if anything happened to him we must carry on.'

'Do you think he has drowned?' asked Holly.

'I don't know,' said Jack. 'He told us himself that Qorx can't swim but that they can float, so perhaps he can survive the river.'

'I do hope so,' said Holly.

'If anyone can it's Hornbeam!' said Jack, as positively as he could. 'He's very strong. Come on! We owe it to him to keep going!'

They dragged themselves from the ground, checked their satchels, and headed out of the Circular Hall, away from the bridge into the tunnel leading to the end wall. Holly reached into her satchel to hold Podge for comfort. She felt very sad. But before she touched Podge, she felt one of her keesceptres. She had an idea.

'Jack!' she cried. 'Let's use a keesceptre to save Hornbeam!'

'What do you mean?' asked Jack.

'Well, can't we make a wish for him to be safe?' asked Holly.

'But we need to a Quadruple Prime for that to work,' said Jack. 'And we don't have one.'

'But can't we try?' asked Holly.

'Yes, I suppose so,' said Jack. 'Anything is worth a try to save Hornbeam.'

'So how do we do it' asked Holly.

'I think you just hold your keesceptre very tightly and make your wish,' said Jack. 'If there is a Quadruple Prime here then your wish will come true.'

Holly pulled a keesceptre out of her satchel and held it very tightly.

'I wish that Hornbeam is saved from the river!' she shouted.

They looked at each other and waited and waited but nothing happened.

'Come on Holly,' said Jack. 'You've tried. There's no Quadruple Prime here. We can't do anything else. Let's go.'

Holly put the keesceptre back in her satchel and stroked Podge. She and Jack began shuffling along the side of the tunnel. The light from the pipe disappeared rapidly, and soon they were once again in total darkness. But the tunnel floor was firm and they couldn't feel any Verdax.

They crept along the wall in silence, Jack in front of Holly, who held onto his satchel strap.

'Do you think the end wall is much further?' asked Holly after a while.

'Hornbeam said it wasn't far from the Circular Hall. We must be getting close,' answered Jack.

'Shall we link arms and feel for the end wall together?' asked Holly.

'Yes, that's a good idea,' said Jack.

He stayed by the wall, and Holly moved to his left. They linked arms, held out their other arms, and started moving forward slowly, waving their hands into the darkness. They felt nothing but air, and without realising it they began to walk towards the middle of the tunnel away from the side. After a while, Jack waved his hand to the right to check where the side wall was. It wasn't there.

'Stop Holly!' he shouted.

'Have you found it?' she asked.

'No,' said Jack. 'I've lost the side wall. Let's move to the right.'

Still linking arms, they shuffled to the right. Jack touched the side wall and breathed a sigh of relief.

'I'll keep touching the side wall, if you feel for the end wall,' he said.

'OK,' said Holly, and they continued forward along the side wall.

Holly waved her hand in front of her. It was getting wet.

'My hand's getting wet Jack!' she cried. 'I think it's raining!'

'Don't be silly!' said Jack. 'We're inside a tunnel. It doesn't rain inside tunnels!'

'Well my hand's still getting wet!' shouted Holly. 'So water is coming from somewhere!'

They stopped walking and Jack held out his hand in front of him. It got wet, and it did feel like rain. He looked upwards and saw a faint glimmer of light in the roof.

'You're right!' he said. 'It's coming from the roof. Look! There's a small hole and light is coming in. The water must be coming through it from the outside.'

Holly looked up and saw the glimmer of light.

'Yes, I can see it,' she said. 'That must be coming from our world!'

Still linked to Jack, Holly turned round and stepped backwards to get a better view of the small hole. Her right Drongle foot hit a wall. She reached back with her left hand; it touched a wall.

'I've found it Jack. The end wall! I've found it.' she cried.

Jack turned and reached forward with his right hand; it touched the wall. 'Yeesss!' he cried.

They unlinked and turned towards the end wall, putting both their hands on it.

'What do we do now?' asked Holly, from the darkness.

'Hornbeam said we should use the keesceptre to open the wall,' said Jack.

'Like we did to get into the Rainbow Factory?' asked Holly.

Yes,' said Jack. 'Shall I try or do you want to?'

'You try,' said Holly.

'OK,' said Jack. 'But you must help me.'

He reached into his satchel, and pulled out a keesceptre.

'I've got a keesceptre,' he said, nervously.

'Right,' said Holly. 'Remember to grasp it firmly. Don't let it be the boss!'

Jack felt for the flat end, and then grasped the other end very firmly.

'I'm ready' said Jack.

'Now shout out your number of toes, and hit the keesceptre against the wall,' said Holly.

'5! 5!' shouted Jack, as loudly as he could, and thumped the flat end of the keesceptre against the end wall.

Nothing happened.

'No,' said Holly. 'Remember you've got your Drongle feet on. They have 7 toes on each foot!

'Of course,' said Jack. He grasped the keesceptre hard.

He screamed, '7!7!' and smashed its end against the wall.

Nothing happened.

'Nothing is happening,' he shouted in a panic. 'It's not working!'

Holly thought carefully, then remembered what Hornbeam had said.

'Jack!' shouted Holly. 'The keesceptre thinks you are a Sorx and they have 3 feet. Remember what Hornbeam said, you must shout "7! Zero! 7!".'

'Of course!' cried Jack .

For the third time, he grasped his keesceptre very firmly. With his other hand he felt for the end wall to make sure he was in the right position.

'7! Zero! 7!' he bellowed.

He thrust his right arm forward, and the keesceptre's flat end crashed into the wall.

Nothing happened. Then something happened.

There was a rumbling sound, and the end wall began to move to the right. Light poured in from the left side and a cloud of dust filled the air. Blinded by the light, Jack and Holly stepped back and shielding their eyes. The rumbling got louder and the wall opened fully, before slowly grinding to a halt. After a short time, their eyes adjusted and they looked out of the opening. They could see the trees at the edge of Woodpecker Woods to the left, and on the other side of the canal were the rhubarb fields. In front of them a grassy bank led down to the canal. Just to the right was the Cow Bridge, and in the distance, an early morning train sped along the valley. And it was raining.

'We are back!' shouted Holly.

'Yeesss! We made it!' said Jack.

They hugged each other, jumped up and down, and cried for joy. As they did so, the rumbling sound started again, and the wall began to move back into position.

They stopped hugging, and ran out onto the grassy bank in the rain. They looked back and watched as the wall slammed shut. It was at the bottom of a steep hillside. Now that it had closed it looked like any other wall, and no-one would know that there was a tunnel to Highlow hidden behind it.

Like a wizard

Jack and Holly sat down on the wet grassy bank and looked around. The rain had stopped, it was just before sunrise, and the morning chorus had begun.

'We never heard any birds in Highlow, did we?' asked Jack.

'No, Hornbeam told us that the Cacawkers had eaten them all,' said Holly. 'I hate Cacawkers!'

Jack looked down to the canal.

'We're on the wrong side of the canal. We need to be on the towpath,' he said. 'How are we going to get across?'

Holly pointed to the Cow Bridge.

'Can't we use that?' she asked.

'No, the farmer keeps it swung closed when she's not using. It's padlocked,' said Jack, looking at the bridge. 'We'll just have to wade across, we can stand up. It's not very deep.'

'I don't fancy that!' shouted Holly.

'You won't have to!' replied a booming voice, that she recognised instantly. She looked to the left, and there, pedarcing his way slowly up the canal, was Hornbeam.

'Jack! It's Hornbeam! It's Hornbeam!' she screamed, at the top of her voice.

Jack turned from the bridge and looked to the left.

'Hornbeam! Hornbeam!' he shouted.

They both stood up and waved their arms above their heads

shouting his name. Hornbeam waved back and laughed his foghorn laugh, as he splashed his way towards them through the middle of the canal. He reached them and stepped out. Holly ran over and hugged his knee.

'Hornbeam is it really you?' she asked.

He touched his head with his hands.

'Yes, I think it's me!' he said, laughing. Jack rushed across and hugged his other knee.

'Are you alright? We thought you'd drowned,' he said. 'How did you escape from the river?'

'Yes, I'm fine, but I don't know how I escaped,' said Hornbeam. 'I felt such a fool when I fell in. I floated for a while but the river was flowing so quickly that I got dragged under. I couldn't breathe and I thought that I wouldn't survive.'

'That's terrible,' said Holly.

Holly and Jack let go of his knees and stepped back so they could see him more clearly.

'Yes, I was very frightened. I felt I was drowning,' continued Hornbeam. 'Then suddenly something happened. It was a miracle. I was pulled up to the surface and soon I was floating very easily. A touch of time later, I streamed out of the tunnel into a much wider river. The flow was less, and I managed to stand up and get onto the river bank. From there I headed for Woodpecker Woods. When I reached the canal, I heard you and Jack talking about the Cow Bridge being closed. So here I am to help you to cross!'

'That's amazing!' said Jack. 'It's great to see you, and you managed to keep your satchel!'

'Yes,' said Hornbeam. 'I managed to save my treasures.'

He took his satchel off and sat down on the grass. Jack

and Holly sat beside him. He reached into it and pulled out 5 Oodax, 7 Yumbax, 3 jigsaws, a keesceptre and 2 bottles of Drointment. He picked up the bottles and handed one to Holly and one to Jack.

'These are for you,' he said. 'They may come in useful. But don't put too much on!'

He laughed his booming laugh.

'Thank you. I won't!' said Holly.

'I hope I don't have to use it, but I already love it!' said Jack, in a gentle Drongle voice.

Hornbeam laughed again.

'We've got something for you,' said Jack. 'We were going to give them to you when we reached the end wall, but of course you fell into the river before then.'

Holly reached into her satchel, and pulled out one of her keesceptres.

'This is for you,' she said.

'And so is this one,' said Jack, handing Hornbeam one of his keesceptres.

'2 more keesceptres! Fantastic! Thank you!' cried Hornbeam. 'My Qorx friends will find them very useful.'

'They will,' said Jack. 'We've already used ours twice. I used one of mine to open the wall at the end of the tunnel, and Holly used one of hers to try and save you.'

What do you mean?' asked Hornbeam. 'How did you try to save me Holly?'

'After you fell in,' said Holly. 'I used one of my keesceptres to make a wish just in case we were close to a Quadruple Prime. I wished that you would be saved from the river. But nothing happened.'

'But I was definitely saved!' said Hornbeam. 'I was about to drown then a miracle happened to stop me.'

He looked puzzled.

'So if you were saved by a Quadruple Prime, where was it?' asked Jack.

'I don't know,' said Hornbeam. 'Let me think.'

He tweaked the little branch on the end of his nose very thoughtfully.

'Tell me exactly what you did Holly,' said Hornbeam.

'All I did was to hold a keesceptre very tightly and make the wish,' said Holly.

'Do either of you have 3 prime numbers that add up to a fourth?' asked Hornbeam.

'I don't think so,' said Holly.

'Me neither,' said Jack.

Hornbeam held his head in 2 of his hands, and thought very carefully then asked, 'What are your birthdays in Hubee time?'

'My birthday in on the 29th of July,' said Jack.

'Which month is July?' asked Hornbeam. 'And what Hubee year were you born in?'

'What do you mean about July?' asked Jack.

'How many months do you have, and where does July fit in?' asked Hornbeam.

'Oh,' said Jack. 'We have twelve months. July is the 7th month, and I was born in the year two thousand and nine.'

'So that gives "29 - 7 - two thousand and nine",' said Hornbeam. 'Unfortunately that doesn't work. Only 2 of them are prime numbers. What about you Holly?'

'I was born on the 23rd of May in the year 2011,' said Holly. 'May is the 5th month.'

'So that gives "23 - 5 - 2011",' said Hornbeam.

He thought about those numbers very carefully.

'Holly!' he exclaimed. 'They are all prime numbers! Let me add them up.'

He closed his eyes and began adding them, nodding his head slowly up and down as he did so. He seemed to add them up several times.

'2039!' he shouted. '2039! 2039! It's a prime number. Holly! You are a Quadruple Prime! That's why your wish to save me worked.'

Holly looked at him in amazement.

Jack just mouthed a silent, 'Wow!'

'That means that any wish you make when you are holding a keesceptre will come true!' cried Hornbeam. 'You're like a wizard!'

Holly couldn't believe what she was hearing.

'You must remember how rare a Quadruple Prime is Holly,' said Hornbeam. 'You are very special.'

Holly felt very proud. She never ever thought of herself as special, but now that Hornbeam said she was, she must be.

Forward to the past

'So can I wish for us to go home?' asked Holly.

'Yes,' said Hornbeam. 'Any wish you make when holding a keesceptre will come true.'

'Is it as easy as that?' asked Holly, not believing what she was hearing.

'Yes, it is, for you!' said Hornbeam. 'But remember not to wish for more than one thing, just in case things go wrong.'

'I won't,' said Holly, who was feeling rather gob-smacked.

'What will you wish for?' asked Hornbeam.

'We're very worried about Mum and Dad,' said Holly. 'They'll think we have got lost. We went into our garden on Tuesday and that was 2 days ago.'

'If we just turn up now and tell them about Highlow, they won't believe us, and we'll be in big trouble,' said Jack.

'So, I want to wish for Jack and me to go back to 2 days ago,' said Holly.

'Yes, you must do that,' said Hornbeam.

He paused and sighed.

'But unfortunately, there will be a problem,' he said. 'If you are able to go back in time, you will forget everything that happened before you went back.'

'Does that mean we will forget you and Lovesome?' asked Holly.

'Yes it does,' said Hornbeam.

'Oh that's so sad,' said Holly.

'But what about everything that has happened since we went into Highlow?' asked Jack. 'Will that never have happened?'

'No,' said Hornbeam. 'Because you are now back in Hubeeland, you cannot change what happened in Highlow time. Remember that Highlow time is very different to time here.'

'So will you still be here in Woodpecker Woods?' asked Holly.

'Yes, I will!' laughed Hornbeam. 'I sure will! I'm not a Hubee!'

'So can we come and see you?' asked Jack.

'Of course you can!' said Hornbeam. 'If you can remember me!'

'I do hope so,' said Holly.

'What's the first thing you will do when you get home Holly?' asked Hornbeam.

'Oh, I want to go and see my pet guinea pigs, Zig and Zag,' said Holly, 'I hope they are OK.'

'I'm sure they will be,' said Hornbeam. 'You've only been away 2 days!'

'It seems much longer!' said Jack. 'So much has happened!'

'Sadly,' said Hornbeam. 'I must be going soon. I've been very lucky so far. No Hubees apart from you have seen me, and I want it to stay like that. I'll help you over the canal, and then I'll say goodbye.'

He packed his satchel, stood up, and walked over to the side of the canal. Jack and Holly stood up, picked up their satchels, and followed him. Hornbeam put his right foot on one bank, then pedarced across, putting his left foot on the other bank.

'That's amazing!' said Jack, looking at Hornbeam pedarcing over the canal. 'That always impresses me!'

'Come on,' said Hornbeam. 'One at a time!'

Hornbeam reached down to one side, picked Holly up with his left and right hands, and lifted her in to the air. He turned and put Holly safely on the towpath. He turned back towards Jack, picked him up, and did the same. Then, lifting up his left foot, he pedarced back to the Woodpecker Woods side. He looked across to Jack and Holly.

'Thank you, young Hubees, it's been a great pleasure!' he called. 'And good luck with your Quadruple Prime!'

He set off walking up the slope towards the trees on the edge of Woodpecker Woods. Then he stopped, and turned back to look at them.

'Goodbye!' he shouted, then laughed his foghorn laugh.

'Goodbye Hornbeam!' shouted Jack and Holly. 'Thank you for everything!'

They watched him reach the woods, blend in with the trees, and disappear.

'Do you think we'll ever see him again?' asked Holly.

'Who knows?' said Jack. 'But we can certainly look for him next time we come down to the rhubarb fields!'

There was a bench just beside them. They sat down to gather their thoughts.

'Shall I use the Quadruple Prime now?' asked Holly.

'Yes,' said Jack. 'Everyone will be looking for us. We don't want to be found.'

'OK,' said Holly. 'What should I wish for?'

'Why don't you wish that we are back at home sometime

341

before we first saw 2:7:3 in the garden? Can you remember what we were doing?' asked Jack.

'Yes, I think so,' said Holly.

She thought carefully then said, 'You wanted to climb the Clock Tree and I wanted to see Zig and Zag. You said we should pick for it. You picked up a snail and asked me to guess which hand it was in. I lost, and we were going to the Clock Tree when we saw 2:7:3.'

'Perhaps you should wish to go back to when I picked up the snail, and make sure you get it right this time,' said Jack. 'We don't want to start all over again! Why did you lose?'

'I picked your left hand,' said Holly. 'You opened your right hand, and there was a snail sitting in a pool of slime.'

'That's amazing!' said Jack. 'If you'd picked my left hand we wouldn't have gone into the garden, and we would never have had this adventure!'

'So, if I wish for us to go back to just before you pick up the snail, will my Quadruple Prime take us back to then?' asked Holly.

'Yes, I think so,' said Jack.

'But you'll still pick up the snail in your right hand won't you?' asked Holly.

'Yes,' said Jack.

'So nothing will change,' said Holly. 'I picked your left hand last time, so won't I pick that one again?'

'Yes, you probably will,' said Jack. 'We somehow have to get you to choose my right hand.'

'Yes,' said Holly. 'That would work. I wish we could do that, but Hornbeam said that a keesceptre might only grant one wish at a time. I can't wish for us to go back and also for me to pick your right hand.'

Jack though about this carefully. Next to him was his satchel with his keesceptre sticking out of it.

'What did you just say Holly?' he asked.

'I said, I wish I could pick your right hand, but I can't do that as well as wish for us to go back,' said Holly.

'But I can!' shouted Jack. 'I've got a keesceptre as well!'

'What do you mean?' asked Holly.

'I can use your Quadruple Prime with my keesceptre to wish that you pick my right hand!' said Jack.

'Do you think that will work?' asked Holly, anxiously.

'Yes, I'm sure it will,' said Jack. 'But I'd better make my wish first, so that it's ready for when we go back. Are you ready?'

'Yes, but I feel very nervous,' said Holly.

'So do I!' said Jack.

'OK,' said Holly. 'Let's make these wishes! You go first!'

Jack took his keesceptre out of his satchel and sat closer to Holly. He grasped it very firmly and said, 'I wish that Holly picks my right hand when she chooses where the snail is!'

Nothing happened.

They waited a while.

'Has is worked?' asked Holly.

'I don't know,' said Jack. 'But I don't think we'll find out until you make your wish.'

'OK,' said Holly. 'My turn!'

Holly grasped her keesceptre in both hands.

'Sit very close to me Jack, if this works I don't want to get back on my own,' she said, very nervously.

Jack moved very close beside her.

'Right, here goes!' she said, taking a deep breath.

She grasped the keesceptre even tighter and shouted, 'I wish that Jack and me were back in Rodley Bottoms just after he picked up the snail!'

The Twice-Upon-a-Time-Day

For the second time in exactly 43 hours plus 5, Jack stretched back up after just having picked up a sleeping snail. He put his arms behind his back, swapped the snail from hand to hand, and then held his closed hands out in front of him.

'You choose,' he said to Holly.

Holly looked at the outstretched hands trying to see if any slime was oozing out between their fingers. There wasn't. She waved her right hand backwards and forwards over Jack's hands, paused for a moment, then put her hand on Jack's right hand. Jack winced, and opened his right hand to reveal a snoozing snail sitting in a small pool of slime.

'I win! Zig and Zag it is!' said Holly, triumphantly, as she set off towards the shed clutching Podge tightly.

Jack carefully returned the snail to a safe spot on the ground and wiped his right hand on his shorts.

'Why do I never win? Holly always wins,' he muttered.

He sighed, took a deep breath, and plodded along the path to the shed.

Both he and Holly were wearing what they had on when they left the house, their T-shirts, shorts and wellies. There were no satchels, no keesceptres, no Oodax, no Yumbax, no empty wooden Perx bottles, no bottles of Drointment and no Drongle feet. Jack didn't have a finger key in his back pocket.

Holly didn't have a Golden Trumpet Medal. Hubee time had gone backwards, and Holly had picked Jack's right hand. Both Quadruple Primes had worked.

Holly waited for Jack outside the shed, and they went in to see Zig and Zag together.

No long before Jack picked up the snail, a Sorx thumped the flat end of a keesceptre on their garden wall. It shouted, '3-3-5!, 3-3-5!, 3-3-5!' in a very high voice. Nothing happened.

In desperation, it hurled the keesceptre at the wall. There was an almighty crack, and the keesceptre dropped to the ground. Suddenly, the stone courses in the wall slid apart to reveal a long dark tunnel.

3:3:5 had a satchel on its back. Just above it, a wobniar soared into the sky. The Sorx let out a high-pitched whistle, and the wobniar slithered back into its satchel. The wall began to close. 3:3:5 picked up its keesceptre and stepped into the tunnel.

'I'll be in big trouble with Four:5:3, the new forager-in-chief,' it said to itself. 'She'll be very annoyed that I haven't foraged any treasure. But at least she's much better than those cowards, the old chief and 2:7:3.'

It turned and dadumed into the darkness, as the wall closed fully.

In the shed Holly, looked into the guinea pig cage and saw Zig and Zag. A little explosion went off inside her head.

'Jack,' she said. 'Do you remember something?'

Jack had a strange look on his face.

'Yes I do,' he said. 'Do you?

'Yes, what can you remember?' asked Holly.

'Hornbeam,' he said. 'What about you?'

'Lovesome,' she said.

They looked at each other in amazement, as the memories of their 2 solars in Highlow came flooding back. They dashed out of the shed into the garden and ran over to the dry-stone wall.

But they were too late. The stone courses in the wall looked like they always did, and there was no sign of any Sorx.

Hornbeam's 5-Point Plan

Hornbeam liked making plans. His 7-Point Plan and his Escape Plan had both been very successful, and he started to make his third and most important plan as soon as he discovered that Holly was a Quadruple Prime.

If Holly's Quadruple Prime wish was granted by her keesceptre, Hornbeam knew that she and Jack would not remember anything. This made him very sad. He wanted them to remember their adventures in Highlow. He wanted them to remember Affable and Lovesome. And, in particular, he wanted them to remember him, because, if they did, they would be able to visit him in Woodpecker Woods, which he would really like.

This plan had 5-points. He spoke each one to himself as put it into action.

'First,' he said. 'Find out what Holly will do as soon as she gets home.'

He had already done this. When she said she would go and see Zig and Zag, he didn't really know what she was talking about, but they were obviously very important to her. So he knew that she would see them as soon as she could.

'Second,' he continued. 'Say goodbye and pretend to walk into Woodpecker Woods.'

He had already done this as well. Jack and Holly had watched him go, and thought he had disappeared.

'Third,' said Hornbeam. 'Sneak back to the edge of the woods so that I can see them, but they can't see me.'

He did this very carefully. He saw them sitting on a bench on the other side of the canal. They seemed to be close enough to him for his plan to work.

'Fourth,' he said, looking into his satchel. 'Get a keesceptre.'

There were 3 keesceptres in his satchel. He only needed one. He reached in, and pulled one out.

'Fifth,' he said, very nervously. 'Use the keesceptre, with Holly's Quadruple Prime, to make a "Remember Wish".'

He grasped the keesceptre very firmly, wrapping all 3 of his hands around it. He had to be the boss.

He looked at Holly and Jack sat on the bench, took a deep breath, and said, 'I wish that Holly and Jack remember everything about their adventures in Highlow, as soon as Holly sees Zig and Zag!'

He then turned, and walked back into Woodpecker Woods.

'I hope that works,' he said to himself, as he disappeared among the trees.

THE END

SOME FACTS ABOUT *THE SORX AND THE QORX*

Here are some facts about *The Sorx and The Qorx*. You may have spotted some of them while you were reading the book.

- The book is laid out in 73 primes. 73 is a prime number.

- Every number in the book, which is a prime number, is written in numerical format, for example, number 23.

- Every number in the book, which is not a prime number, is written in word format, for example, number fifteen.

- The word wobniar is rainbow backwards.

- The word keesceptre is an anagram of keep secret.

- The word deesceptre is an anagram of deep secret.

- The name Super Bremmin is an anagram of prime numbers.

- The name Telecar is an anagram of treacle.

- Not including the official publication stuff on page 2 and the words on the front cover, the back cover and the spine of the book, there are 80147 words in *The Sorx and The Qorx*. Although this was not planned when the book was being written, 80147 also happens to be a prime number!